I0633250

Medicine Man

Ibeh Liedstrand-Nwokocha

Copyright © 2016 Ibeh Liedstrand-Nwokocha

HATCH
PUBLISHERS
Breivik
Vesterålen
8450 Stokmarknes

All rights reserved.

This book is a work of fiction. It is not intended to be historical fiction. References to real people, events, establishments, organizations, or locales are intended to provide a sense of authenticity, and are used fictitiously. All other characters, and all incidents and dialogue, are drawn from the author's imagination and are not to be considered as real.

The art work 'Horizon' by Ragnhild Adelheid Holten is duly licenced for this publication and remains the property of Ragnhild Adelheid Holten.

A catalogue record of this book is available from the National Library of Norway.

ISBN 978-82-93475-00-2
(paperback)

ISBN 978-82-93475-03-3
(ebook)

ISBN-13:

Version 2.0

This book is copyrighted material and must not be copied, reproduced, transferred, distributed, leased, licensed, or publically performed or used in any way except as specifically permitted in writing by the publishers, as allowed under the terms and conditions under which it was purchased or as strictly permitted by applicable copyright law. Any unauthorized distribution or use of this text may be a direct infringement of the author's and publisher's rights and those responsible may be liable in law accordingly.

To Ellen, the beautiful rock on which everything is built,
and to the fallen, forgotten and nameless who find themselves in this book.

Ten percent (10%) of author royalties from this book go to the *GLK Student Fund*, www.glkstudentfund.com. *GLK* is listed by *GlobalGiving*, the first and largest global crowdfunding community for nonprofits, www.globalgiving.org.

ACKNOWLEDGMENTS

Special thanks to Professor Jane Bryce, Luke Finley, Nwabugo Ubochi, Kelechi Nwokocha, Vivian Nwofor, Lukas Mwaijega and Ragnhild Adelheid Holten.

Many thanks to family and friends for all their support, including: Ellen, Leo, Noah, Jaja, Lucille, Emeka, Uzodimma, Samantha, Roy and Hege.

Some inspiration was drawn from the spirit of the works of Dr Patrick Iroegbu of Grant MacEwan University in the areas of social, cultural and medical anthropology.

FOREWORD

When we meet Obioma as a child in 1983, he is threading his way through the chaotic centre of rush-hour Owerri, with its cacophony of traffic, people, market traders and amplified music, in search of 5.00 Naira. This is the price of entry to the school's effort at winning a French song competition, instigated by the charismatic Mr Success. One of the key ways the novel tracks the expansion of crime and the growth of corruption in the succeeding years is through the value of money, and Obioma's quest for a paid errand that will earn him his 5 Naira signifies the relative stability and shared values of an era that is about to end. Not that this earlier time is in any way perfect.

Even for a country whose post-Independence history has been as turbulent as Nigeria's, the ten years covered by this novel - 1983-93 - will be remembered as a period of unprecedented social change. The novel is not, however, a record of the political upheavals that marked this period, so much as a dramatization of their effects and consequences on ordinary people in a particular place. Though dates are important: it starts with a prologue dated Weds 27 May, 1993, before taking us back to 1983, forward to 1985, 1987, 1990 and eventually full circle to 1993 again, the date markers are those of an individual life rather than a national or political entity. The one exception is Dec 31 1983, the date when a short-lived democratic inter-regnum, begun in 1979, was once again replaced by military rule, which lasted a further 15 years. But the individual life we mainly follow is that of Obioma, a boy of ten in 1983, twenty by the time the story ends, and in this respect the novel could be described as a bildungsroman or coming of age story. But the place, Owerri, is equally important in the narrative; one of the novel's greatest strengths is the way it evokes the smell, feel and shape of that eastern town, and the concerns and ambitions of its inhabitants.

Further strands woven into the narrative are that of the rural village, Umuwe, from which Obioma's family hails, and the story of Nneka, Obioma's childhood sweetheart. In the former, Obioma's uncle, Iwuagwu, is a figure of resistance to the corruption that is worming its way into the very heart of a traditional way of life that has sustained Nigeria's sense of its own humanity up to that point.

Though the novel is in English, the use of proverbial sayings as epigraphs to every chapter (most, but not all, Igbo and given in the original language), is a metatextual device that signifies the alternative morality and wisdom to which Iwuagwu adheres and for which Obioma had been marked out by the deity, Agwu, whose call he fails to answer. These sayings offer a benchmark against which the degradation of national values can be measured. The same metaphysical frame of reference informs Iwuagwu's classification of people into four types, recalled by Obioma towards the end of the novel. "Ndi oma", the good; "Ndi miri miri" the benign but essentially passive onlookers; "'Ndi nkemu nkemu", the indifferent and selfish, who inevitably become "nde ojo" , bad people, "vile and entirely disconnected from the positive forces of life; people who take actions that hurt others and would never dream of preventing harm, but rather only of causing it." Obioma is forced to ask himself to which category he belongs. The disease infecting the body politic has already gone global, with: 'Cartel leaders in Europe, Asia and South America, even motorcyclists in North America… along with respectable suited bankers in large skyscraper-infested cities, quiet dainty hamlets in Switzerland and others in picturesque vacation islands,' all forming part of a global network of violence, crime, and corruption. Obioma, spade in hand, has become a truth-seeker.

Jane Bryce, Professor of African Literature and Cinema
University of the West Indies

PROLOGUE

"Nde mmadụ kpọkọta nkume, nkume aghọọ chi akpaalaokwu"

"When people gather stones, the stones become deities"

(Traditional Igbo proverb)

1:15am Wednesday 27 May 1993

The sound of pounding feet, along with stirring church hymns and renditions of gospel songs, things normally reserved for Sunday masses, now serenaded the usually dead, sleepy early-morning streets of Owerri.

Obioma joined one of the swelling crowds of hundreds marauding through the city. Toppled, burning cars lit up the sky in their wake. Obioma felt as though he sat on a comet, perhaps somewhere around its tail, observing the collection of loosely connected people flow forward in such destructive harmony that they acquired their own gravitational pull, drawing others in.

The road eventually straightened, and it became apparent where they were now headed. Obioma sprinted ahead, side-stepping the broken bottles and other debris that littered the great Nnamdi Azikiwe Road. He imagined the mass digging that would ensue when they got to their destination. *What would they find this time?*

PART 1

1 SUCCESS

"If the palm of the hand itches it signifies the coming of great luck for someone"

(Traditional Lesothan Proverb)

Owerri, South Eastern Nigerian, 1983

Like most ten-year-olds who plied the Nnamdi Azikiwe Road to and from school, Obioma drifted about in a naive haze of childish thoughts. With his gaze mostly fixed to the skies, he leaped over large drainage gutters and miraculously navigated his way onto the great road from the busy side streets near his home. From high above, Nnamdi Azikiwe Road must have looked amazing, Obioma thought as he traced the slow progress of a passenger aeroplane slogging across the almost clear morning sky. It dipped in and out of the modest scatterings of white clouds that hung high above him until it disappeared beyond the horizon.

"This road used to be called Douglas Road. Some people still call it that, but Douglas was a deeply unpleasant man," Obioma remembered his uncle saying before launching into his recurring lamentations about the notoriety of H.M. Douglas, and how this British colonial District Commissioner of Owerri in the late 1800s either incarcerated or killed dissenting locals to get this road, and many of his other projects, completed.

The main arteries of the city of Owerri pumped vigorously from well before dawn. Whetheral Road half surrounded the old city, marking its perimeter, and a handful of main roads ran through Owerri, but the great Nnamdi Azikiwe Road cut through its very heart and ran three miles south through the middle of the city. The road started just a stone's throw from

3

where Obioma lived, by the Old Market. It ran past churches, dwellings and shops, a handful of banks, bus stations, a primary school and a few more dwellings, then past the city's New Market, a secondary school and a colossal timber market. The road then acquired a new name, Aba Road, and was said to stretch a full two hours' drive out of the city to Aba, another sprawl of slightly rusting iron rooftops but twice as large as Owerri.

One of Obioma's first memories was of donning his tan leather sandals early one morning and slipping out of his home undetected. Minutes later he had found himself lost and bewildered on the long, busy stretch of road. He had no memory of how he had got home again. Five years on, the road had become the central route of his daily commute to school, and Obioma shuffled along the road's edges with the carelessness of someone who knew every inch of it very well.

Luminously bleached white shirts peeking out of men's two-piece suits, the brilliant tones of women's wrappers and blouses, and the school uniforms worn by Obioma and his fellow pupils, caused a pleasant riot of colour. Well-polished shoes and sandals and the tyres of an array of vehicles relentlessly pounded the sturdy tarmac of the great road. A young boy who looked about six years old clung with both hands to the railing of the stairwell of what was apparently his home.

"*Biko, achọghịm ị ga school ta,*" the boy cried out, as his mother untangled his grip, half helped by the boy's fascination with the robotic arm of a nearby bright yellow SULO truck lifting two rubbish containers simultaneously. The boy's further cries were drowned out by the cacophony of bleating cars trapped in long tailbacks on either side of the road.

When Obioma got to the junction with Mbaise Road the expectant stares of election candidates, trying their best to look appealing, beamed down from wall-mounted posters. Below them, hordes of stooping project managers pleaded with tradesmen clutching carpentry and masonry equipment, portable ladders, helmets and shovels of every variety.

"It is a tradesman's market. Any tradesman you see here after seven o'clock in the morning is either very lazy or a very rich person," Obioma remembered his mother saying once.

Not too far away, gospel music blasted from various radios and large amplifiers mounted outside a handful of record and electronic appliance shops. The radio relays were punctuated by jingles warning of the curse of the deadly 'ember' months – the months of September, October, November and December. These months always brought with them a wave of fatal road accidents in the run-up to religious and end-of-year festivities, as people rushed around making reckless last-ditch efforts to rack up money to cover the planned excesses of the holidays.

A conspicuous kiosk doused in electric-blue paint stood further along on Obioma's way to school. His mind spun at the thought of the cold and the sweet taste of the frozen mix of artificial colour, vanilla essence and cheap industrial saccharin that came in the shape of the lollipops he regularly bought from that kiosk. A short distance ahead, the intricate metal mesh of his school gates beckoned.

Bonjour, bonjour mes amis…
Comment, comment allez-vous
Tu es tres, tres, tres, tres
Et vous, et vous
Tu es tres jeolousi
Merci beaucoup

Various renditions of the one-versed song cascaded from classrooms and floated through the corridors, hallways and verandas of Obioma's primary school. Obioma knew this was no ordinary day.

Mr Success had his back to the class, etching out the French song on the large blackboard in beautiful calligraphy. He was writing at more than five times the speed that Mrs Añara, Obioma's teacher, usually wrote with. In no time he was done and he turned to the class, his face brimming with intense energy.

"My name is Success."

Success looked to be in his late twenties, his smiley round face complementing his tall, gangly frame. He had so much energy that he appeared to be constantly in motion, and his carriage reminded Obioma of the twitching, jerking movements chickens constantly made with their heads. Success's darker-than-usual skin tone glowed as the sun-rays splashing through the window panes fell on him, presenting an even more striking impression.

Even before Success had opened his mouth Obioma had known that he was cleverer than anyone he had ever met, including Mrs Añara, the middle-aged woman who sat behind a large desk at the front of Obioma's classroom, whose floral-patterned three-piece outfits, bowed head-ties and spectacles that magnified her eyes to three times their actual size gave her the appearance of a wise old owl perched on a large tree branch.

Success was even cleverer than the cleverest person Obioma knew: Kalu, his classmate who sat beside him on his right-hand side. One of nature's one-offs, Kalu could read a page from a book and recite that page verbatim, even weeks later. Obioma always felt privileged to be Kalu's friend, to sit beside him in class and seem almost as clever as him when he was awarded second spot after Kalu, though only in the class performance reports. Kalu had been named Pupil of the Year each of the past four years, for the entire school. But now even Kalu sat silent and glued to the enigma that had walked into their class that morning.

"If you sing this song well enough, you and your teacher will be going to France to represent your school," Success said when he had finished writing on the blackboard.

Obioma and the twenty-nine other ten-year-olds in the classroom rummaged through their brains for as many references to France as they could muster. A tall metal tower, and other images from the rare 1982 World Cup trading cards that were doing the rounds in the school at break time. Michel Platini raising his muscular left leg to strike a ball. Then, finally, Jean-Jacques, or rather Ginjaki, as he was called – the Cameroonian boy in the adjacent classroom who spoke French, and whose family had narrowly escaped a mistaken deportation to Ghana.

After a few seconds taking in the strangeness of the proposal and their new visitor, Obioma and his classmates gave in to the usual instinctive scramble to reproduce in their notebooks what was written on the blackboard.

"Stop writing and listen, all of you," Mrs Añara shouted at the top of her voice, inspiring the pin-drop silence that her classroom was known for.

With that, Success started to sing. His astonishingly light singing voice floated across the classroom.

"In a week from today all classes will compete to represent your school, and the class that wins will go on to compete against the winners of every school in the state. In a month, the class that emerges the winner across the nineteen states in the country will go to France with their teacher, all expenses paid." This was what Success said right after he had finished singing. It caused heads to pan across the room towards the poster-sized map of Nigeria on the wall of the classroom, tracing the broken lines demarcating the nineteen states of the country.

Success sang the song a second time and then a third, before encouraging the pupils in Obioma's class to join in, and by the fifth rendition Obioma and his classmates could sing it coherently. This was when, to gleeful excited gasps, Success declared, "You sound like French angels. I think you have a very good chance.

"But, listen up. To take part in the competition, you must come along tomorrow with your administrative fee of five naira. Make sure you hand it over to your teacher, Mrs Añara, first thing tomorrow morning." When Success had finished instructing Obioma and his classmates, he walked to the back of the class and repeated himself. And when he was satisfied that everyone understood, he disappeared to the adjacent classroom.

2 DURU ANYỊ ỤLA

"Agbakọọ nyọọ mamịrị, ọ gbọọ ụfụfụ"

"When people urinate on the same spot, it foams"

(Traditional Igbo proverb)

That afternoon

> *Duru anyị ụla, duru anyi ụla*
> *Duru anyị ụla, duru anyị ụla*
> *Eze Jesus, duru anyi ụla*
> *Duru anyị ụla*
> *Amen*

The slow and poignant prayer-song imploring Jesus to guide them home safely always instilled calmness in what would otherwise have been a free-for-all dash by the pupils to escape the school gates. Since the adoption of the song many years ago, the three-thousand-strong procession of pupils would calmly file out of their various classrooms into the vast, open school compound, all heading for home. Even the scramble to find relatives, friends or neighbours before the trek or ride home had a certain type of order to it. Obioma could not remember a day that the song wasn't sung. In fact, he looked forward to hearing its eerily soothing melody. Not only did it signal the imminent freedom to aimlessly wander the streets outside his school's gates, but it somehow had the power to embody different things at different times. That afternoon, as Obioma skipped out of his classroom singing, with Nneka's hand clutched in his, and as the dusty hamatan winds blew across the school from the distant Sahara Desert to the north, the song provoked nostalgic thoughts of past December holidays in Umuwe, his father's ancestral village, a long bus ride away from Owerri. Obioma wished Nneka could join him there for this year's holidays.

Obioma always sat as close as possible to Nneka in class. She bore a radiant gap-toothed smile that enthralled him. Nneka finally came round to understanding and reciprocating Obioma's desire to always be in her company after almost a year of his pulling her hair-plaits and pouring fistfuls of sand down her navy-blue school dress, and his bizarre energetic and sustained campaign to establish her nickname in school as 'Sunshine'.

That afternoon, as Obioma, Nneka and the other children emerged from their classrooms singing, and as gusts of wind twirled crisp dead leaves and shaved blades of sun-baked grass up into the air, a completely new ambience began to settle over the school. The closing prayer-song, which had been sung for decades, was suddenly being abandoned and replaced by the new French song. It started as a mishmash of renditions sung at the same time by the students as they emerged from their classrooms. These repeated recitals eventually merged into one another, growing louder and louder, overpowering and completely drowning out the cacophony of traffic sounds that constantly oozed over the school fence from the adjoining great road. Obioma, Nneka and the mass of other children who were supposed to be homebound instead swarmed and congregated at the foot of the largest structure in the school compound, a one-storey classroom block that also housed the headmistress's office. Arms now wrapped around each other in a sort of human chain, Obioma, Nneka and Kalu fused on to the other pupils and swayed gently from side to side with the rhythm of the song. Teachers on their way home stopped and joined in, and the headmistress, who had now emerged from her office and was standing on her front balcony, waved her hands about like a symphony conductor, with far less grace but a great deal of glee.

3 OLD MARKET

"Chọwa ngwere mgbe ọ nọ n'elu ana, tupu ọ banye n'ogologo ọhia"

"Look for the lizard when he is on open ground, before he enters the tall grass"

(Traditional Igbo proverb)

That afternoon

Obioma's stroll through Owerri seemed aimless even to him. He watched with a sense of desperation as bank notes and coins were crumpled, folded or tossed into cash registers, as shopkeepers concluded exchanges with customers.

Obioma's father was easy when it came to prising money out of him, but he was away for a few days. Obioma's mother, on the other hand, was of the tough-love persuasion. Situations of great want and need were, for her, good opportunities to teach hard lessons. Obioma heard her asking why he didn't anticipate things, and save the fifty-kobo coins he got from time to time as pocket money. Or why he had not done what prudent children would have, and put away the twenty naira he had received from his uncle who'd visited a few months previously, rather than wasting it on *quiniquini* and *puff puff* snacks. Obioma was sure his mother would even be determined that he lose out on going to France just for the sake of a lesson in savings. Unclear on how best to avoid this, he took a detour, not heading straight home but instead strolling down the ever-busy Nnamdi Azikiwe Road, en route to the Old Market.

The market must be at least ten football pitches wide, Obioma reckoned. It spilled out onto the surrounding Nnamdi Azikiwe Road, School Road and Ekeonunwa Road. Nwokorie Street, hosting the market's open-air section, was no longer accessible by car, and the other roads were barely passable at the points where they intersected with it.

Obioma weaved through the makeshift stalls of shoe-shiners and cobblers staked out at the top end of School Road, just off Nnamdi Azikiwe Road. His anxiety grew almost as intensely as the rumbling in his stomach, until he caught a whiff of the invisible but powerful chilli mist hovering over traders selling huge basins full of assorted fried meats, all seductively bright red from the concoction of marinades in which they were cooked. His stomach churned as he struggled to tear himself away from standing and gaping at the marvel, and from the heavy price tags sticking out of the basins.

Further along, hawkers carrying trays of *akwa ọkụkọ* and *ọgazị* (boiled chicken and guinea fowl's eggs) on their heads encroached dangerously onto the road, besieging the cars and buses that snaked through.

Street performers bellowed through their acts over the sizeable crowds that gathered around them. A tall, thick-set magician, whom everyone knew as Nakwaecheki, had apparently just cured a man of impotence, a concept Obioma struggled to grasp. The formerly impotent man stood beside Nakwaecheki, clutching his bulging crotch area with both hands. Two weary-looking and heavily pregnant women stood right next to him, the magician gesturing towards them as he told the crowd of how they had been standing there several weeks earlier, worried about the fertility problems that had plagued them for years.

A pile of nails and razor blades lay on a mat beside Nakwaecheki's briefcase, which was placed right in the middle of the huddle of people around him. A boy standing next to Obioma talked in low tones to another of how the magician swallowed and regurgitated the razor blades and nails at the start of his act.

Nakwaecheki retrieved sachets of tablets and small bottles of potions from his briefcase which he handed out, in exchange for naira notes, to the stream of people stepping forward from the huddle around him. Obioma overheard some of the conversations with the magician, mostly conducted in low tones: people questioned him about dosage and claimed to be buying the potions and tablets for barren and impotent distant relatives back in their villages. Obioma watched for a while as Nakwaecheki's stash of cash, which he stuffed into his briefcase, grew rapidly. When he could no longer bear the sight of the money he could not have, he headed for Moses' shop on the off-chance that Moses might have a five-naira-paying errand for him to run.

"Nda Moses, good afternoon," Obioma greeted the shopkeeper loudly as he stepped into Moses' bookshop, the quiet calm contrasting with the scene outside. Moses sat on a stool deep inside his shop, engrossed in a book, far away from the pandemonium.

The word 'stampede' played havoc with Obioma's mind whenever he visited Moses' shop. Obioma knew that it would be deeply offensive to utter the word in Moses' presence, but it sat on the tip of his tongue, for reasons he could not comprehend.

'Stampede' was the nickname that mean-spirited children and teenagers taunted Moses with. They would sometimes appear outside the shop and pelt it with stones. Even though Obioma had not seen this for himself, he knew that Moses had once roamed the Old Market naked, carrying a large sack and obsessively collecting only yellow pieces of paper. It had also been said in the past that Moses would intermittently and abruptly jolt off in any direction in a frenzied sprint, shouting, "Stampede!".

Obioma's mother had grown up in the same neighbourhood as Moses and attended the same primary and secondary schools. She would always speak about him with great admiration. Moses was said to have been a very bright and clever mathematician. He had lectured at University of Lagos before he lost his mind. Some speculated that his state of mind had not been helped by years of smoking grass with the students he was supposed to be teaching. Obioma did not believe that particular rumour, since he had never seen or heard of anyone collecting discarded blades of grass other than for compost.

Obioma's father was less complimentary. "The man is a lunatic," he had once said with an air of irritation when the subject of Moses came up as they ate dinner. Obioma knew that his father did not like Moses, and that it had something to do with the very familiar and companionable tone with which Obioma's mother spoke about Moses.

Moses' bouts of insanity were said by Obioma's mother to have plagued him well after the loss of his teaching job in Lagos and his return to Owerri to live with his mother, only tailing off after his elder brother started sending him medicine from the United States. Moses now sold second-hand books from his mother's old fabric shop, a shop she was too old to carry on minding.

"Ndaa Moses, good afternoon," Obioma called again, this time more loudly.

"Nnọọ, Obioma, *school O gbasa go*," Moses responded with an uneasy smile on his face when he finally lifted his gaze from his book.

"*Ee*," Obioma answered lazily, nodding and sheepishly focusing his gaze on the peeling tip of his brown leather sandals.

"*Mama gi kwanu?*" Moses asked, as he always did, his focus already back on his book as he said it.

"*O di mma*" (She is well), Obioma responded.

Obioma had not been to Moses' shop in months and, as Moses briefly got up from his stool to remove books from the chair he intended Obioma to sit on, Obioma noticed how fat he had become. A strange sort of fatness, not at all like the healthy layers of fat Obioma's father was amassing around his stomach area, having recently landed a very enviable role at his workplace. Moses seemed to have swollen up as if pumped full of air like a balloon, his cheeks, belly, legs and arms puffed up and his eyes staring into his book like two dark beads looking out from two slits in his face.

Moses' head was clean-shaven and he was dressed in black from his shirt down to his socks and shoes. Even though he had changed so dramatically, his shop hadn't. His ceiling-high bookshelves, covering the four walls of the shop, were stacked full. Other long, cage-like bookshelves, which had formerly held the rolls of cloth sold by his mother, hung down from various points in the ceiling like chandeliers, all now stocked with books labelled according to their subject areas. Everything was as it had been before except for an obituary poster bearing an old woman's picture, pasted over some books on a shelf behind where Moses was sitting. Obioma hadn't noticed it at first.

"*Ndo*" (Sorry), Obioma said, after about two more minutes of sitting quietly, arms folded and shoulders propped up in the vacant chair in the corner of Moses' shop. This was what Obioma saw his father do whenever they went to pay condolence visits to people who had recently lost someone very close.

"Thank you," Moses responded as he stared out of the shop reflectively, watching the streaming herd of passing people.

Obioma continued to sit quietly in his seat for a while. When he thought it was no longer too soon or too insensitive to change the subject, he announced to Moses that he was going to France.

"Really? How come? When?" Moses questioned him, trying to force out another strained smile, in an apparent attempt to show solidarity with Obioma over his exuberant announcement.

"I am taking part in a singing competition and the winners will go to France next month," Obioma explained.

"That sounds good," Moses drawled, before folding his arms, closing his eyes, tilting back and resting his head on the bookshelf behind him. It was at this point that Obioma decided against asking for any paid errands. Instead he whiled away a few more minutes looking up 'France' in one of the volumes of an old encyclopaedia set which took up a significant portion of a shelf at the front of the bookshop. When he had had enough of looking at pictures of the Eiffel Tower, Obioma departed.

4 NWOKORIE STREET

"Love is a despot who spares no one"

(Traditional Namibian proverb)

That afternoon

The open-air wing of the Old Market, running along the entire one-mile length of Nwokorie Street, was always fully occupied by traders. They lined the middle of the road, sitting back-to-back, their wares laid out on mats and raised platforms in front of them. Between them and the wooden stalls that flanked the sides of the road, shoppers snaked along two narrow paths running parallel to each other. Some overzealous traders heckled, cajoled, implored or tugged on the limbs of the steady stream of would-be customers. Obioma tentatively edged forward with the other shoppers. The blend of pleasant and not-so-agreeable smells hung in the air as traders sold all manner of fish, grains, vegetables and fruits.

Halfway down Nwokorie Street, about two dozen young men with bulging arms leaned over, energetically winding manual grinders fixed onto small benches, pulverising seeds and grains for a fee. A cluster of women sat next to them with trays and chopping-boards, cutting *ugu* and *ukazi* vegetable leaves and selling pre-chopped and soaked *olugbu* leaves from large covered basins. It was after Obioma had squeezed past them and a shopper ferrying a goat on his shoulders that he saw Nneka and her mother. Both were sitting, shielded from the scorching sun by the black brocade wrapping cloths of Nneka's mother. Their wares – three large basins of *egusi* seeds – were rested on a large mat in front of them. Nneka was engrossed in some arithmetic, counting on her fingers as she worked out the change to give a waiting customer. Her mother was also just about to complete a sale.

"Aunty, good afternoon. Ndaa Agnes, Ndaa Stella, Ndaa Gladis, good afternoon." Obioma greeted Nneka's mother and the other women sitting behind and on either side of Nneka and her mother, each tending to large basins heaped full of various grains and seeds. Obioma settled into his seat, a low vacant stool beside Nneka, under what was left of the shade of the large piece of cloth draped over the heads of the women.

"*Ikom*" (Lover). Nneka's mother's response was delayed but cheerful.

Obioma remembered how she had called him *Ọpara m`* (my first son) the day before – the name she was more in the habit of using for him.

"Even though my husband is long dead and no one speaks out for me anymore, I have a son, yes, a son, at last, to add to the daughter I have. My in-laws can no longer say that I am unable to produce a son," Nneka's mother had added the day before, in one of the downward mood swings that Obioma had noticed plagued her every other week. It was during these times also that she told and retold of her plight at the hands of her in-laws, to the women who sat alongside her and sold groceries in the market. How her husband had died in far-away Arochukwu, when Nneka was still very young, and how her in-laws had set about stealing Nneka's inheritance and everything they owned.

"We were lucky to come out alive," Nneka's mother had explained, as she always did, wiping the black lace hem of her wrapper across her face to soak up streaks of breakaway tears. Her ever-present wide, gap-toothed smile had disappeared, and she had frantically stood up, wrapping and rewrapping the worn, all-black mourning outfit that she still wore most weekdays, eight years after her husband's death. Obioma had noticed that Nneka didn't seem to remember much about her father or his family, or how her mother had had to bundle her in a blanket in the middle of the night and trek through several villages before boarding a bus to Owerri. She, too, listened to her mother's stories as though they were tales about unfamiliar people in far-flung places.

This afternoon, however, Nneka's mother's was back to her usual cheery self and her intermittent smiles had reappeared – especially when a balding, middle-aged man stopped in front of her stall for no other reason than to compliment her on how good her children looked.

"*Ha bụ ejima*" (They are twins), Nneka's mother responded as Obioma looked on.

"When she gets a little older and if she continues to take on your great attributes, I will marry her," the man continued. "I mean, it's a big shame you only have two children. Those things are built for at least six," he concluded as he leered at Nneka's mother's cleavage.

Obioma flared his nostrils and bowed his eyebrows at the man from where he sat. He had long ago noticed how the compliments Nneka's mother received seemed to centre either on her ample bosom or on people wanting to marry Nneka. Obioma glanced across to Nneka, who was still obliviously counting the kobo coins a customer had just handed her. He knew that if she had heard the man's comments she would have vehemently shaken her head and told him to find someone his age.

"Customer, even in about ten years' time, when she is no longer a child, she will still be too young for you. Are you buying anything today, sir?" Obioma watched as Nneka's mother responded with a forced smile on her face. The man shuffled on.

Obioma was not sure what to make of some of the other customers who deliberately overpaid Nneka as they flattered her. Some said that she should be on television, advertising creams, soaps and clothes. Others suggested Nneka be sent to America immediately to act in films. Nor was Obioma pleased with the handful of men, and women, who asked Nneka's mother how much money they would need to give in order for her to betroth Nneka to one of their children: requests that did not seem serious but which Nneka's mother played along with. It had not been until one rainy evening the previous year that Obioma had realised that there was no need to feel threatened by them. That evening, Nneka's mother had once again been in one of her sad moods and Obioma had expected the usual monologues recounting her experiences at the hands of her in-laws.

"You should never allow yourselves to be broken apart," Nneka's mother had said in hushed tones that evening, as they'd huddled under a family-sized umbrella while a heavy downpour pelted loudly down on them.

"I may be saying to people now that you are twin brother and sister, but in the future when you are older, if it is something you want, you should get married and have kids of your own.

"So we shall keep acting like you are brother and sister until such a time comes," Nneka's mother had concluded.

Obioma had noticed that there was none of Nneka's vigorous head shaking, and this had pleased him very much.

"I learnt that you are going abroad to sing?" Nneka's mother asked Obioma excitedly, snapping him out of his deep thoughts.

Obioma nodded, though not as enthusiastically as she had enquired. Teasing him, Nneka leaned forward into Obioma's view, clasping a crisp five-naira note between her thumbs and index fingers, and, accompanied by a smug look on her face, she wriggled her head and torso in a gleeful celebratory jig.

"*Nneka ozuola*" (That's enough), Nneka's mother snapped.

"*I chọtala five-naira gị?*" Nneka's mother enquired. Obioma shook his head, telling her that he was going to his mother's shop to ask her for the money.

"*Papa gị kwanụ?*" she enquired, apparently sharing Obioma's unspoken scepticism about his getting the money from his mother.

"*Ọ gara Lagos*" Obioma responded.

"OK, *bịagharịa… Ọ bụrụ na o nyehị gi five-naira*" (If she doesn't give you the five-naira, come back to me), Nneka's mother finally proposed, as expected. She did not know this, but Obioma had once gotten into trouble at home for taking money from her to buy a football.

Obioma's mother had told him in confidence that Nneka's mother had never been good with money and that that was why they continued to live in just one bedroom. She had mentioned that this was also why Nneka's mother found it hard to pay Nneka's school fees, and why she had a makeshift stall on Nwokorie Street and not a proper store in the main market. She had warned that he was not being a true friend if he continued to take money from her, because she needed it even more now that her husband was dead. This had stuck with Obioma, and he vehemently refused any money she offered him.

Obioma said his farewells anxiously and fleetingly, hopping over the mounds of *egusi* and leaving Nneka's mother to explain to a puzzled Nneka why he had left so soon. Nneka, who was engaged with another customer, stood up from her low stool and looked after him worriedly, her face ridden with guilt.

5 MAMA'S STOCKFISH

"Aka aja aja n'ebute Ọnụ mmanụ mmanụ"

"Soiled hands bring forth oily mouth"

(Traditional Igbo proverb)

Obioma left Nwokorie Street and entered into the immense network of rows and columns that was the market proper: an intricate and windowless maze made of corrugated zinc roofing sheets, wood, fabric, cardboard, concrete and just about any material that could be propped up. Whatever you were looking for – onions, grains, baking ingredients, rolls of cloth or already-sewn apparel – there was an aisle for it. And, in some parts of the market, whole groups of aisles were dedicated to just one item. Rolls of fabric were sold across four aisles, each stretching for at least twenty-five metres. Traders sat in front of each other on the narrow aisles, as would-be customers wandered by.

The snug shops, most of them no bigger than a small single room, offered a cosy and warm reprieve from the elements on cold mornings and evenings, especially at the height of the rainy season and during the cold evenings of the hamatan. In the heat of the dry season and toasty hamatan afternoons, the hundreds of small oscillating fans employed to cool the shops had no hope of getting their one job done, as they mostly recirculated baking hot air.

The pungent smell of dried fish filled the air as Obioma approached aisle 14, an unusually broad but short aisle which was part of the original build of the market, and the only one where *okporoko* – stockfish – was sold. Obioma's mother owned a large shop on this aisle. It had initially belonged to her brother, Festus. He had suddenly died several years earlier, collapsing in the middle of a motor-park while waiting to board a bus to Onne, the seaport town where he bought large bales of stockfish. Obioma remembered him only vaguely, but he always featured in his mother's morning prayers.

"Let my enemies watch me prosper," Obioma's mother had repeatedly said that morning during one of the prayer meetings she insisted that the family have every morning before they each left the house.

"Protect us, oh Father, because our struggle is not against flesh and blood, but against the principalities, powers and demons in high places…" Whenever this was said, it usually meant that his mother was having a particularly bad week at her shop, probably due to her long-running feuds with the other traders on her aisle.

Obioma could always tell the precise moment his father had had enough of the praying. His amens grew successively louder – his polite way of signalling to Obioma's mother to wrap things up. This rarely worked, even when he started saying them well before his mother had completed her prayer verses.

Obioma's mother carried on sometimes until Obioma's father got fed-up enough to quietly slip away to work, something Obioma knew his father would answer for in the regular late-night arguments his parents had as they lay in bed. Obioma remembered a time when the prayers went on for so long that they *all* had to leave his mother kneeling on the living room floor rather than risk being late. When they returned later in the afternoon, they found her there, still praying.

"The enemies," Obioma mouthed to himself that afternoon, as he walked past the other shops that sold stockfish on his mother's aisle. There was no one in sight, but Obioma could hear the murmur of conversation from deep inside the shops as some of the traders took advantage of the lull in trade to converse with each other. A number of the shops were closed, their owners having left early or not bothered at all to open up that day.

Augustus sat on a stool in front of his shop, three stalls away from Obioma's mother's shop, as he always did – arms folded, staring blankly ahead in seemingly deep reflection – but when he noticed Obioma's approach his eerie gaze followed him, prompting Obioma to run past Augustus's shop as quickly as he could.

Augustus had a face that Obioma believed could never endear him to anyone, a fat, round face riddled with folds of skin, all settled in a perpetual grimace. It was Augustus's face that Obioma saw whenever his mother talked about principalities and demons. This mingled with the other demons that Obioma had witnessed wreaking havoc in *Evil Dead*, a film he deeply regretted staying up to watch once when his parents were away.

Obioma knew that Augustus had once told Obioma's mother in an altercation that her brother had died because he was greedy, that Festus had amassed stockfish bales that he couldn't possibly sell in twenty years but still wanted more, and that he died trying to bolster his supplies.

Obioma knew that, barely a month after Festus's death, Augustus and four of the other traders on the row had offered to buy up his late uncle's stock and take over his store for a fraction of its value. His mother had refused the offer and had given up her *mamaput*, her canteen business, on the other side of the city to take over her late brother's store. Apparently, this had angered Augustus and the other scheming traders, so they ensured Obioma's mother was refused membership of the Owerri Stockfish Sellers' Association, which they controlled. At least, this was how his mother put it.

Tales about Augustus's latest ploys to undermine Obioma's mother's business often dominated weekend lunch and daily dinner-table discussions at Obioma's home. Obioma believed that this was also what his parents often talked about deep into the night, as they lay in bed in their bedroom, their inaudible murmuring floating into his room, punctuated by his mother's dry cough which flared up every now and again.

The night before had been the same. Obioma had caught the gist of their discussion as he left the toilet cubicle wedged between his room and his parents'. Obioma's mother believed that the other traders on the row were angry because she would not abide by their price-fixing rules. They would not give her membership of the association, yet they expected her to abide by their policies. Almost all of the traders on the row had to go to Aba to buy stockfish more expensively from middlemen, so, the week before, they had sent the most docile amongst them to sheepishly ask Obioma's mother to give the entire aisle access to her supplier, a long-running associate of her late brother whom she had maintained contact with, who owned ships that went to Iceland and Norway.

Many times, Obioma's mother had told of how her brother had met her current supplier by pure chance. The father of a good friend of Festus had once worked on a Norwegian ship. Months before Festus's death, Festus made his first trip to Norway with him and had met with the owners of the largest stockfish production business in Scandinavia.

Obioma's mother would talk of the acres of coastal land her brother described, all lined with wooden racks many metres tall and wide on which thousands of cod, halibut and other fish hung in the open air. It was a place cold enough to keep the fish from rotting but not so cold that they became frozen, and after a few months they would become as dry as wood: stockfish.

Obioma's mother would mention during this discussion how her brother had agreed with the people he met in Norway to buy stockfish in larger quantities at a much cheaper price. He had planned to become a wholesaler, selling stockfish to traders all over the south-east of Nigeria and beyond. Obioma's mother would go on to claim that the wholesalers from Aba, who sold fish to the other traders on the aisle, had overheard her brother talking to the captain of one of the ships that delivered stockfish to Onne, and had immediately informed the other traders on her aisle, claiming that Festus planned to put them all out of business. Obioma's mother would also tell of how the traders secretly met to discuss Festus's association with the importers, and how Augustus and a few other traders approached a witch doctor to put a stop to Festus's plans.

"This is when they decided to kill Festus," his mother would conclude with a steely look on her face, a look that stayed with Obioma and which made Augustus's already scary face even more terrifying. This was also why Obioma took his mother seriously when she warned him and his sister never to greet or talk to any of the other men and women who sold stockfish on the aisle, or even to their children.

Obioma eventually arrived at the entrance to his mother's shop, which was bustling with activity in stark contrast to the rest of the aisle. Several large, middle-aged women dressed in rolls of silver- and gold-threaded wrappers arrived and left with their bulging shopping bags. Some ran large eating houses in Owerri, and arrived with one or two servants who did the heavily lifting and carrying for them.

Obioma wriggled in between the women and was soon engulfed in the invisible concoction of fumes from the perfumes they wore and the ever-present smell of dry fish from the thousands of stockfish stuffed into every shelf, corner and crevice in his mother's shop.

He tip-toed and shimmied his way through the crowd of women, his eyes expectantly fixed on the large ceiling fan that dangled in the middle of his mother's shop, which, despite his longing for fresh air, blew back stale-smelling, fishy gusts. His stomach began to churn painfully again. He spotted his mother at the far end of the shop. Her frazzled look was exacerbated by the beads of sweat which rolled off her forehead, and by her scattered hair, which she normally combed into a neat afro style but which at that time floated awkwardly and haphazardly with every gesture and movement she made. The calculator in one hand, the wad of naira notes in the other and the head-tie secured around her skinny waist were all sure signs that she was too busy to be approached.

Sebastian, her second cousin who had recently become her assistant, was not faring any better at the other end of the shop. His diminutive stature was almost cloaked by the large women and their servants hovering over him, as he counted and recounted wads of cash handed to him.

Obioma retreated to the quiet back room of his mother's shop, his stomach churning and a bout of dizziness momentarily overcoming him.

This room was also full of stockfish, though, rather than being stacked individually on shelves, the large broad fish were stuffed into bales and piled high on top of each other. The largest haul of stockfish yet lay in the shop's basement store area, which Obioma's late uncle had had specially built a few years before he died.

Obioma had only been down there on a handful of occasions. The ceiling of the basement was not very high, but the space stretched at least two shops beyond his mother's shop area on each side. It was also where his mother kept all of her money. Festus always dealt in cash and never used banks, and Obioma's mother followed suit. A large safe, bolted to the floor and reinforced with steel and concrete, stood just at the foot of the narrow stairs that led up from the basement to the back room. Inside the safe itself, old, crumpled naira notes, neatly gathered and organised into 10,000-naira wads, sat in large plastic bags.

Obioma half considered going down to the basement to get a five-naira note. His mother would never notice, he was sure. But at that moment the fate of Cletus Oyeima, the most recognisable pupil in his school, came to his mind. Cletus was known for having the latest toys and gadgets, which he regularly brought to school. During break periods, pupils would flock around him at the canteen area at the far end of the school compound known as Choppoint – a place where a handful of local caterers were permitted by the school to sell their wares: small tin-cups of *jelloof* rice and *moi moi* bean pudding, and the deep-fried pieces of flattened baking dough mixed with chilli and salt known as *dieti*.

On a typical afternoon, Cletus usually bought a handful of *dieti* slabs, two or three bottles of Fanta and tins of rice and *moi moi*. He stuffed his face full until he was almost sick, and what was left was either snatched out of his hands or given away to the scores of begging pupils that constantly hung around him like flies. This was until one hot Tuesday afternoon in January when the headmistress appeared at the balcony of her office and began to ring her large iron bell frantically.

Obioma remembered that day like it was yesterday. Pupils were ushered out of their classrooms by their teachers and instructed to line the balconies of the school buildings that overlooked the large field in the middle of the school compound. Minutes passed as the pupils looked expectantly out onto the middle of the large empty playing field, a barren stage of scorching hot sand and various patches of dry grass. Moments later, the headmistress made her way down the stairs and out onto the middle of the field.

The scorching sun, the wraps of brocade around her and the large head-tie sitting on her head all forced her to mop up gushes of sweat from her forehead and the top of her cleavage.

"Good afternoon, children," she bellowed out at the top of her voice, a greeting that bounced around the buildings that surrounded the large patch of playing ground.

"Good afternoon, madam," the pupils responded resoundingly.

"Good afternoon, children," she shouted out again even louder.

"Good afternoon, madam," they responded even more loudly.

"I have decided to follow Jesus, I have decided to follow Jesus, I have decided to follow Jesus, no going back, no looking back," she sang loudly, gesturing for a clap-along, which took off instantaneously.

"Now your turn. One, two, three, go!" she prompted.

"I have decided to follow Jesus..." the pupils responded, clapping in rhythm.

As Obioma and the other pupils sang the lines, the headmistress waved her arms about in a sort of dance right where she stood. The singing carried on for a few more minutes until a tearful woman whom Obioma recognised as a trader from the Old Market walked to the middle of the field to join the headmistress. When the headmistress caught sight of the woman, she raised and dropped her arms at the conclusion of the last verse of the song, causing an eerie and ominous silence to fall upon the school.

"Do you know why I have asked you to sing this song?" the headmistress barked out, to the clueless faces that surrounded her.

"I said, do you know why I have asked you to sing that song?" the headmistress screeched.

"No, madam," a handful of students eventually responded in a mis-timed chorus, causing a lingering murmur.

"It is because some of you have decided to follow the devil," she barked sharply.

"As young as you are, you – yes, you – you have decided to follow the devil." She gesticulated accusatorially, pointing in turn at different sections of pupils in the balconies around her.

"This woman, Mrs Oyeima, lost her husband three years ago. She is a trader in the Old Market, toiling to make sure her family is taken care of, but her son Cletus has been stealing and squandering all of her money.

"But, as you know, 'many days for the thief, but one day for the owner'.

"Cletus was caught red handed yesterday stealing over two hundred naira. *Two hundred naira.*

"Cletus has stolen over one thousand naira from his own mother this term alone. You all know him and have probably been eating that money with him. His mother has brought him here today to show you what happens to thieves, so that nobody repeats what he has done. Mr Nwankwo, bring him out here."

Obioma remembered a strange hush falling over the school as Cletus was led out to the field, naked, from the back of one of the school buildings. His face was doused in luminescent robin-blue powder and the rest of his body was painted with dark charcoal. Shivering in the baking sun, Cletus initially stood alongside his weeping mother, who blew her nose uncontrollably. Obioma and the other pupils looked on as the middle-aged and usually mild-mannered Mr Nwankwo stood guard gingerly behind Cletus, looking like an imposter in his new school-disciplinarian role. His flogging cane slipped from his grasp on at least two occasions, and his knees seemed as though they were going to buckle from all the attention directed around where he stood.

Dissatisfied that Cletus was not visible enough, the headmistress walked over to him and led him further out into the centre of the field, with Mr Nwankwo in tow.

"Stand there where they can see you," she instructed sternly, before gesticulating to the pupils all around to clap in rhythm again.

"*Cletus onye oshi, oshi adịghị mma, Cletus onye oshi, oshi adịghị mma*" (Cletus the thief, stealing is not good). Obioma listened and watched as the headmistress sang this over and over again to the rhythmic claps. When she was convinced that she had repeated the chorus enough times for the words to be memorable, she instructed the pupils to sing.

As the pupils sang, the headmistress picked up the flogging cane that had once again slipped from Mr Nwankwo's hand and, to the soundtrack of the pupils' stunned and frightened voices, she held Cletus by his shoulder while her right hand delivered at least twelve stinging strokes of the cane to his bare, charcoal-painted buttocks.

When Cletus could not take any more strokes, he bit at her hand and made a run for it. Obioma and the pupils watched Cletus's unsuccessful attempt to circumnavigate the ring of teachers that quickly closed in on him as he ran. They dragged him back to the headmistress kicking and screaming, and that afternoon he would receive a further twelve strokes of the cane.

The events of that afternoon meant that Obioma quickly discarded any thoughts of raiding his mother's safe for the five naira. But he did give in to his hunger, and took advantage of the fact that he was alone in the inner room to tear off a chunk of dried fish which was protruding from one of sealed bales of stockfish placed in the corner of the room – a sizeable piece which he struggled to chew. Obioma wrestled with the piece of fish, clutching on to it with both hands as his stomach growled even more loudly. This was when his mother walked into the back room with one of her customers.

"*Mma*, good afternoon." Obioma greeted her nervously with a mouth full of fish and his hands hidden behind him. He was sure that his pathetic attempt to conceal the chunk of stockfish in his hands had not worked. The woman who accompanied Obioma's mother into the inner room smiled at him in a way that let Obioma know that he had not succeeded.

"Obioma," his mother began. She sounded more embarrassed than annoyed, but he still expected a telling-off from her, as well as an exact estimation of how much the chunk of fish he had just bitten was worth.

"Did you not see the *garri* and *egusi* soup I left for you at home? Do you want people to think you are not being fed well?"

"*Mma*, I came straight here," Obioma responded, but his mother had already disappeared down the hatch into the basement, and in moments had dragged up a 45-kilo bag of stockfish. Obioma took this opportunity to spirit away the chunk of stockfish which he held in his left hand behind him, into the pocket of his school shorts.

"Norway cod, 50 to 70cm, full bale, 45 kilo," his mother said in between her momentarily heavy breathing.

"*Ego ole?*" the woman enquired.

"Twenty thousand naira total," Obioma's mother announced after an elaborate and protracted series of punches into her calculator. Obioma watched as the woman shook her head disapprovingly, before inspecting the large bale of stockfish which Obioma's mother dragged in front of her for a closer look. The woman broke a small piece from one of the fish protruding from the bale, chewing on it while maintaining an expressionless face.

"I'll give you fifteen thousand?" the woman eventually offered, saying that the fish was average and that if she went any higher, she would incur a loss at her eating house.

"*Mba*, eighteen thousand, last price." Obioma watched his mother respond in her conclusive, almost annoyed tone. She had broken an even larger piece of fish from the same bale and stuffed it into her mouth, rebutting the woman's comments about the quality of her fish and lamenting the loss to her own business if she sold at a lower price.

"Seventeen thousand, five hundred," Obioma watched the woman counter-offer, and after some initial reflective slow shaking of the head, Obioma's mother nodded. The woman loosened one of the many layers of expensive wrapping cloths around her waist and untied a bulge at one end of the lacy wrapper to reveal folded wads of naira notes.

Obioma's mother counted and recounted the money offered to her and momentarily disappeared back down the hatch to store the money in her large safe in the basement. By the time she resurfaced, Obioma had negotiated a ten-naira fee with the woman for the service of carrying the bale of stockfish back to her eating house, a thirty-minute walk away.

6 OCDA

"Į guzo ọtọ na-agụ ngwere ma ọdụ ekweghị ya"

"The lizard would like to stand erect, but his tail will not permit him"

(Traditional Igbo proverb)

Two weeks later

The pristine engine of the brand new Peugeot 504 saloon car ground to a halt as the first light of dawn began to show, but not before Obioma's father had revved it repeatedly until everyone awake in their neighbourhood peeked out of their windows to see how beautiful it looked. The car's silvery body and chrome bumpers gleamed and sparkled even in the dim morning light, and the two gold-frilled flags of the national green-and-white colours and the Nigerian coat-of-arms hoisted at the front of the car's bonnet fluttered regally in the dry morning hamatan winds.

"Papa Obioma, fine motor," one of their neighbours, a trader, remarked as he padlocked the latches to his live-in shed, which stood alongside the run-down five-storey building that Obioma and his family lived in.

The large building had ten flats, five on either side of a concealed staircase that ran down the middle. Obioma's family lived in one of the two flats on the top floor of the building. There were eight such buildings on the cul-de-sac, and a few others dotted around the neighbourhood. Shabby live-in sheds made from corrugated zinc roofing sheets, like the one Obioma's neighbour had just stepped out of, carpeted the pockets of land

25

around the tall apartment blocks. These sheds eventually merged with the Old Market, about quarter of a mile away.

Still seated in the driver's seat, Obioma's father looked disdainfully at the shed beside their building as his neighbour disappeared in the direction of the Old Market.

That should not be there, he thought, his stern gaze focused on the large, fading red *X* marked on the side of the shed. Underneath it was the acronym *OCDA*: Owerri Capital Development Authority. He knew the mark had been made on the structure about three years earlier, *when the government considered people living in the area to be human beings*, he lamented to himself. Anywhere else and it would have been swiftly demolished along with the others, particularly in the well-to-do neighbourhoods on the outskirts of the city.

His gaze shifted to the thick, peeling electricity cables that draped down into some of the other sheds, dangerously criss-crossing the balcony of one of the two flats on the ground floor of his building. Another trader had just moved in to one of the second-level flats, Obioma's father suddenly remembered. The flat had only recently been vacated by a Ghanaian optician and his wife, who had decided to move back to Ghana of their own accord, rather than be caught up in the wave of mass deportations that was going on. It was common knowledge that the newly arrived trader was storing all manner of goods in his home and in one of the sheds downstairs which he had also rented: noisy livestock and large quantities of near-rotten, foul-smelling foods, which he regularly ferried back and forth between his shops and his home in a large van. There were also rumours that he was constantly drafting in relatives from his village to assist in his shops, with as many as five sleeping in a single room.

"Illiterate traders," Obioma's father muttered under his breath to himself, before remembering that his wife was one. The details of a big row he had had with her about moving away from the neighbourhood came rushing back into his mind.

"They have started selling land in Ikenegbu. We should make plans to move," Obioma's father had said as he and his wife lay in bed late one evening. "How much money do you have these days in that safe of yours at your shop?" he remembered adding, even though his wife had remained silent.

"That does not concern you," Obioma's mother had eventually responded in an angry tone that, in hindsight, he knew he should have taken as a sign not to press any further; but he had.

"What do you mean, it does not concern me?"

"Julius, it's my money. It does not concern you."

"It does concern me. You are my wife," Obioma's father had insisted.

"If you want to buy land, use *your* money to buy land," Obioma's mother had suggested, knowing that he made less in a month as a driver for the state civil service than she took in a week at her shop.

"Leave your job and open another store in the New Market. The stockfish we have will be more than enough for both stores," Obioma's mother had concluded, a suggestion she had made many times before. Obioma's father could not imagine anything worse, and with that thought his gaze settled back on the dilapidated shed that had prompted his deep pondering. He decided it was time to get out of his car and head towards his apartment block.

The day had not fully dawned yet, and Obioma's father stumbled up the closed stairwell in near-pitch-black darkness with two large carrier bags in his hands. Every time he reached a new flight of stairs he placed the bags he was carrying down by his feet and gave the light switches yet another fruitless try, though he knew that the city had just suffered a power outage which was unlikely to be repaired by NEPA, the electricity authorities, for hours.

He got to their flat, unlocked the front door and made his way to the refrigerator, in the corner of the dining room, which was cordoned off from the living room by some hanging curtains. Obioma's mother emerged from one of the bedrooms carrying a kerosene lantern.

"It is already morning: NEPA has just taken the light," Obioma's mother said.

"The Commissioner's wife gave us some meat. Some pork and beef," Obioma's father responded.

"We have not seen you in a week," his mother said.

"First I had to go to Port Harcourt and collect the Commissioner's new car, then I drove him to Lagos for the Ministers' Conference, and when we got back I had to drive the Commissioner to…"

"It has still been a week since your children saw you last," Obioma's mother insisted, interrupting him. Obioma's father decided it was better not to say anything else. He silently transferred packets of meat wrapped in cellophane bags from the carrier bags into the freezer compartment of their refrigerator. Obioma's mother announced that she was going back to bed and headed back to the bedroom, as the sudden buzzing sound of the fridge announced the return of electricity to the neighbourhood.

Obioma's father checked his wristwatch. It was quarter past five in the morning, which explained why there was none of the usual citywide fanfare and cheering that usually greeted the restoration of power. His mind returned to the real prospect of yet another row with his wife that morning.

She is resentful that I am no longer begging her for money, Obioma's father concluded as he pondered the changes that had occurred in recent months. Things were finally looking up at work, especially following his recent promotion to chief driver to the Commissioner for Industry, Chief Dr

Lewis Amamuta. For over fifteen years, Obioma's father had languished as a pool driver at the secretariat. Now he no longer ran pointless errands, ferrying boxes of files and insignificant civil servants here and there for a measly salary. He was pleased with himself that a year ago, he had finally saved up enough money, and plucked up the courage, to drag a medium-sized goat, a bag of rice, a bale of stockfish and three thousand naira to the Assistant to the Head Secretary of the Commissioner, to ensure that the latest of the eleven applications he had made over the previous seven years for one of the three roles of driver to the Commissioner was placed at the top of the pile. The move had paid off and his new salary, including all the extra allowances, was almost triple his old monthly intake. Now all he needed to do was to remain at the beck and call of the Commissioner and his wife, and the gifts would keep coming in. He was almost halfway through payments for a second-hand car, a twelve-year-old Datsun 140J saloon – a former taxi which had no front passenger door following a crash, but which Obioma's father knew could be fixed in no time. He imagined the look on his wife's face when he finally got custody of his car, making all her mockery and nagging worth it. Next will be a plot of land in the suburbs, he thought.

7 GAME OF MOSQUITOS

"Anaghị ata ọkukọ uta ọ bụrụ na nri ghere oghe"

"The chicken is not to blame if the food is left uncovered"

(Traditional Igbo proverb)

That morning

When Obioma awoke that morning he could hear his sister talking to his mother in the next room. Obioma had no particular strong thoughts about his younger sister, Ogechi, who had just turned six years old, and whose life revolved around plaiting the hair of old dolls with no arms and legs. The constant painful itch of the mosquito bumps on Obioma's legs, arms and face, already scratched raw, epitomised something more profound about how Obioma now understood the world worked. Obioma remained within the confines of the apparently not-so-secure mosquito net which was draped over four metal posts welded on to his small bed. A crisp twenty-naira note lay beside him, placed there by his father, who had tiptoed into his room earlier that morning, having just returned from a week-long work trip.

But these things could not stop Obioma's mind from dwelling on the events of the evening before.

After dinner with his mother and sister, he had taken the short stroll to Kalu's house. They were sitting on the fading floral carpet that spanned the length and width of Kalu's living room when Success's face appeared on the TV screen. It was the local television station's news programme.

"The police are still trying to calculate just how much this man swindled from a number of schools in cities around the south-eastern region of the country, including Owerri," the newscaster said, as a cropped picture of Mr Success's round and reluctantly smiling face beamed out from the television set.

"Is that the same guy you were telling me about?" Kalu's father, who lay sprawled on one of the large couches in the living room, had been distracted from his newspaper by Obioma and Kalu's surprised gasps.

"Yes, that is the guy, Pa," Kalu responded.

"Very clever man indeed," Kalu's father said.

"*Ego ole ka ọ napụrụ?*" (How much did he swindle?) It was very much like Kalu's father to laugh at a time like this, Obioma thought to himself. He had laughed when his neighbours' car was stolen, branding them stupid for not using a steering wheel lock. He was apparently pleased when the shop adjacent to his had been broken into and robbed clean, as it meant less competition for him. He had looked on with indifference from a distance when the roof of one of his neighbours' houses had been blown away in a rainstorm, while other neighbours had rushed to help them salvage their furniture. Kalu's father reminded Obioma of Augustus and all the other traders on his mother's aisle.

Headteacher after headteacher appeared on the news programme giving accounts of Success's ill-fated visits to their schools. Obioma watched as Kalu set about calculating how much Success had stolen, while Kalu's father offered guesses as to how many schools and pupils there were in the states that had been hit by Success's scam.

"Don't forget Aba – there are at least fifty schools in Aba," he highlighted.

As Kalu concentrated on his calculations, Obioma remembered how the intense rehearsals of the French song had continued right up to the day marked out for their school singing competition. So taken in were teachers and the headmistress that a large marquee and sound system had been installed on the playing field in the centre of the school. A large luxurious bus had been booked to ferry the winning class to the state finals, three days after the school heats.

The day on which Mr Success was supposed to arrive to officiate the school heats passed unremarkably, except for the growing unease in the school as the hours ticked by without any sign of anything happening. No one had heard from Mr Success after his last brief visit to collect the administration charge from the school's headmistress. Even so, despite Mr Success's no-show, teachers continued to oversee the usual rehearsals for a few more days. After about a week, things began to unravel. In the middle of afternoon recess, a lone uniformed policeman appeared at the school gates and was watched closely by pupils as he made his way up to the headmistress's office. Minutes later, teachers began to gather at the headmistress's office, cramming the passageway and balcony area. Their apparent emergency meeting that afternoon lasted only minutes, and as the policeman left the school premises teachers briefly stood outside on the field in small groups, speaking in hushed tones.

The characteristic authoritative tone of Mrs Añara's voice vanished for at least a week after her return from the brief meeting. Like the teachers in the other classrooms, Mrs Añara mentioned in passing that there would be no trip to France, but she did not explain why. As the days passed, pupils stood in groups during break time sharing accounts from relatives, friends and neighbours about Mr Success's visits to schools across the city. The police were now looking for Mr Success.

Rumours began to circulate that he was from a far-flung state in the west of the country; others reckoned that he was from as far away as Cameroon, and that he had now fled back there. Rumours also began to spread that Mr Success was now moving around the country dressed as a woman.

"How much?" Kalu's father bellowed as he grew impatient with Kalu counting and double-checking his sums on a writing pad strewn with calculations.

"Twenty-one million, nine hundred and sixty-one thousand naira," was the figure Kalu finally announced that Mr Success had got away with. This was greeted with a rapturous cheer from Kalu's father, followed by a protracted fit of laughter.

The memory of the hearty, mocking laughter that spewed out of Kalu's father now caused Obioma to break out of his pondering and proceed with the delicate job of locating the mosquitos' point of entry into his net, accompanied by the itching of his bumps and the buzzing sounds of mosquitos still trapped inside the net. He soon discovered and tied a knot in a large tear in one of the corners of the old netting, before setting out to hunt down the remaining insects one by one. After some brief manoeuvring and clapping, the dirty deed was done and he rubbed his bloodstained hands clean against the sides of the shorts he had slept in.

8 ONE NAIRA FROM EACH CITIZEN

"Wisdom is like fire. People take it from others"

(Traditional Hema proverb, DRC)

As the weeks rolled by, the hamatan winds grew stronger and dustier, the days and the nights colder. The school term was drawing to a close. As anticipation of the various approaching end-of-year festivities grew, thoughts faded of a trip to France that was never to be. Christmas carols took over, constantly blaring from the speakers on the great road.

On the very last day of school, Obioma, Nneka and the other pupils took advantage of a morning free of lessons to play in the low-hanging cool morning fog that had settled over the school playing field. Obioma held Nneka's hand tightly as they ran through the fog. As they did so, Obioma thought about the long, unpaved dusty village roads that stretched for miles, roads he would soon be running and playing on. He and his cousins would often race barefoot down the earthy stretches of road, cutting through the fog just as he now did with Nneka. He wished Nneka could be there with him too.

"I wish you could come to the village," he said aloud, slowing down their running pace.

Nneka smiled as she wriggled out of his grip, disappearing deeper into the thick fog. Her bright gap-toothed smile lingered in his mind as he gave chase, the rapid but light sound of her unique loping gait giving her position away. He caught up with her in no time.

"Do you think your mum will let you come?" Obioma asked her. She shook her head, her frown suggesting she had taken his question as a slight.

32

"Do you think your mum will let you stay with us here, instead of going to your village?" Nneka responded sharply. Obioma knew from the handful of times that she had met his mother that Nneka did not like her. This was not helped by the snide remarks Obioma's mother regularly made, like the suggestion that it was time for a re-plait of Nneka's hair or that she needed a new, less shabby school uniform.

"Well, do you?" Nneka demanded before wriggling free from Obioma's grip once again.

After an unsuccessful search for Nneka through the thick blanket of fog, Obioma walked back to the mound of sand next to their classroom block. He remembered that rainy day that Nneka's mother had sat him and Nneka down, and how they had agreed to keep up the act of brother and sister until it was time to reveal to the world that they planned to get married. He also remembered what had happened that very night when he had broken the news to his parents as they sat around the table to eat supper. He had announced that he had joined another family and Nneka was now officially his sister.

"My young man, you are only ten and you are already taking a wife," his father had quipped, Ogechi sniggering along with him even though she didn't understand what was being said. Obioma had been shocked that his father had already seen through the plan, but his father was the least of his worries.

Predictably, his mother had reacted just as she always did when matters of grave importance arose — she had convened an emergency family meeting right there at the supper table. After a lengthy session of negotiation, it had been agreed that Obioma could spend time with Nneka and her mother at their stall, but only for a maximum of three days a week.

"So you can also play with the boys around where we live and not turn into a girl," his mother had explained. Additionally, Obioma could refer to Nneka's mum only as 'Aunty'.

Though far from ideal, this was a far better deal than Obioma had thought he would get. With a firm nod, Obioma had agreed to the terms, delivered in serious tones by his mother, against the backdrop of his still-sniggering father and sister. Obioma was sure he would never get his mother to agree to him spending the entire holidays with Nneka and her mother.

Interrupting Obioma's thoughts, Kalu walked up and sat beside him.

"I have been thinking about Success," Kalu announced. Obioma thought that it was not at all unlike Kalu to still be contemplating the legacy of Success's actions long after it had completely departed the minds of other children and adults alike.

"There are eighty million people in Nigeria," Kalu announced to Obioma, pointing intently to a table in a book he retrieved from his school bag as he spoke. "What if we were to get one naira from each one of them?"

"Like Success?" Obioma responded, a thought that was not immediately agreeable to him.

"Not quite, but what if we sold something that every single person needed?"

"Like what?" Obioma asked.

"I'm not sure about that yet."

9 RIPE AND READY

*"Ihe aghutara na eze̖ ad*i̖*ghi̖ eju O̖nu̖"*

"No one gets a mouthful of food by picking between another person's teeth"

(Traditional Igbo proverb)

Two weeks later

Ten thousand acres: that's how much land Kalu believed was necessary to plant enough palm trees to produce the quantity of oil needed to sell to everyone in the country. This included the land required for the buildings and open spaces where the palm fruits would be converted to oil.

Palm oil. Everyone uses palm oil, Obioma suggested enthusiastically that last day of school. This struck a chord with Kalu and in just moments they had hatched the basic details of their new ambitious joint venture.

Kalu and Obioma planned initially to build wooden safe-boxes to save up the money they needed for their plans. After that they would buy land in Ohaji, a far-flung rural area at one of the state's borders. Obioma and his father often travelled there to buy palm oil, pounded yam and *garri* in bulk.

"Land here is very cheap," Obioma's father would often remark as the public minibus they travelled in sped past acres of forest area. This was news that was very much welcome to Kalu. After the land was acquired, Obioma and Kalu planned to plant palm trees across most of it, and when the trees reached maturity and bore fruit it would then be time to make the palm oil.

Kalu told Obioma how he had witnessed his maternal grandmother making palm oil in the village on many occasions. He brandished a hand-written note of the process which he had jotted down from his recollections.

Break apart the large thorny palm fruit bunches, each holding hundreds of palm fruits. Cook palm fruits in very large cast-iron pot under wood-fire, until softened and cracking open. Transfer in batches to large mortar and pound with pestle until juices start to run out and they are a mushy mess. Strain in straining cloth and then collect strained juices and pour back into large cast-iron pot. Boil again. Scoop bright red oil floating on the top of the water and place in an oil container.

"We will need at least five hundred old women for the amount of oil we are after," Kalu continued. "We will ask them to bring their own cast-iron pots, large mortars and pestles, sieving cloths and stools."

Obioma imagined the elderly women working in a football-pitch-sized field. Then he realised that they had not accounted for the heaps of firewood needed to cook the palm fruits. Trucks would also be needed, to send the oil to the distant markets. These would need to be either bought or hired. They would need to save a lot more money than they had initially planned.

This was why Kalu rekindled the errand-running arrangements he had with his oldest brother Benjamin, despite the fact that he had grown uncomfortable with some of the chores. At twenty-two, Benjamin was twelve years Kalu's senior. They were half-brothers. Benjamin was the first and only child of his father's first wife, who had died during childbirth.

Kalu had always been aware of Benjamin's ruthless streak. But ever since Benjamin had bought a rubber-vulcanising business, which he ran from a work-shed off the Owerri–Aba highway, his cutthroat tendencies had climbed to greater heights.

Helpless customers would regularly roll into the compound of his work-shed with punctured tyres, and Benjamin would always be on the ready with a number of nails in his pocket to discreetly make a couple more punctures to the deflated tyre tubes, warranting the need to buy and install brand new tyre tubes, which he in turn sold for a profit. Customers who had to leave their cars with him for collection at a later time would always have their vehicles vandalised, with Benjamin substituting all their new tyres for older ones and selling the newly acquired tyres to other customers. When business was slow, Benjamin would pay Kalu to strategically litter doctored nails along the highway in the vicinity of his work-shed. This was the last straw for Kalu, who walked away from his brother's crooked business practices. Now that he needed the money more than ever, Kalu had agreed to a fee of ten naira to clean his elder brother's room, a shack made entirely of corrugated zinc roofing sheets that was annexed to the old bungalow Kalu lived in with the rest of his family. He also agreed to clean his half-brother's old 1962 Vespa 150 GL, a scooter Benjamin had bought a year after he started his vulcanising trade.

"I think that one is ready," Benjamin leered at a group of teenage girls walking by that morning, as he idled in his armchair outside his shack next to Kalu, who was hard at work cleaning his brother's scooter.

"Do you know her? What is her name? Where does she live?" Benjamin enquired, interrupting Kalu's vigorous scrubbing of the tyres of his scooter.

"Which one?" Kalu responded grudgingly, knowing exactly where his brother's enquiries were leading.

"The one in the middle in red – are you blind?"

Later that day, Benjamin set his brother off on a new task.

"This is for you, if you get the job done," Benjamin said, grinning and brandishing a ten-naira note.

"That's not enough. Her father used to be a boxer. I will be pulverized if he finds out," Kalu protested, half hoping that what he had just said would lead his brother to abandon the venture altogether. Instead, another ten-naira note appeared out of Benjamin's bulging wallet. The sight of it prompted Kalu to begin, in his mind, to concoct further tales that he could deliver to his brother which might extract even more money from him.

"They did not want to come, so I gave them ten naira, which they refused, but then I offered them twenty naira and they agreed to be here at six o'clock like you said."

This was of course a lie. Kalu had actually only offered them five naira, promising more next time if they kept quiet about the arrangement. This meant that, in the end, almost twice as much money found its way into his new safe-box. Kalu knew very well that the teenagers he lured to his brother's shed did not need money to agree to come. They came because Benjamin was the only person his age who owned a scooter and who had a shed all to himself. A shed with a black Hitachi music system, which had twin cassette players, a turntable and various amplifying and equalising components, all stacked up next to a tall fridge-freezer in one corner. They came to watch dubbed pop music videos on his Sanyo 21-inch black-and-white television and the JVC VHS video player that sat on a low table adjacent to Benjamin's king-sized bed. There were only three other people who had video players in the entire neighbourhood.

Kalu knew that Benjamin's inept people skills meant that he had come to rely on him, Kalu, to satisfy his insatiable appetite for teenage girls. Kalu would often walk straight into the girls' homes, charming fathers and mothers alike with his manner and successfully delivering his message to his target.

10 EXODUS

"Anụ n'enweghị odu,chi ya na achụrụ ya ijiji"

"God swats flies for an animal that has no tail"

(Traditional Igbo proverb)

One week later

The old motor-park beside the Anglican Church in the centre of Owerri was filled with restless, sun-beaten commuters. Hordes more trooped into the motor-park with their luggage from the main road; Obioma, his father and Ogechi were amongst them. The usually plentiful ramshackle commuter minibuses were nowhere to be seen, and the long wait for everyone meant a bumper sales afternoon for the young boys and girls who hawked peeled oranges, *udara* fruits and trimmed sugar-cane from trays balanced on their heads. The same could be said for the men and women clutching several bottles of ice-cold soft drinks and cellophane bags of chilled water, all retrieved from their banks of coolers stashed under the far corners of the brick fence that surrounded the motor-park.

Since the close of schools in early December, Owerri had been steadily emptying itself out into the small motor-park and other departure points around the city, as people escaped to their respective villages for the Christmas break.

"Mineral water." Obioma's father spotted a hawker frantically calling out and swimming against the tide of bodies rushing into the motor-park.

38

When he was close enough, he swiftly grabbed two bottles of Fanta from the tall, lanky woman before taking the temperature, with the back of his hand, of the sweaty bright orange bottle.

"This Fanta no cold," Obioma's father complained in pidgin English as he studied the unfamiliar long and wide tribal marks on the hawker's cheeks.

"All of them, dey like that," she responded quickly.

"How much?" Obioma's father enquired hastily as it became apparent that the lady was contemplating handing the drink instead to an outstretched hand behind him.

"Ten naira."

Obioma's father promptly paid and hurried off to the far end of the motor-park, suitcase in hand. Obioma and Ogechi, each carrying a bag on their heads, were not too far behind him. Using their bags as seats, they all soon settled down under the sparse shade of an almost leafless mango tree and prepared themselves to be there all day.

It had already been a great year for the Eze family. Obioma's mother had announced that morning that it had been her most successful year of trading yet. She also seemed pleased that she was going to have a few weeks of peace and quiet on the home front while her husband and children were away. Ogechi finally had a new doll with all four limbs intact. For Obioma, the disappointment of not going to France was well and truly behind him, particularly given his new venture with Kalu and the various payments he had received for helping customers carry stockfish from his mother's shop – windfalls quickly added to the money in his safe-box.

"Julius, thank you for a job well done and for taking on all the extra work for my wife," the Commissioner had said to Obioma's father earlier that week in his office. Then he gave him a personal cheque for one thousand naira and the news that, on the recommendation of his wife, he had drafted in another driver, a young single man, to temporarily relieve Obioma's father from his duties, increasing his paid Christmas leave from one to three weeks. This was so that he too could be with his family over the holidays, the Commissioner explained.

The Commissioner and his wife meant well, but the gesture was completely misplaced, Obioma's father felt. He had deliberately shortened his usual three-week Christmas leave because of the opportunities that came with being a commissioner's driver at that time of the year – a time when fundraisers, anniversaries and luncheons were strategically staged up and down the country to rope in crowd-drawing celebrities and dignitaries, as well as well-off visitors from the diasporas temporarily home for Christmas. As early as September, the Commissioner's secretaries were swamped with the task of combing through heaps of invitations, whittling them down to the lucky few that the Commissioner would be gracing with his presence.

A week after the list was compiled and well before responses to the invitations were sent, Obioma's father got hold of the final list.

"Good morning sir, I am calling from the office of the Honourable Commissioner of Industry, Chief Dr Lewis Amamuta. Please can you confirm your car parking and security situation in case it is decided that the Commissioner will attend the opening of your bicycle assembly plant."

Obioma's father knew that whoever answered the phone would immediately place him on hold and scramble off to find the most senior person available.

"Good morning sir, this is Chief Engineer Okeke here, managing director of Allied Works."

"Good morning to you sir. I am Mr Eze, official driver to the Commissioner. I just want to confirm that there will be dedicated parking and security arrangements for at least two official cars, sir."

"Definitely, definitely, so the Honourable Commissioner is definitely coming?"

"I cannot confirm that absolutely at this stage, sir, we are still working on the shortlist, but I will try my absolute best."

"Please do, and of course I will see you personally when you arrive here with him."

"Ok sir."

All of his hard work was for nothing, Obioma's father grieved. He imagined how his temporary replacement would be handed brown envelopes stuffed with cash at each occasion he attended with the Commissioner, together with all the other gifts surplus to requirements that would be passed to him by the Commissioner's wife.

Besides all this, Obioma's father enjoyed sitting in the brand-new air-conditioned Peugeot 504 saloon car, ferrying the Commissioner and his family. He liked how the Commissioner's wife always treated him like a house guest, especially as drivers were typically invisible and treated the same as other live-in staff such as cleaners, gardeners and housekeepers. The Commissioner's young children, whom he dropped off and picked up from school, had come to refer to him as Uncle Julius, which was particularly pleasing to him.

This was why Obioma's father sat under the mango tree indifferent to the crowds of people that continued to pour into the motor-park, and oblivious too to the epic ruckus developing right next to him.

"This is the middle," Obioma yelled after a protracted period examining the bottle of Fanta his father had handed to him and his sister to share. Obioma picked up a pebble from the baking ground and marked the bottle at the spot.

"That's a lie." Ogechi shook her head vehemently. "*This* is the middle, drink to *this* point, *this* is the middle,"she insisted, snatching the bottle and pointing just above the scratch that Obioma had made with the stone.

"No, this is the middle," Obioma said, wrestling it back, and a shouting match ensued.

"That's a lie! You are being sly. You are always trying to be sly."

"Father, isn't this the middle?"

"The bottle is slim here at the top, so it looks like it's not the middle, but it is the middle," Obioma explained, handing over the bottle to his father under the untrusting and watchful gaze of his sister.

"He is right, Ogechi. That *is* the middle," Obioma's father finally concluded, after a careful inspection. "Ogechi, if you still don't agree, you could always have the first drink."

"Ogechi, you can have the first drink," Obioma offered almost immediately after his father had spoken, seeing the cleverness of the suggestion.

Just then, the bursting crowds in the motor-park were once again prompted to another frantic guessing game as a bus approached.

"Afo Enyogugu!" the young male conductor finally yelled, his upper torso dangling dangerously out of the half-shut slide-door of the minivan as it swerved into the motor-park compound.

A section of the crowd was immediately thrown into frenzy and scrambled to board the vehicle. In no time it was packed full of passengers and ready to leave, with the conductor at the last minute squeezing a couple more paying customers into the mass of squeezed, complaining bodies on board the van.

Obioma and Ogechi and their father waited one more hour before their bus arrived, an old yellow Mitsubishi Delica minivan which approached the compound tentatively. Obioma's father recognised it before anyone else in the motor-park did.

"That is definitely Donnatus," Obioma's father said as he sprang to his feet and raced towards the van, his bag in tow and Obioma and Ogechi in pursuit. The van pulled into the compound and slowed to a creep, but the conductor did not yell out the van's next destination to the rushing crowd. Instead, he scarpered off to the far end of the motor-park for some snacks and a drink. The driver emerged from the front of the car.

"My vehicle is faulty. It's not going anywhere," he announced at the top of his voice, warding off the approaching crowd.

"Donna *kedu?*," Obioma's father called out to his old classmate.

"*Nwannem*" (My brother), the man responded. "How far?"

"How is business?" Obioma's father enquired.

"Good afternoon," Obioma and Ogechi greeted Donnatus almost in unison as they caught up with their father.

"Afternoon. Junior. *Nne*, you two are growing fast," Donnatus responded, before turning back to Obioma's father. "Business is good, we thank God. Congrats! I heard you got a promotion."

"Yes, a few months ago now. I am working with the Commissioner for Industry, but I am on leave now until January."

"Wonderful. Are you going home? What of Mrs – is she going with you?" Donnatus asked, looking over Obioma's father's shoulder towards a tall, slim woman in the distance whom he, for some reason, had judged to be Obioma's mother.

"She is looking after the shop and will join us on the twenty-fourth," Obioma's father responded. "What about your van – are you fixing it today?"

"There is nothing wrong with it," Donnatus replied, the frown he had worn when he got out of his van momentarily returning to his face. "I just needed to catch my breath. We have been at it since five o'clock this morning. Plus some kids broke my wing-mirror earlier, rushing onto my van."

Donnatus ushered Obioma's father, Obioma and Ogechi to the front passenger seats of his van, before disappearing to the back of the van with their bags.

"Are they paying for it?" Obioma's father responded, as he observed the chunky, broken wing-mirror placed on the dashboard of the van.

"No. The bastards ran off as soon as they realised what they did. Let me urinate and come back, then we go," Donnatus said, before rushing off.

In no time, Donnatus emerged from an area of the motor-park overgrown with shrubs.

"Conductor, *loaduo moto*!" Donnatus barked out to his young conductor, who raced back to the car, munching on some biscuits and sucking out the last drops of fluid from the Coca-Cola bottle in his hand.

"Ebube Junction!" the conductor eventually yelled out after swallowing the last morsel of food in his mouth, and another mad rush towards the van ensued.

The mix of shabby one-storey buildings and bungalows that lined Owerri's roads were soon replaced by a tarred single carriageway flanked by trees and bushes. The van coasted up and down the undulating minor hills and, as it swerved to avoid the scores of potholes, it creaked under the strain of twice its capacity of passengers.

Ogechi diligently counted the large electric poles that lined the road, providing a running commentary on which ones were straight or crooked, and which ones looked old or new. Obioma tracked the progress of an aeroplane flying high up in the sky in roughly the same direction as they were travelling, half listening to his father and Donnatus as they briefed each other on which of their other classmates had died, were back in the village, had moved to Lagos, had been given chieftaincy titles, or had got ridiculously rich.

When the aeroplane finally disappeared and Obioma grew bored of the discussion between his father and the driver, he envisioned the vast palm-oil tree fields and the multitudes of jerry cans filled with palm oil. He imagined that the eighty million naira he and Kalu planned to make would be stored in an enormous metal safe-box, many times bigger than the wooden one his mother kept her money in, and that it would be buried deep under a portion of the palm-oil field. Then he changed his mind and imagined it to be made of concrete, buried in the ground somewhere on the palm-oil field, with a slit made of rubber which money could be pushed through, but which prevented water from entering.

The day's light had already began to fade when Obioma felt the light tapping of his father's hand on his head, and his father's voice asking him to wake up. He felt the chill of the cold hamatan evening as he, his sister and his father stepped out of the van and onto the side of the expressway, before the backdrop of a dense forest of tall trees. This was 'no-man's land'. The ever-present sound of crickets chirping seemed to almost drown out the heavy-duty engines of the handful of large touring motorcycles for hire. They appeared and vanished into paths and small dusty roads that cut through the dense bushes flanking the barren and lonely stretch of expressway, the only man-made objects for miles around.

The second leg of their journey involved hiring the services of a generously bearded man and his 1971 Honda SL 125 Enduro, which weaved through the intricate network of lonely, dusty roads and past the many mud-huts and bungalows dotted here and there on the way to Umuwe.

Ogechi sat at the front, straddling the motorcycle's petrol tank, taking the brunt of the rushing cold and dusty hamatan air, her eyes watering more profusely than those of the others as she grasped tightly onto the stem of the motorcycle's handlebars and tilted her head down.

Obioma was squeezed in between the fat, bearded motorcycle rider and his father, who managed to hold on to both his and Obioma's bags, even as the motorcycle dangerously tilted and swerved into and out of the maze of village roads.

Umuwe, Obioma's father's ancestral home, was made up of nine hamlets, all clustered around the very wide road that the motorcycle turned into, which also ran through a series of other villages. This was where Obioma would spent the majority of his long school holidays, staying with Iwuagwu, his father's only surviving brother, and his family.

Everyone here addressed their seniors with the title of 'Dede', even if they were older by only a few months. Obioma's uncle, Iwuagwu, often remarked that this had the magical effect of constantly reminding people that what came out of their mouths needed to be dignified and respectful.

"This is why Umuwe is always harmonious," Obioma remembered his uncle insisting.

The motorcycle slowed down when they arrived at Ama Egwu, Obioma's father's kindred village – partly because the roads and paths were even narrower and more intricate, and partly because the rider, who hailed from another area, was struggling to hear Obioma's father's directions over the high-decibel rattle of his motorcycle's engine.

Obioma smelled the various aromas of the soups being cooked in the compounds as they slowly rode past them. Distant dim lights from lanterns placed on dinner tables and flames from open-air cooking wood-fires flickered through the hedges and vegetation all around like welcoming beacons.

Obioma remembered how long days at the farm and happenings at the various village markets would be recounted over the same flickering kerosene-powered light. He thought about how adults conversed, conveying poignant and sensitive thoughts in confusing proverbs and idioms involving domestic and wild animals. Like the one about the tortoise who, when bandits came to his home to capture him, pleaded for a few minutes in which to trash his own house, explaining to the hoodlums that he wanted people to know that he had not given in to them without a struggle. It was a proverb Obioma had heard his uncle tell and tell again without any particular context.

Umuwe was a world away from the city of Owerri, Obioma thought. It did not have the tangled mesh of electric cables that dominated Owerri's skyline, roping across the city, indiscriminately weaving in and out of buildings in a mindless tangle. It did not experience the loud but short-lived euphoric citywide roars of jubilation that greeted the first brief flow of electricity through those cables. Neither did it have a network of decaying water pipes underneath its surface, and the puzzle of only a handful of buildings in the city experiencing the only occasional spurt of running tap water. Like the bungalow at the top end of Obioma's cul de sac in Owerri; its occupants initially saw this as good fortune, until, during one particular dry spell, they were besieged by about a quarter of the city carrying buckets or large jerry cans in wheelbarrows.

As the motocycle turned in and out of small dirt roads, Obioma remembered how the rainy season in Umuwe brought with it the tradition of dragging out all manner of containers and vessels of all sizes – anything that could hold water. All were strategically positioned under corrugated zinc roofs or sturdy wide-leafed shrubs. In the dry season, Umuwe residents would first raid the wells, streams and ponds before they dried up. Later, just as in the rainy season, water containers would again be dragged out of mud-huts and bungalows as loud cheers greeted the arrival of water tankers, days overdue.

Obioma saw his uncle's flickering lantern ahead.

PART 2

11 IWUAGWU

"Agwa ọjọọ nọkaria otu ọnwa, ọ bụrụ omenala"

"A bad habit that lasts more than a year may turn into a custom"

(Traditional Igbo proverb)

Minutes later

Bare-chested, with his patterned wrapper tied around his thin frame, Obioma's uncle was leaning over a stone in the centre of his compound, conscientiously sharpening his machete. This was almost exactly how Obioma remembered seeing him last.

As their motorcycle came to halt at the entrance of Iwuagwu's compound, Obioma's uncle walked up to them with his usual purposeful gait and broad smile. Tiny heels pounded the ground as Iwuagwu's two grandchildren, Obioma's second cousins, also emerged from amongst the bungalows and mud-huts that made up Iwuagwu's large compound.

"*Dede m, Dede m!*" screeched the young children as they hugged their arriving relatives, tugging and pulling at their bags. Obioma, expecting this, held his bag well over his head, the sound of colliding coins in his safe-box revealing the reason for his caution. His cousins eventually disappeared into one of the bungalows, as quickly as they had first appeared, along with his sister and the rest of their bags.

"*Dede.*" Obioma watched as his father greeted his older brother, and as they seized each other's hand in a handshake. Obioma knew this was as far as their pleasantries would go during their trip to the village. They were always at war with each other. This was why Obioma reluctantly dragged his bag towards the compound in very slow, deliberate strides, taking in the warm orange hue that emanated from the kerosene lantern hanging from a low branch of the *oha* tree, under which Iwuagwu had been sharpening his machete. The faint shadows of the tree's canopy and Iwuagwu's bungalows cast haphazard shapes on the barren compound grounds. A stream of smoke gushed out of a vent in the thatched roof of a mud-hut at the far end; the kitchen.

Obioma knew that his cousin's wife, Iwuagwu's daughter-in-law, was hard at work cooking the evening's dinner – *oha* soup, undoubtedly, given the aroma that hovered over the compound. The other end of the compound was like an abyss of pitch blackness: the portion that bordered the many miles of sprawling bushes and trees which marked the boundary between Umuwe and the neighbouring village. Obioma knew that his father's small mud-hut was somewhere just before those monstrously tall shadow-like trees. This was where Obioma's father would mostly be during their stay in the village, keeping out of his brother's way. The mud-hut was Obioma's father's old childhood room, now a family inheritance along with a sizeable chunk of the adjoining forest. The hut marked where Obioma's compound would have begun had they lived in the village.

These days, Obioma's father mostly returned to cocoon himself in his hut, browsing through stacks of old lifestyle magazines he had collected during the 1960s and 1970s. When he was not doing this he'd be listening to his small medium-waveband transistor radio. Obioma's father also regularly played his stash of vinyl records of highlife music on his old turntable, emerging occasionally at meal times to briefly check on his children, who lived in the main bungalows with their uncle and younger relatives. Obioma's father never attended kindred meetings, despite the fact that Obioma's uncle regularly made a point of strolling to his brother's hut to inform him of a meeting session commencing in the kindred's gathering place.

As Obioma waddled his way towards his uncle and father he overheard their exchanges, which were, unsurprisingly, building up towards one of their big rows.

"Julius, didn't your wife return with you?" Obioma heard his uncle ask his father with an exaggerated air of concern. Obioma had previously observed that something about his uncle's tone regularly rattled his father into a snapping response, and it was no surprise that evening to hear his father's annoyance ringing through in his voice.

"No, she is looking after the shop. She will join us on December twenty-fourth, just like last year."

Obioma knew it was time to quicken his pace towards his father and uncle.

"*Dede*, good evening," Obioma said as he seized his uncle's outstretched right hand with both of his.

"Nwagwu, *kedụ ka ị dị?*" his uncle responded, referring to Obioma by a name he had insisted on calling him weeks after Obioma's birth.

"The boy's name is Obioma. My wife and I named our son Obioma," Obioma heard his father sharply interject from the pitch blackness halfway across the compound, as his father headed to his hut. Unlike the year before, Obioma's father did not turn around that evening and walk back to confront his brother about his insistence on calling his son by the name 'Nwagwu'. Instead, he drifted into the darkness towards his retreat.

Like 'Iwuagwu', 'Nwagwu' was one of a handful of select traditional names usually given at birth to devotees of Agwu, the female patron deity of health and divination. It denoted a calling that was said to be indicated well before birth by the vivid and mesmerising dreams that plagued pregnant mothers and other relations of the child. Obioma remembered his uncle explaining this to him many years before, and he had learnt that his uncle had approached his parents about it shortly after he was born.

After extensive training, male devotees of Agwu would usually become Dibia: traditional doctors specialising in all sorts of practices, from soothsaying and clairvoyance to bone setting and mending, which Iwuagwu practised.

Obioma had been told how, just before he was born, Iwuagwu had pestered his pregnant mother and father with talk of signs that Obioma had been selected by Agwu to be her devotee, that the two-headed, blue-faced dog that constantly visited Obioma's mother in her dreams, muttering indecipherable messages to her, was, in fact, Agwu in one of her physical manifestations announcing that Obioma was to become her devotee. Obioma's uncle regularly recalled how he had rightly predicted to Obioma's parents when his mother was only weeks pregnant that Obioma would be a boy. Obioma had heard about how his father desperately hoped that he would turn out to be a girl, just to finally silence his meddling brother.

Despite all this, as Obioma walked to his uncle's bungalow to set down his things he knew that all that mattered on his trip to the village was being able to collect a substantial amount of money for his safe-box, particularly as he would need to match Kalu's contributions to their new palm oil venture.

12 THE APPRENTICE

"Nwata kwọzie aka ya o soro ndị okenye rie nri"

"A child that washes his hands well will learn to eat and dine with elders"

(Traditional Igbo proverb)

About two weeks later

A week before Christmas Day was an Nkwo Day, the last day of the Igbo four-day week and the last Nkwo in the traditional seven-week month. It was a day when the loitering goats and chickens that besieged the sleepy, deserted rows of wooden stalls and pegged shelters at the centre of Umuwe were chased away, as the market transformed into a place of frenzied trading.

Obioma firmly held on to the right leg of the screaming young man, pinning it firmly down to the caked bare earth. Iwuagwu glanced at Obioma with quiet pride as he pressed down firmly on the man's other leg with one hand, his free hand tracing the contours of the bones in that leg.

"It's broken in two places, *here* and *here*, but the bones have now been set in place. *Don't* move your leg!" Iwuagwu said sternly, as the young man winced in anguish.

"Healing will take time," Iwuagwu continued, "but I will first have to secure it in place." From this, Obioma knew to swiftly hand his uncle four short strips of manicured wood and coils of raffia twine. This sort of display of intuition greatly gladdened Iwuagwu. Earlier that morning, when

50

Iwuagwu had put him on the spot with a series of quizzes, Obioma had correctly responded that that very day was the fourth and final week of Onwa Ede Ajala, the twelfth and penultimate month of the Igbo year and the month that saw the end of the *okikie* ritual. This was a thing lost on many adults and young children in Umuwe, some of whom now gathered around the thatch-roofed stall held up by four pegs where Iwuagwu and Obioma plied their medical trade, one of many erected over the bare, dry red earth that spanned the entire village market.

This was where subsistence farmers with surplus-to-requirement crops and their regular trading counterparts congregated. They gathered amidst a contagion of smells, a sea of colours which ebbed and flowed, as the various patterned wrappers and costumes the women and men wore clashed gloriously with the bright yellow, green and red peppers on trays and tables, the brown, gold and silver shades of fresh and dried fish also on display, and the bristling afternoon sun. People poured in and out of the market, and this was how it would continue until just before dusk. Young boys and girls who lived in the vicinity of the market or who had accompanied their parents to shop or to sell deserted their guardians and gathered around Iwuagwu's surgery stall like flies, for the voyeuristic pleasure of seeing Iwuagwu's orthopaedic patients scream and squirm through their treatment.

Iwuagwu had initially been worried about Obioma's commitment to the job, fearing that deep down Obioma preferred to be in the position of these other children – free to mill about in an endless childish bliss, devoid of any real responsibilities. In fact, in the past this had very much been the case. A simple errand to get beverages from a nearby stall would have seen Obioma wander off for ages, and when he returned he would be full of implausible tales as he made excuses for his gratuitous gallivanting.

But Iwuagwu noticed that things had changed following Obioma's latest return to the village, observing the boy's new impatience to run errands and his prompt return. Iwuagwu also noticed how diligently Obioma dragged his new safe-box out from its hiding place, stuffing every single kobo he came across into it. This was why Iwuagwu now attached monetary gain to all the tasks he gave Obioma to do, particularly as this newfound interest in the work ran far deeper than running errands swiftly. Iwuagwu now often overheard Obioma murmuring various mnemonics he had devised for remembering the days and weeks of the month of the various traditional markets they attended. He also used these systems to remember the names of the various shrubs, roots and barks used in the preparation of medicines, and in what order and quantities these concoctions needed to be applied.

Obioma was like another boy altogether. His uncle remembered how just months ago he had had to regularly threaten Obioma with floggings and damning reports to his mother to get him to do even the most basic of chores.

Iwuagwu recalled how difficult it had been, years before, to come to the arrangement of their current apprenticeship, how the sustained lobbying of Obioma's parents, before and well after Obioma's birth, had not worked, and how, three years ago, he had adopted a more direct approach as he and Obioma trekked through the bush from family farmlands miles away from the compound. It was a trip he had purposely delayed until just after dusk, prompting the need to walk with touch-lights in the pitch-black moonless night.

"Do not step there," Iwuagwu said to Obioma in an alarmed tone, as they negotiated around a tall tree. Obioma was seven years old at the time.

"Pius's body once lay there," was the reply Iwuagwu had prepared for Obioma's puzzled look.

There were many stories about Pius's tragic death, and that evening Iwuagwu set about telling Obioma a version he was sure Obioma had no knowledge of. He talked of how Pius, their distant relative, had been called to the service of the Agwu deity just as Obioma had been called at birth, and how all his life Pius had refused this call, as a result suffering protracted bouts of mental illness. His misery had finally ended when he hung himself from the very iroko tree they were standing under. It was a cautionary tale of what happened to people who tried to escape the calling of deities.

"Agwu *bu mma iwu abuo*" (Agwu is a double-edged blade), Iwuagwu remembered continuing as they lingered in the dense bush. "Agwu is caring, kind and merciful because she is, after all, a female spirit, but she can be destructive and fiercely menacing too." Iwuagwu recalled having to temper his pitch to his young nephew, who looked visibly shaken. Obioma immediately stepped away from the spot where he had been standing and shone the torch he carried up at the tree, as if expecting to see Pius still hanging there. But this restraint did not last; it was not compatible with the plan, and Iwuagwu and Obioma's conversation about the deity dominated their entire trek back to the compound that evening.

"*Ara* Agwụ" (The madness of Agwu), Iwuagwu said, punctuating the brief silence that lingered after they exited the bush onto the long untarred road that led back to the village compound. "She uses it to torment the lives of those whose life choices go against her wishes, especially those who refuse her calling. Plagues of nightmares, illnesses, misfortune and insanity are deployed by Agwu to bend them to her will."

Iwuagwu told of how, as tradition would have it, Luffas Okere, a midget, and specialist in these matters, had to be called to climb up the tree and cut Pius down, because it was bad luck for anybody of normal height to touch Pius's body. This bad luck extended to anyone socially engaging with

Pius's immediate family until there was news that someone somewhere else had taken their life in a similar manner.

"Agwu is never, ever wrong."

Iwuagwu then told Obioma about Dr Ejike, the popular university-trained village doctor. Ejike's mother, just like Obioma's mother, had had vivid and strange dreams: visions of Agwu in the many forms and shapes she took. Iwuagwu explained to Obioma that, like his parents, Ejike's family had been afraid of the responsibilities that came with having such a child and, because of this, they had sent Ejike to Lagos to live with a family from his maternal home when he was ten years old. Ejike's parents had wanted Ejike to be an engineer, to learn how to build bridges and roads like the people he was staying with, but, instead, Ejike had returned as a medical doctor.

Iwuagwu had known that his plan had worked the following morning when his brother angrily approached him with accusations of frightening his son with stupid stories. Apparently, Obioma had approached his parents as they slept in his father's old hut, informing them that he wanted to start his training to be a healer with his uncle.

It was critical to win over Obioma's mother. This was why, three years ago, Iwuagwu had staged his stunt when Obioma's mother was present in the village, and used the opportunity of conflict with his brother to gather Obioma's parents to make his case.

He had known Obioma's mother would soften when he mentioned that, in addition to teaching him traditional medicine, he planned for Obioma to be a medical doctor like the well-liked Dr Ejike, the only university-trained medical doctor in Umuwe and even as far as Iyiala, twenty miles away, where Obioma's mother came from. Iwuagwu had known that she would see reason when he told her that Dr Ejike would be involved in his training from the very beginning, as he now regularly worked with Iwuagwu.

Iwuagwu had also been certain that Obioma's mother would be completely won over when he showed her several wads of naira notes fastened together by thin strips of palm leaves – a portion of his life savings which he had explained would pay for Obioma's university education and all the other costs of Iwuagwu's plans for Obioma.

13 ADANNA THE GREAT

"Where a woman rules, streams run uphill"

(Traditional Ethiopian proverb)

That evening

With dusk fast approaching, Obioma loaded the last of their bone-bending paraphernalia onto the bicycles that he and Iwuagwu had cycled to the market with that morning. Traders bellowed their farewells across aisles and the revving of various engines intensified as they scrambled to get their wares off the display tables and onto the back of motorcycles, into cars and vans.

Obioma and Iwuagwu did not immediately set off on their thirty-minute cycle home to Ama Egwu. Instead, they were headed for Umuwe Secondary School, a sprawl of new buildings beyond the vast football pitch that separated the market from the school. Iwuagwu was invited to attend a town meeting there. Obioma could not understand why Iwuagwu insisted on his attending a meeting that apparently would not include anyone his age.

Obioma had first heard of the meeting when the local town crier arrived with his *ogele* gong outside Iwuagwu's compound three evenings ago. "His Royal Highness, Eze Anthony Osondu summons to a meeting official representatives of the elders of each of the nine hamlets that make up Umuwe," the crier announced, beating his *ogele* intermittently as he reeled off details of the meeting.

Obioma had only seen the reigning Eze of Umuwe a handful of times.

The very first time, almost exactly a year before, Iwuagwu had pointed him out at the Nkwo market in Umuwe. The introverted tall and lanky man, whose mannerisms revealed no clues as to the high office he held, seemed no more important to Obioma than the conflict-shy market attendant who occasional stopped by market stalls to cajole traders to clean up the litter in front of their stalls.

The nine hamlets that made up Umuwe, including Ama Egwu, Obioma's village, had not always been joined together as one and presided over by an Eze, Iwuagwu had once explained to Obioma. Rule by monarchy was a very rare thing in almost the whole of Igbo-land and key decisions were generally taken by a committee of elders. Iwuagwu had also explained how the British colonial rulers had joined the nine hamlets together and called them 'Umuwe autonomous communities', a name borrowed from the historic co-operation of just three of the nine hamlets. And, as in other places they colonised, to make ruling easier for them the British had then installed an Eze to rule over the nine villages. Iwuagwu had also explained how some autonomous communities like Umuwe chose to replace dead or retiring Ezes by election, while others automatically installed the eldest son of the exiting Eze.

All these things were brought to mind for Obioma because of the woman who stopped by their stall just as they were about to leave for the Eze's meeting that evening. Lolo Adanna Akuoha slowed her brisk walk down the aisle when she spotted Iwuagwu and Obioma.

"You must be Nwagwu," she stated as she shook Obioma's hand, cutting him short halfway through his greeting.

"*Isi ukwu Kedụ.*" She greeted Iwuagwu with a nickname – Big Head – that Obioma had never heard. She was neither fat nor skinny and her neatly cut, short jet-black hair, which looked like it might have at some point been weighed down under a head-tie, was peppered with strands of grey. Obioma watched as his uncle and the woman embraced each other warmly and spoke with the familiarity of people who were already in the middle of a deep conversation.

"Adanna, how much are we looking for?" Iwuagwu asked.

"Approximately six million naira" she responded, as her face stiffened.

"Will evoking Nkuchi Nkwu be enough to raise that amount?"

"Not anywhere near, unless we are prepared to wait five years to complete the work. We will need donations from abroad and we need to see how much we can get out of those thieving bastards in government. But Nkuchi Nkwu could raise about two million naira," Lolo Adanna concluded as Iwuagwu fell silent in apparent worried thought.

"I will need your help to snuff out any opposition tonight. I hear Okoro and some of his friends abroad are not happy about our plans," she added.

"Say no more. I will do my part, let me not delay you any longer," Iwuagwu said, and with that Lolo Adanna Akuoha resumed her brisk walk down the aisle, disappearing round the corner.

"That is our real Eze," Iwuagwu said to Obioma as they cycled the short distance to the school compound. Lolo Adanna Akuoha was a recently retired principal of Umuwe Secondary School and the wife of the late Chief Rufus Akuoha. Obioma now understood that she and Iwuagwu must have been very close when they were younger, just as they seemed to be now, but Iwuagwu had never discussed this.

Lolo Adanna Akuoha was also daughter to none other than Major Henry Okubi, who had hailed from a neighbouring kindred in Umuwe. Iwuagwu had mentioned that he had died in the Biafra war, but not before flying missions to airfields in Port Harcourt and Benin, single-handedly taking out three expensive enemy aircrafts and almost half a battalion of enemy soldiers. As with her father, there were many stories about Lolo Adanna Akuoha. Obioma had heard one about how she loaded students of Umuwe Secondary School on to at least five buses for a trip to Owerri to protest the fact that they were studying under the shade of trees because of the lack of funds to rebuild classroom blocks damaged by storms as far back as the mid-1970s. When she got there, she had the students sing hymns and folk songs outside the Commissioner's office until he came out to meet them.

Another tale was of the time she slapped a male clerk in the Local Government Chairman's office for laughing as he tossed back her application to contest the Ezeship of Umuwe because she was a woman and there had never been a female Eze. Unlike on her trip to Owerri with the students, she did not get her way, but she got what she considered was the next best thing: the freedom to determine who would become Eze and the new title of Chair of the Umuwe Welfare Association. Earlier that week, when the town crier had arrived with his gong to announce HRH Eze Anthony Osondu's invitation to village heads, those in the know had understood that it was really Lolo Adanna Akuoha summoning them.

The new classroom blocks, as well as the large staff building where the meeting was to take place, had the slick appearance of the new banks that had recently been build in compounds along the Douglas Road in Owerri, with their smoothly plastered and painted walls and expansive tinted glass windows. With no dedicated Umuwe town hall, this was where all Umuwe meetings were held. Obioma could hear, somewhere in the compound, the hum of the generator that powered the bright ceiling- and wall-lamps that lit up the long corridors leading to the large staff-room.

Many of the elderly and middle-aged men who represented the

committees of the nine Umuwe hamlets had arrived and were already seated.

Obioma eventually settled quietly in a chair beside his uncle, in the front row of a bank of seats facing a high table. This was the seat in which Obioma eventually nodded off to sleep until it was time to go home, but not before he had heard snippets of Lolo Adanna's latest venture: plans to tax every household by commandeering a portion of their palm tree harvest, evoking Nkuchi Nkwu, to pay for a borehole that would supply clean water to the nine hamlets of Umuwe.

14 MONEY TREE

"You learn how to cut down trees by cutting them down"

(Traditional Bateke proverb, DRC)

The next day

Obioma's time at Dr Ejike's clinic was a far easier affair. That day, before his first ever session, Obioma walked up the pineapple-plantation-flanked path that led from near where Iwuagwu's compound was to Dr Ejike's clinic – an old bungalow which, despite the coats of paint poured over it, betrayed its age.

Obioma felt that he needed a break from pretending to fully understand the intricate relationships between the various deities and paranormal entities that Iwuagwu insisted he needed to understand – Chukwu, said to be the global all-creating entity, and Chi, which Iwuagwu depicted as a tiny personal god that lived within everyone who was ever born, overseeing their navigation through life. Obioma's mind also wrestled with the concept of the many other themed, stand-alone deities whom Iwuagwu explained had to be placated and negotiated with during one's life's journey – Agwu, the deity of divination; Ekwensi and Alushi, whom Iwuagwu referred to as the testers, who presided over chaos, war and change; Njoku, the deity of Yam, responsible for prosperity and nobility; and Ndichie, a collective manifestation of dead people, which Obioma imagined, terrifyingly, as large crowds of ghosts who roamed about together and spoke in one loud eerie chorus.

Time spend at Dr Ejike's clinic was also much more profitable for

Obioma's safe-box. Iwuagwu was paying Obioma ten naira to visit Dr Ejike's clinic twice a week and to follow him about for around two hours each time he visited.

A modest stream of people entered and exited the clinic's small front yard. A door-stop held the large mahogany doors open and, as he stepped through them, Obioma caught the first whiffs of a mixture of detergent, paint, and the sort of smells that Obioma occasionally perceived oozing out of the wounds that Iwuagwu's patients sometimes had. In the pale-green front room, people sat quietly on banks of benches arranged in rows, many hunched over in their seats and one stretched out on his back across the entire length of one of the benches. Obioma recognised some of them.

"Good morning," he tentatively mouthed in a catch-all greeting as he stepped into the room, not entirely sure if it was within etiquette. The response was a momentary bout of murmured returned greetings, like those of someone who had just been disturbed in their sleep, and the dragging of feet against the floor.

"Can I help you?" a voice thundered from behind a file-cluttered desk at the front of the room. The stocky middle-aged man, judging from his accent, was not from anywhere near Umuwe.

"I am here to see Dr Ejike." Obioma approached the desk.

"You are Nwagwu, right?" Obioma eventually nodded his assent. "Please go to Room 5 over there." The man gestured Obioma towards a corridor that ran through the entire length of the house.

Death and Dr Ejike's clinic were not very far apart. Obioma knew that many of the people sitting on the benches in the front room were actually relatives of people being treated there, and that people tended to die, or seemed close to it, whenever they needed to attend the clinic.

"No. People stupidly go to Okoro and his charlatan traditional medicine practice first, and by the time they realise their mistake and arrive at the clinic, it is often too late," Obioma's uncle would often say whenever people made such a suggestion.

Dr Ejike never smiled, whether it was around his clinic, or in the company of villagers outside it, but it was understood that he was a kind man. The boy, not older than six, who lay on a table in the middle of Room 5 tore his eyes away from the large needle in Dr Ejike's hand and affixed them intently on Obioma as he entered the room. The boy's mother was by his side, holding his hand in a tight grip.

"Nwagwu, *kedụ*", Dr Ejike's mouth mumbled from behind his face mask.

"*Dede*, good morning" Obioma responded.

"Wash your hands over there, just in case you need to get something for me." Dr Ejike pointed to a plastic contraption on the wall hanging over a sink: a large, decapitated jerry can with a makeshift tap affixed to its base. It was when Obioma reached the vantage point of the sink that he saw the bloodied, gaping and jagged laceration on the boy's leg that Dr Ejike was just about to sew up.

15 CHIEF ALUSI

"A sị na onye afọ ukwu, riri nnukwu nri, kama o nweghị onye ma ihe o riri"

"All you can tell from a big belly is that the owner has had a lot to eat, not what he had

to eat"

(Traditional Igbo proverb)

Two days later in Owerri

Chief Alusi was the fattest person Kalu had ever seen; he was also the richest. The only other people considered to be richer were the Queen of England, King Fahd of Saudi Arabia, Michael Jackson, and perhaps Chief Arthur Nzeribe and Chief Emmanuel Iwuanyanwu, who both also owned helicopters. This was why Kalu found it hard to believe when his older brother Benjamin announced in their living room that the Chief was coming to their home to visit him.

That morning, Kalu had woken up to the familiar Saturday morning sounds: a medley of songs that his two younger sisters, Obiageri and Chisom, belted out while plaiting each other's hair in the living room; the scraping sounds from the local knife-sharpener's grinding stone; and the sound of splashing soap-water and rigorous scrubbing by his mother, as she gave the house a thorough clean.

"Mpa, good morning," Kalu greeted his bare-chested father, who stood in the veranda of their bungalow, his ample belly hanging over the

patterned wrapper tied around his waist, waiting for the wet cake of white shaving cream on his face to do its job.

It was well into the middle of December, and more than half of the city's inhabitants were away at their ancestral villages in far-flung rural areas. Kalu's family, like most of the people still around in the neighbourhood, were indigenes of Owerri. This meant they never left Owerri. Kalu lost his train of thought for a moment as he surveyed the deserted verandas of the shabby tower blocks that dominated his neighbourhood's skyline.

"Why is Chief coming to see Benjamin?" Kalu asked his father.

"Your brother is joining Chief Alusi's business; you already know this," his father responded.

Kalu had indeed spent that entire week unsuccessfully interrogating his brother about the details of his connection to the Chief, partly out of an overwhelming sense of envy about his brother's apparent good fortune, but mostly because he believed his brother was a fundamentally bad person, and such things were not supposed to happen to them.

For as long as he could remember, Benjamin had been known all around the neighbourhood as a troublemaker, often getting into fights and regularly being rebuked for his unruly behaviour. Kalu remembered visits from the parents of the various children Benjamin fought with. They arrived demanding compensation from Kalu's parents, for drugs and clinic visits on account of injuries Benjamin had caused, or for clothes torn in the fights, or to replace windows Benjamin had broken with his wanton stone-throwing. Similar stories were also told about his father by some older relatives.

Even though these stories were told as though from an era long past, Kalu recognised the cruel streak that marked the personalities of both his father and his brother, the impulses that he had avoided being at the receiving end of, so far. These impulses were at the heart of the mocking quips and the disappointed looks his father often gave his mother as she prepared to leave the house, because she opted to attend church instead of joining Kalu's father at their shop in the market. They were also connected to the vitriolic monologue he had once aimed at visiting Jehovah's Witnesses.

"Jesus loves who? Rubbish. My friend, listen: the world is just as you see it, nothing but earth below, nothing but sky and space above. We are no different to that gecko over there on the wall," Kalu's father had said to the ambushed and fidgeting Jehovah's Witnesses, whom he had initially warmly welcomed into his living room, even offering them malted biscuits in a saucer.

It had all been carefully planned out, and Kalu understood this to be entertainment for his father – a way to fill his free Sunday afternoon.

"Someone has to educate you fools," Kalu's father eventually sneered, his indulgent toothy grin eventually turning into a mocking, bellowing laugh

– a laugh Benjamin had inherited from his father. It was this laugh that had finally forced the Jehovah's Witness visitors to decide to cut short their visit and flee, but not before they had witnessed Kalu's father smack the wall-gecko to a mushy pulp with his slipper to make his point.

As they fled, Kalu had watched his mother's eyes cloud up with tears as she withdrew quietly to the bedroom she shared with her husband. She had previously welcomed the canvassers herself, as distant comrades and relatives-in-Christ.

Kalu had heard from his mother how, two years into secondary school, Benjamin had slapped and punched his mathematics teacher before running away and scaling the school fence. There was also talk that Kalu's father had done a similar thing during his time in school. For Benjamin, that was said to be the last time he attended school. What had followed shortly after Benjamin's departure from school was a string of visits from neighbours and police officers, who accused Benjamin of being involved in a number of burglaries and thefts in the area. Kalu remembered watching his father, on those occasions, retrieve his mother's large bible from the living-room shelf where she kept it. He would dramatically swear to Benjamin's innocence in front of the police, convincing them each time that Benjamin was being framed by envious neighbours and insidious enemies. He also handed them money to aid their pursuit of the real culprits.

Then came the day when a close friend of Benjamin was lynched – dowsed in kerosene and set alight on the road adjacent to where Kalu lived. Kalu had seen it happen. An armed robbery had gone wrong which, rumour had it, might have involved Benjamin and his friends. In the end, only one of them was captured by a mob of vigilantes who, after giving him a severe beating, set him alight. That morning, as Kalu watched the charred, dark figure stagger about, slump and become lifeless, he had begun to believe that this was how his brother would eventually meet his own end. Kalu knew that his father had also come to the same conclusion, and that this was why he had arranged for Benjamin to become an apprentice with a vulcaniser friend of his.

Even though Benjamin had learnt the vulcanising trade in less than a quarter of the time it normally took, he had also proceeded to steal and sell all of his father's friend's equipment, squandering all the money in drinking and gambling houses and on the young girls he paid to visit his shed.

In the end, Kalu's father had had to replace his friend's equipment, as well as funding the purchase of new tools for Benjamin's new vulcaniser business.

When Kalu eventually broke out of his train of thought, he found himself staring at the gunk of facial hair and shaving cream that had been wiped off his father's face and which now littered the balcony floor. Kalu's mind settled on the idea that his father and brother were almost one and the same.

"What will Benjamin be doing for Chief Alusi?" Kalu pressed his father, as his father scraped the last smudge of shaving cream and hair off his face.

"Chief Alusi has his fingers in many pies," his father responded in a very rare foray into the use of English language. Kalu had noticed his father did this when he did not know what he was talking about. Kalu was sure about this because it was also what his brother had said when he had posed the same question. However, unlike his dad, he knew his brother was being cagey.

Everyone knew that Chief Alusi owned many buildings in the city and that he rented them out to civil servants, traders, banks and other businesses. Kalu had assumed that his brother would be a caretaker, just like the men who attended to the tall blocks of flats around where they lived. But perhaps Benjamin was being hired because he was a troublemaker. He would be well placed to harass and terrorise tenants who refused to pay their rent or who damaged property and didn't fix it.

Anticipation over Chief Alusi's visit grew as that Saturday wore on. Kalu mobilised his sisters in fetching water from a compound a few streets away whose taps, miraculously, functioned. As designated by his mother before she left for the market, Kalu's key job was to ensure that the large metal water-barrels in their veranda were filled with water, that all the drinking bottles in the fridge were topped up, and that the large bath in the bathroom was full to the brim, for flushing the toilet.

Kalu's mother returned from her impromptu dash to the market laden with a basin of additional groceries for her cooking. The menu that day was to be all-accommodating – *egusi* soup with assorted pieces of meat and pounded yam, long-grain foreign rice with fish, as well as a meat stew. Kalu's father placed several bottles of Guilder, Star and 33 in the fridge to cool, together with a keg of palm wine, delivered by his cousin and tapped by a specialist in a village about two hours' drive west of Owerri.

When the time drew sufficiently near, Kalu's family changed into their best outfits, normally reserved for special occasions like weddings and baptisms. Obiageri and Chisom were handed over to their next-door neighbours, where they would spend the rest of the day and evening, conveniently out of the way.

By the time the off-white clock that hung from the wall over the standing black-and-white television set in the living room struck four, the appointed time of Chief Alusi's arrival, Kalu's father had already exhausted all of his stories relating to the Chief. Like the one about Chief Alusi's fifth Chieftaincy ceremony which Kalu's father had attended about fifteen years ago. Citing it as the most lavish event that he had ever been to, Kalu's father made a point of listing all of the livestock killed to provide food during the ceremony. As he did so, Kalu's mother would intermittently appear from the kitchen, large spoon in hand, enquiring whether the Chief had arrived yet.

Some time after they had got bored of waiting and lounged idly in the armchairs and sofas in their living room, Chief Alusi's driver loudly revved the brand-new-looking lime-green Mercedes Benz 300CD Turbo as it pulled in to one of the parking spots close to Kalu's family's bungalow. Kalu watched from the vantage point of their porch as his father and Benjamin rushed out to greet the Chief.

The top of Chief Alusi's traditional silver cap was the first thing Kalu saw as he emerged from the other side of his car. Short and pot-bellied, the Chief wore a pale-blue short-sleeved brocade shirt and loose trousers of the same material. Walking with a slight limp, and resting his frame on a dark-brown sculptured walking stick the same colour as his sandals, Chief Alusi smiled warmly at Benjamin, who rushed over to him ahead of his father. Scores of neighbours stood gaping brazenly in astonishment from their balconies; others peeked out more cautiously from behind the corners of their curtains.

"Chief. Good evening, sir," Kalu's father said reverentially, as he clasped one of his hands on the other, before offering his conjoined hands to the Chief for a handshake, stooping slightly as he did so.

"*Kedụ afa gi*, young man," the Chief said, smiling and offering his right hand as he caught sight of Kalu emerging from behind his father.

"*Aha m bu Kalu*," Kalu responded, as he mimicked his father's stoop, clasping his left hand around his right wrist, just as his father and brother had done, before shaking the Chief's hand.

He hung back to gape at the Chief's car along with a handful of neighbourhood children as Kalu's father and brother ushered Chief Alusi and his driver into their bungalow.

Kalu studied the glimmering Mercedes Benz emblem which sat at the front end of the bonnet. With his fingers, Kalu traced the equally glittery thin chrome panel decorations which ran from one end of the car to the other on both of its sides. At the back, the Chief's decorative animal-skin chieftaincy fan sat on display on the mantle behind the car's back window. *Chief Stephen Alusi, Nwadinamba of Illoba*, it read. Two elephant tusks lay on either side of the large fan.

Kalu had, on a few occasions, seen the Chief's car drive past, and on some of those occasions he had seen split-second glimpses of the Chief sitting in the passenger seat of the car. Kalu had also seen the distinctive green-and-yellow-painted helicopter the Chief was believed to own fly past. Chief Alusi also appeared in snippets of news reports on local television, sitting in state boxes alongside other dignitaries and celebrities. These recollections prompted Kalu to wonder even more bemusedly what Chief Alusi would want with Benjamin.

16 THE APPRENTICE 2

"Money can't talk, yet it can make lies look true"

(Traditional South African proverb)

Minutes later

Chief Alusi's driver was already seated at Benjamin's old school-desk-and-chair combo, which Kalu reckoned must have been dragged out from their storage shed at the front of the raised bungalow balcony. He had already begun his assault on the huge mound of pounded yam and the large bowl of *egusi* soup which Kalu's mother had no doubt rushed out to him as soon as he sat down.

"Good afternoon," Kalu greeted as he walked past the driver towards the living room.

"*Nnoo*," the driver mumbled as he took a swig from a frosty bottle of bright-orange Fanta, in between hoovering up large morsels of food.

Inside, the Chief had already made himself at home, sprawled across the family's entire green three-seater couch. His small leather bag, which he clutched under his right arm like a lady's purse, rested on one end of the couch, while his silver hat was placed delicately at the other end. Chief Alusi leaned over the long coffee table in front of him, his concentration pouring through his tiny half-rimmed glasses and onto the various sheets of paper placed before him.

He signed his signature here and there, checking and double-checking. Benjamin stood by the side of the large couch looking over the Chief, and Kalu's dad and mum sat expectantly but quietly in the two armchairs on the other side of the coffee table.

"This is now done," the Chief eventually announced, his eyes flicking across the room searching for Benjamin, before he realised he was standing over him.

"The Embassy should issue you a visa to travel," the Chief concluded.

"Yes Chief," Benjamin responded promptly mid-sentence.

"Pick up your flight tickets from our Lagos office and..."

"Yes Chief," an edgy Benjamin cut in again.

"I will meet you in Brussels," the Chief added, grinning as he handed the papers he had been poring over to Benjamin.

Kalu manoeuvred his way to Benjamin's side and briefly caught a glimpse of one of the documents being handed back to him: *Embassy of Belgium in Nigeria*, it read.

The realisation hit him that his brother was indeed working closely with Chief Alusi, and that the job was far more important than that of a rent-collecting agent.

"Fifty thousand naira," Kalu's father mouthed loudly in disbelief. Engrossed in Benjamin's documents, Kalu had failed to notice that Chief Alusi had just handed a cheque to his father.

"Oh wonderful! Thank you, Chief!" Kalu's father and mother's chorus of "thank you"s continued, building up to a point where Kalu's mother began to clap in exuberance, performing an impromptu celebratory jig.

"Chief, now you must eat," Kalu heard his mother order when her dance had tailed off, as she gave the coffee table an unnecessary wipe down.

"Yes. The main event," the Chief chuckled, making himself even more at home. With his glasses folded and back in their gold casing, he loosed the drawstrings of his trousers, collapsing back into the couch in a momentary cosy stretch.

Chief Alusi's assault on the enormous feast laid out in front of him by Kalu's mother was indiscriminate. He hopped from pounded yam and soup, to *jeloof* rice, to rice with stew, and back to pounded yam as he engaged in relaxed conversation with Kalu's father and brother.

Chief Alusi told anecdote after anecdote of his various business exploits and engagement with dignitaries and celebrities, as bottles of beer and cups of fresh palm wine were filled and emptied.

As Kalu sat in the corner watching, he continued to wrestle with what the Chief could have seen in his brother. He had heard that the Chief, on a handful of occasions, had visited Benjamin's vulcaniser business. Kalu wondered if this was where they had first met.

"So how old are you, young man?" Chief Alusi said as he picked at his teeth with a toothpick, his assault on the spread of food beginning to wane.

"Ten years old, sir," Kalu managed to respond, startled by the question and abruptly sitting up from his slouch on the living room floor.

"One of my sons is about your age," the Chief told him. "What class are you in now?"

"Primary four sir, at Progress Primary School, Owerri, sir," Kalu responded promptly.

"How did you do in your exams this term? What position did you take?" the Chief enquired further.

"First, sir. I came first, sir."

"First in your class? That's brilliant!" the Chief said.

"No. First in my school, sir," Kalu corrected.

"First in your school, really? Wonderful!' the Chief smiled, glancing towards Kalu's mother and father, as if not entirely believing their son's claims.

"How many pupils are there in your…?" the Chief asked.

"Two thousand, nine hundred and forty-three," Kalu responded before the Chief could complete his sentence.

"Is this guy serious?" the stunned Chief asked, glancing at Kalu's father.

"Kalu, go and get your report card and show Chief Alusi," Kalu's father ordered.

As Kalu rummaged through his personal papers at the bottom end of the huge suitcase in his room where his best clothes were also kept, he relished the opportunity to upstage his brother.

"Wonderful, excellent, very good, oh very good indeed," the overwhelmed Chief gushed as he read through the pages of Kalu's report card. "You are one bright young man. When you finish school you should come and work for me, maybe travel overseas like your brother. I have my fingers in many pies."

"No sir."

"No?" The Chief was stunned. "What do you plan to do?"

"I am saving money to buy ten thousand acres of land to plant palm trees and to build a palm oil factory."

"You are planning to take over the palm oil market?" the Chief enquired, staring down at Kalu. Kalu nodded silently, prompting a thunderous and protracted fit of laughter from the Chief.

"My oh my. Mr Obi, you have some really ambitious children here. That's an incredible plan for someone your age, but I don't doubt that you will achieve it," the Chief said. "Look here…" He reached for his brown bag, unzipping it. "I like your plan and my offer for you to work for me still stands. In fact we could be equal partners in the venture. This is one thousand naira to add to your savings and get you started." The Chief smiled broadly as he handed Kalu a wad of crisp twenty-naira notes from the stash of money in his bag. Kalu's father and Benjamin looked on with amazement; they had never even heard of Kalu's plans.

"Thank you sir," Kalu responded as he clasped the large wad of notes with both hands and headed immediately to the safe-box under his bed in his room.

17 NINTH CIRCLE

"Between true friends even water drunk together is sweet enough"

(Traditional African proverb)

Days later

Professor Nwachukwu's bicycle glittered in the sun as he rode into Iwuagwu's compound one hot afternoon. Through the gap in the curtains of the bungalow he was in, Obioma saw him arrive and watched as the Professor's slender frame gingerly dismounted from his shimmering chrome bicycle, as if it were a large and unstable horse.

Obioma concluded that the bicycle definitely did not need cleaning. He also now realised why the Professor had scratched his head for a long time when Obioma accosted him on the balcony of his mansion a week earlier to sell his ability to accomplish "any errand or chore, no matter how hard".

At that moment, Obioma felt a slight twinge of guilt. He had more or less bullied the mild-mannered Professor into his carefully crafted agreement to "clean and grease his bicycle for a fee" the next time the Professor visited his uncle, which he knew was imminent as the Professor regularly visited Iwuagwu.

"Nwachukwu *kedụ̀?*" Obioma heard his uncle bellow from the far end of the compound, as Iwuagwu dragged out two of his most comfortable lounge seats.

Nwachukwu's visits were very well-rehearsed routines. Obioma emerged from the bungalow, delicately balancing two kola nuts on a saucer surrounded by beads of alligator-pepper, and took quickened strides

71

towards where his uncle and his guest were settling into their seats. A keg of that morning's fresh palm wine would shortly follow, retrieved by Obioma from a cool corner of the mud-hut kitchen where Iwuagwu had had a delivery boy place it.

Obioma then dragged off the Professor's bicycle to a short distance away, but within sight and earshot of his uncle's conversation with his guest, soapy water and sponge at the ready for the scheduled bicycle clean.

"Thomas Sankara is at it again," Obioma heard Nwachukwu announce as he unlatched the straps of a tan leather bag which moments before had been fastened to the back of his bicycle.

"Listen to this." Nwachukwu thumbed through a copy of the *New African* which he retrieved from his bag, translating loudly into Igbo as he skipped along the columns of the magazine.

"All men in Burkina Faso must go to the market as well as enter the kitchen to prepare meals for their families… A man can no longer marry more than one wife in Burkina Faso… Forced and arranged marriages prohibited… Female genital circumcision prohibited… Three more female ministers appointed… Ten million trees to be planted…

"All very sensible things," Iwuagwu added as he glanced towards the mound of earth heaped next to the mud-hut kitchen, the spot where his wife was buried. "Ikom would have liked him a lot."

Obioma had only vague memories of his aunt – a tall, soft-spoken old woman with a patterned wrapper around her waist. Her bare breasts drooped down and swayed gently as she walked around the compound in her slow, tired gait. Obioma remembered how he and his cousins would troop into her kitchen with locusts, praying mantises and green caterpillars, all hunted down in the endless rows of tall corn-stalks in the vast farmlands that Iwuagwu and his wife kept. Her mud-hut kitchen also hosted the bitter ends of the fist-sized snails that emerged in the dead of night after the relentless week-long heavy rains. They, along with wild mushrooms, found their way into the buckets that Obioma and the other foraging children dragged along with them during their regular aimless wandering through the forests and bushes, pickings they now presented to Chidimma, Iwuagwu's daughter-in-law, who now did the majority of the cooking.

"Did I tell you her mother was one of the women who organised the famous Ogu Ndem riots in 1929? They travelled to Oloko to protest against the warrant chief's actions to restrict women from local government," Iwuagwu continued to Nwachukwu, snapping Obioma out of his nostalgic thoughts. "The foreigners who controlled them must have known something that we did not realise then. Perhaps, if given power, women would not as easily be blinded by high office, greed and power as most men inevitably are."

Obioma had heard the story many times before. Iwuagwu's mother-in-law had been directly responsible for burning down at least five court houses during the riots, he'd once said.

Obioma always found Iwuagwu and Nwachukwu's meetings spectacles to witness, not least because both men were the unlikeliest of close friends. Even more so, they were the least likely of men to be engaged in what amounted to a book club. Obioma concocted various pretexts to be in the vicinity of their meetings.

As accomplished and renowned as Iwuagwu was in his bone-mending and local custom knowledge, he could not read or write. Professor Nwachukwu, on the other hand, had written books that filed whole bookshelves.

The Professor and Iwuagwu had known each other when they were teenagers, but only for a brief period. Back then, they were not close friends. Iwuagwu had talked vaguely about how Nwachukwu and a handful of other boys spent their free time roaming the vast forest areas around the village, chiselling out holes in the sides of tall rubber trees and tapping buckets of natural rubber, which they sold to contractors servicing the World War II allied effort. This rubber-tree sap would eventually be turned into the tyres that carried various vehicles and aircrafts.

Nwachukwu's father was the only person in the village to serve in the contingent of allied soldiers from Nigeria who fought the Japanese on the Burmese eastern front. Iwuagwu had once mentioned this to Obioma when they stumbled across a series of graves near Nwachukwu's mansion in the village. Iwuagwu told about the jubilation and merriment that continued for a full month when Nwachukwu's father finally returned safely from the war, and how people would gather at Nwachukwu's house to listen to his father tell stories about their passage through India to the war front, the deadly encounters with the Japanese, the British officers who managed their regiments and battalion, and the various shrapnel wounds that Nwachukwu's father bore from the war.

Obioma heard how Nwachukwu's father spend all of his military discharge payment on entertaining visitors, and how it wasn't very long before hardship set in. In the end, Nwachukwu and his family packed their belongings and headed to Ghana, where Nwachukwu's father worked as a factory foreman. This was where Nwachukwu did the rest of his growing up, where he married and had children, only finally returning to Umuwe in 1975, just after the death of his wife in Ghana.

"What else have you got for us today besides news about Sankara?" Obioma heard his uncle ask.

"But we have not finished discussing the last one," Nwachukwu replied as he sat cradling a book bound in rich red paper. Obioma strained his neck until he could read the title – *Comedy*, the same book Obioma remembered they had been discussing some days previously, when Nwachukwu had last visited the compound.

"You still haven't explained what you meant when you said that this was just a bad reaction to Dante's realisation that in this life and after, there really is no order," Nwachukwu stated.

Nwachukwu's words made no sense to Obioma. In fact, Obioma found that he always needed to concentrate a great deal to understand Nwachukwu, who spoke Igbo with a funny twang and with many English words, the way that some people spoke when they had been away for too long.

Nwachukwu also did not express himself with proverbs, as most people his age in Umuwe had a habit of doing. Obioma reckoned that, having lived away for so long, Nwachukwu probably did not know many proverbs, and his embarrassment at this must be the reason why he said very little in meetings and conversations with groups around the village.

On the contrary, Iwuagwu, could go for days solely conveying his thoughts in proverbs and idioms and citing obscure *omenala* and local customs, a thing that Obioma knew delighted and interested Nwachukwu – so much so that Nwachukwu would from time to time jot down Iwuagwu's statements in a little red notepad he always carried with him in his tan leather bag.

Obioma reckoned that this keen interest in cultural and local matters had greatly endeared Nwachukwu to his uncle, but ultimately both men were friends because of their mutual disdain for Okoro, a self-proclaimed traditional doctor and one of Obioma's older second cousins. Okoro was regularly accused by them and others of causing the death and suffering of many who regularly sought help at his dubious traditional medicine practice.

"But which of Dante's circles of hell do you think Okoro belongs in?" Obioma remembered Iwuagwu and Nwachukwu's conversation earlier in the week as they discussed the red book Nwachukwu now cradled in his hands.

"Surely he should be running the ninth circle?" Iwuagwu responded.

The previous meeting's discussions were even more entertaining than those of the present meeting, even though Nwachukwu found it challenging to translate.

Obioma listened keenly as the two men rowed humorously about which of the vividly described circles of hell Okoro belonged in. Nwachukwu reckoned Okoro was destined for the eighth circle, to which the spirits of thieves and imposters were banished. There they were perpetually afflicted with different debilitating diseases, combined with the never-ending terror of a centaur who had fire-breathing dragons on his shoulders and an equine back covered in snakes, the snakes on the centaur's back biting the thieves and imposters, causing them to shift-shape into painful amalgamations of various animals.

On the other hand, Iwagwu believed Okoro belonged to the ninth circle, reserved for traitors who were plagued by the wrath of biblical giants and encapsulated in frozen lakes. Here, a multi-coloured three-faced beast, Satan, wept from his six eyes as each of his three mouths chewed perpetually on a prominent traitor.

Obioma steeled himself to look into the red-covered book Nwachukwu was reading from, hoping that the words were as vividly depicted in pictures.

18 HEADLESS CHICKEN

"Ọchụ nwa ọkụkọ new ada; nwa ọkụkọ new mnwe mnwe ọsọ"

"A person who chases a chicken is due a fall; the chicken is a master of the dodged

escape"

(Traditional Igbo proverb)

Days later

Umuwe was bustling with life the day before Christmas as more relatives arrived back from across the country and beyond. Motorcycles, cars, trucks and lorries pounded the network of narrow untarred roads in and around the village, more than in any other period of the year.

Children idly hung around the compound entrances and along the village roads in anticipation of returning relatives. Great cheers would greet a successful spotting, and help would be at hand to drag suitcases, large bags of rice, goats and chickens into the compounds. Music and merriment were abundant in the air.

Earlier that day, Obioma's mother had eventually made the decision to close her shop and head down to Umuwe. On the other hand, Obialor, Obioma's cousin and Iwuagwu's only surviving son, was not returning that year from Sokoto State in the north of the country where he worked as a road builder. Despite this, Obioma, Ogechi and their second cousins' protracted wait, well into the night on 24 December at the foot of the compound, was not in vain. They still dragged in two large live chickens and half a bag of rice, courtesy of a neighbour who was returning from the Sokoto area in a chartered open lorry that did the rounds in the south east, dropping off workers from the north.

Still in the clothes he had worn for two nights, the neighbour handed Obialor's wife a brown envelope of cash and passed on a verbal message. They were on a contract to finish a road and her husband would now be back in Easter, she was told.

Apart from the livestock and grains, the message that Obialor was alive and well was of great relief to Obioma. During the previous Christmas, Obialor had related a number of stories about some young Muslim men in the north who had felt slighted in one way or another by a Christian southerner, which sometimes resulted in them decapitating the southerner and parading the head around cities there.

Iwuagwu's daughter, Ezinne, was also not coming back home from Lagos, where she worked as a trainee nurse, but this was largely expected as she had rarely returned in previous years.

That year, Obioma did not participate in the endless feasts served at house-crawls that his second cousins and sister made with other visitors, reacquainting themselves with relatives and friends in Umuwe. Nor did he join in the impromptu jaunts into neighbouring villages by young boys his age, who gate-crashed dozens of marriages, chieftaincy ceremonies and death remembrances, hoovering up their food. Instead he accompanied his uncle to rummage through the forests and bushes for roots, leaves and barks from rare trees. They opened up for their bone-mending surgery sessions, tending to people who dropped in with minor sprains and dislocations. After that, they would call at a handful of patients' homes to check on them. The contents of Obioma's safe-box continued to grow, so much so that he contemplated building a bigger box.

Obioma could now perfectly recite the procedure for mending fractures, whether transverse, spiral, oblique or comminuted breakages. He could recall by heart most ingredients and which shrub or tree was required to make potions or ointments for their treatment. This was a significant achievement given the short period of time he had to take in the information.

An animated Iwuagwu related all this to Obioma's mother in Igbo, in an update he insisted on giving her to ensure she remained on board with the plans they had agreed upon. But Iwuagwu could not elicit the reassuring look of approval that he was seeking from her until Obioma's involvement with Ejike the doctor was mentioned.

"Dr Ejike told me that Obioma is well on his way to perfectly locating and reciting the major bones of the body in both English and Igbo. He has also lent Obioma some of his books. The white man's medicine might be erronously limited to physical ailments and completely bereft of an understanding of the impact of the layers of the cosmos on well-being, but those who practice it still do good, and command the utmost respect."

This was what Obioma's mother wanted to hear, and she showed her appreciation and support in her typical style – by reminding Iwuagwu that he was to let her know immediately if Obioma ever stopped being co-operative. She said this with a threatening glance towards Obioma that could only mean one thing.

Iwuagwu did not talk with Obioma's mother about the aspects of Obioma's apprenticeship programme that concerned rituals and initiation ceremonies. He did not talk about planned trips to shrines in Arochukwu, Igbo Ukwu and Enugwu to further Obioma's education, things he was planning for after Obioma had mastered bone-mending practice and after he had exhausted all of his own knowledge of the fundamentals of Igbo medical practice. He did not talk about the long list of rituals that he knew she would object to, like the Itu Anya ceremonies that would have to begin soon to start the process of opening Obioma's eyes so that he could become clairvoyant, seeing things well beyond ordinary human perception. A succession of other rituals would see Obioma increasingly entangled with the cosmos. Some would include potions, as well as the blood of dogs and other animals, dropped into Obioma's eyes, amidst incantations to various deities. Iwuagwu knew that these were not things which Obioma's mother, being a church woman, wanted to hear.

Iwuagwu recalled his long, tedious debates with Obioma's mother many years ago, when she was a lot chattier, when you did not have to plan ahead and prepare to speak to her. This was when she and his brother were only just courting. She had humorously called Iwuagwu a devil worshipper for admitting to occasionally conversing with Ekwensi, the deity she preferred to refer to as the devil – the association also made years earlier by the meddling missionaries who had brainwashed her and many others. She did not realise that Ekwensi was not the devil, nor even in the category of *muo ojo*, bad spirit, but that he was actually a deity of conflict, deception and war. She still did not realise that traditional doctors like Iwuagwu did not worship the deities they dealt with, but rather sought to placate and pacify them, and negotiate favourable terms.

Early on Christmas Day morning, Iwuagwu shunned the village-wide ritual of attending Christmas Mass at the Catholic parish church, preferring to use his time to forage in the bush for medicinal plants. Obioma joined his parents at the Catholic Church diocese compound, a full seven-and-a-half-mile walk further than the parish church attended on regular Sundays.

As noon approached, those who had attended Mass began to return and the Christmas Day celebrations began in earnest.

Steady streams of smoke snaked out from all compounds, as the

Christmas cooking that had been suspended during Mass recommenced. Obioma stood, overwhelmed with nerves, gawking at the large chicken whose life he had been tasked with taking. This was to be his first ever kill – not counting the scores of *ndanda* (ants) and *ngwere* (lizards) he and his friends had respectively scorched with rays from magnifying glasses and pummelled with pebbles.

Obioma was somewhat comforted by the fact that he had seen a chicken killed many times before, and as soon as he managed to tuck and pin the struggling large bird between both his knees, he sliced quickly into its plucked neck area.

"Steady – don't let go of it. Slice quickly so the animal doesn't have to suffer more than it needs to," his uncle calmly instructed as Obioma's other relatives looked on. His young sister and second cousins, standing some distance away, buried their heads in their laps as blood spewed haplessly out of the bird's deep wound. Obioma remembered images of the previous year's unfortunate incident. Next door, a boy of about his age had let go too soon and the headless chicken ran amok around the compound and into one of the bungalows, covering the walls and furniture of the house in blood. They had all gone over to peer at the spectacle and were eventually roped into doing the cleaning as penance for their voyeurism.

The chicken tucked between Obioma's knees eventually gave up its ill-fated fight, and in minutes its dead carcass was soaking in a large basin of hot water, waiting to be plucked by Ogechi and her much younger cousins, something that was Obioma's old job. The soaking bird gave off the familiar stale smell which Obioma associated strongly with Christmas Day.

19 EMILY NWANYI N'EBI EGO

"To be without a friend is to be poor indeed"

(Traditional Tanzanian proverb)

Later that day

For Iwuagwu, Christmas Day was always a very sober and sterile affair, and it was mostly spent reclining on his lounging chair underneath his *oha* tree, watching the day drag by.

Obialor was not around this year, and neither was the crate of Guinness stout he usually travelled back with from the north. Obioma's father, in a welcome move and a rare sighting the day before Christmas, ventured out from his mud-hut enclave with Iwuagwu's bicycle and bought two crates of soft drinks and a crate of large bottles of Guilder beer. Now, a large, warm bottle of Guilder accompanied Iwuagwu in quietly seeing out this slow day on his lounge chair – at least until closer to lunch time, when Obioma's father decided to spend his usual full hour fiddling with cables and portable batteries to set up his turntable and amplifiers in the dry, open air. All manner of furniture had been carried out of the huts and bungalows and arranged for twice the usual number of people by Obioma and his younger relatives.

Iwuagwu endured a measured session of idle talk with his brother until it was finally time to savour the hoped-for triumphant success in recreating Iwuagwu's deceased wife's special Christmas dish. Iwuagwu's daughter-in-law and Obioma's mother had made their usual attempt to recreate the special stew and the large pot of white fluffy rice, but they did not come close. Iwuagwu had given up trying himself.

Obioma, his sister, and their second cousins played their part, ensuring that the sporadic sounds of children laughing and the impromptu frenzy of heels pounding against the ground in carefree play were heard from time to time.

This made Iwuagwu feel that he had perhaps taken his dead wife's presence for granted. He feared that, with his stubborn personality, he must have seemed to be perpetually whinging. His wife had scolded him for his stubbornness, sometimes humorously and other times less so.

Iwuagwu now hoped that he had not spoiled her enjoyment of Christmas throughout their time together, with his pontificating about how it was not in the Igbo nature to have a celebration that was reserved only for immediate family. He found it strange that it was the only day in the thirteen-month Igbo calendar year that no visitor was expected to drop in, at least not until after it could be reasonably expected that the first plates of foods had been dished out and consumed.

The rowdy children around him were definitely not guilty of his petty folly, Iwuagwu thought, as Obioma and his young relatives affectionately cradled the whole bottles of soft drinks handed to them.

The rare 1978 recordings of songs by Okwuamara Dancing Group which played from Obioma's father's turntable prompted Iwuagwu from one recollection to another. This had been his wife's favourite dance group and, for as long as he or anyone could remember, on Christmas Day she had pestered Obioma's father to play the record over and over again. Iwuagwu remembered this as he heard the protracted grainy silence from the old vinyl plate, as it sat spinning on Obioma's father's turntable, before the music began.

"*Emily Nwanyị N'ebi Ego.*" The rhythmic and soulful voice of the female lead singer would then emerge, followed by the voices of the many women who sang in the background, along with the sounds from the *udu*, *ọkwa* and *ogele* that they played.

Iwuagwu gazed in quiet contemplation at the mound of earth which remained heaped on the spot where his wife was buried, just next to the kitchen – a mound of earth he imagined was preventing her from getting up and performing her usual graceful jig to the song, egged on by the rhythmic clapping that would break out all around. This was ultimately why, nowadays, Iwuagwu preferred the traditional kindred day celebrations. These were to occur days later and, as chair of the committee that organised it, he personally presided over its preparations. Amongst other things, this meant there was no time to sit pondering about what had been lost.

20 KINDRED

"Nwoke Obioma, g'arụ ọrụ ya ọfụma"

"Man must always be happy in order to perform well"

(Traditional Igbo proverb)

Five days later

The kindred day was a feast like no other in the year. This was a time originally intended for women across Ama Egwu to kick back and not involve themselves in any chores. It was also a time when anyone with a connection to the kindred was invited to feast and make merry with their relatives. This meant women who had long ago married into families in distant towns, cities and villages returned with their husbands, children, grandchildren and great grandchildren, and in-laws. All roads led to Ama Egwu in Umuwe that day. The compounds of the Eze extended families – the bearers of Obioma's surname who literally made up the entire population of Ama Egwu, were besieged by distant relatives.

Iwuagwu had managed the occasion for over two decades, and the day before the celebrations he recited to himself from memory his itinerary of 'things remaining to do', as he had always done.

Just after dark he dispatched the town crier to remind the males in the kindred to gather early in the morning. At dawn, hundreds of boys and men assembled at the meeting point: the *obiri ama*, the mud-hut located amongst trees beside a pond at the intersection of the four main roads in the village.

A commemorative shot or two of strong schnapps in libations to the ever-growing body of departed ancestors and the governing Ndichie deity would follow, before Iwuagwu split the men and boys into various teams, appointing a captain for each.

The youngest in the kindred were usually assigned to fetch firewood in the bush and nearby forest and to assemble the necessary pots and pans and utensils in commandeered kitchens up and down Ama Egwu. Obioma and a number of other boys his age were in this group. And, following their jaunt the year before, they were warned not to take a detour from their duties to seek out *udara* fruits, which were in season at that time and hung tantalisingly from very tall trees scattered across the forests where they retrieved their firewood.

Those known to be savvy and experienced in trade, for striking good bargains, were assigned to market duties, and they ventured off with the kindred purse to buy the necessary food items. There were also teams of butchers, who killed scores of chickens and goats as part of preparations. The cooking group prepared all manner of foods ancient and modern, from *jelloof* rice and red chicken stew to *agbono*, *oha* and *egwusi* soups. Others made large portions of oil-bean salad, and washed and prepared alligator-pepper and hundreds of garden eggs and kola nuts.

A group of men were tasked with ferrying in guests by bicycle, motorcycle and car from their main stations of arrival, and the young boys who had previously gathered firewood and who were part of the folk music group went home to pick up their various musical instruments to serenade the relatives arriving from far-flung destinations.

Iwuagwu would every year dust off his *opi* flute and join Obioma and other boys his age and older who played the *ekwe*, the wooden drums which were beaten with two large sticks, the metal gongs known as *ogele* and *igbugbo*, the large clay *udu*, and the spear hung with bells called the *oji*.

Alongside the kindreds was the popular vocalist nicknamed Ireoha, or 'tongue of the people'. While Ireoha sang and Iwuagwu would use his flute to narrate ancient stories and folk songs, while women, many very elderly, who had once called Umuwe home but who now had well-established homes in other places, ate, danced and sang songs, all transported, like Iwuagwu, across many decades to more simple times.

21 COUP D'ÉTAT

"Onye n'enweghị ego adịghị enwe enyi"

"A poor person does not have rich friends"

(Traditional Igbo proverb)

The next day

The hours during the build-up to New Year's Eve came and went by like any others in previous years. Adults lined the main roads in Umuwe with cast-iron gongs tipped with gunpowder. Children and teenagers, hours ahead, vandalised any loose-lying motorcycle wheels they could find, ripping away their metal spokes, the tips of which they crammed with copious amounts of phosphorus sesquisulfide, together with potassium chlorate harvested from the tips of matchsticks. They stuck nails into the mesh of powder and laid out their arsenal, waiting for the appointed time. Others swiped or wangled various strengths of white carbide blocks from mechanics' shops, laid them on leaves and waited with large perforated tin-cans and small wood-fires.

The intermittent flurry of loud explosions and dim flashes of light which all of these devices caused kicked off just as the sun disappeared on New Year's Eve, intensifying at midnight before tailing off in the early hours of the morning, exciting and entertaining the young, irritating the old and scaring the life out of pets and livestock.

After the merriment, the 'happy new year' chants, and the poignant libations and hopeful remarks made with cups of gin, whisky and schnapps. Like most people, Obioma retired from the chill of the early-morning hamatan, in his case to the front room of his uncle's bungalow with the usual anxious anticipation about what the new year would bring.

He waited patiently for sleep on a stack of mattresses. His mind settled on the prospect that by that exact time the following year, he and Kalu would be gazing upon acres and acres of growing palm fruit trees. He imagined the cacophony of sounds from hundreds of old women pounding cooked palm fruits in large mortars with hefty pestles.

His thoughts were interrupted by the familiar sounds of screeching from his father's small transistor radio. It was a mystery to Obioma why his father religiously woke up so early to fiddle with his small transistor radio, and why his mother let him, given her no-nonsense temperament and the intermittent piercing squeaks that accompanied the unstable medium-wave transmission which rang across the neighbourhood.

"This is Bush House," a stern voice would announce, prompting a brief flurry of music, a little like a speeded-up version of the sort of music played by church organs in early morning Latin Mass at the Owerri Asumpta Cathedral or at St Paul's parish church not too far from Obioma's home.

This time, the irritating shrieks were not just muffled sounds confined to his father's small mud-hut at the far end of the compound, temporarily amplified by a gust of wind. In Obioma's sleepy haze it felt as though his father's radio had grown legs and begun to draw closer and closer. Then Obioma heard the sounds of his father's dragging gait, which seemed quicker than usual, and finally a knock on the front door of the bungalow he slept in, which also housed Iwuagwu's bedroom. Obioma knew something serious must have happened. The old clock hanging on the wall in the front room had not yet struck four in the morning.

"*Gịnị mere?*" (What happened?), Iwuagwu enquired, as Obioma's father called out Iwuagwu's name repeatedly.

Iwuagwu rushed out before Obioma could untangle himself from the layers of bed-clothes he had wrapped himself in, unlatching the series of bolts wedging the door shut.

"*Coup d'état. Nde army emela coup,*" Obioma's father announced tensely from behind the door. Obioma was not sure what a coup was at first, until he recalled his previous vacation in Umuwe, months before in August that year, when an animated Professor Nwachukwu had made an impromptu visit to Iwuagwu one afternoon to inform his uncle that there had been a coup in Upper Volta led by Thomas Sankara.

By all accounts at the time, it seemed as though it was a good thing. Obioma remembered Nwachukwu mentioning how the Sankara fellow had made a number of announcements about a handful of changes he wanted to happen: a name change for the country, although Obioma was not sure why this was desirable; a great deal more planting of trees and food crops; and vaccines for kids, which did not sound palatable to Obioma, as it entailed painful injections. Nevertheless, at the time, Iwuagwu and Nwachukwu had seemed cheerful about the news.

This time, Obioma noticed that there seemed to be an air of grave concern hanging over Iwuagwu and his father, as they digested the news in silence and waited for a protracted bout of signal interference to clear from the buzzing transistor radio.

"This could mean war," Iwuagwu said under his breath.

""I must go and warn my friend, the Commissioner," Obioma's father said loudly.

This caused Obioma to revisit Iwuagwu's tales of the various times in the past when villagers had had to abandon their homes and hide in the bush. He feared that this could be one of them. That would also mean, thought Obioma, that their diet of chicken, fish, goats, rice, yams and sumptuously cooked vegetable soups and *fufu* would suddenly be replaced by lizards and rats, hurriedly roasted over quickly assembled bare fires as people hid up and around trees. That is, if these things were to be found at all, as the same tales about old wars suggested that lizards and rats also had a habit of making themselves scarce during these periods.

An anxious Obioma continued to stew in his various assumptions of what a coup was, as his father and uncle kept their silence and waited impatiently for the waves of static to clear from the radio. When it did, the station they were listening to had stopped giving bulletins and was instead playing marshal music non-stop. Obioma looked on as his father borrowed his brother's bicycle and cycled off into the still pitch-black early morning.

PART 3

22 LAGOS BOY

"Ike gwụrụ mma, awụghị na ọ nyụrụ nkọ"

"The knife can be worn down, but it cannot be blunted"

(Traditional Igbo proverb)

1985

Nobody, including members of Kalu's family, heard from Benjamin for almost a full year after he had moved to Lagos to work for Chief Alusi.

Kalu sometimes imagined Benjamin in a sharp suit, strolling in and out of smartly decorated offices in tall buildings mostly made of glass. Other times, he pictured Chief Alusi and Benjamin getting on aeroplanes bound for Europe to negotiate the purchase of fleets of large air-conditioned buses for Chief Alusi's transport company or luxurious vehicles for the many car showrooms the Chief owned up and down the country.

Benjamin's occasional calls to Mr and Mrs Abiali, the only people in their neighbourhood who owned a telephone, had suddenly stopped many months ago. The scores of traders Kalu's father knew who plied the Owerri–Lagos route on a weekly basis had never seen Benjamin in Lagos. When his family called the phone number Benjamin had left behind, it would ring until it got tired and switched itself off, and they found that the people who answered Chief Alusi's phone always gave ambiguous responses, and would neither confirm nor deny if they were breathing air.

For months, Kalu's family waved off concerns over Benjamin's silence with the excuse that he was probably abroad and very busy. But as it approached almost a full year since his departure with no contact from him, Kalu's mother began to fear the worst. Kalu watched his father maintain a stoic calm over the matter, as though he knew that Benjamin would eventually surface one evening at their house by the Old Market with a large scar across the side of his face.

It was very late into the night. Kalu's siblings were already asleep. There had been a power outage across Owerri, and Kalu's mother answered the light, timid tapping on the front door of their bungalow with caution. Kalu, who stood close by, saw the look of alarm on his mother's face when Benjamin stepped from the pitch-black darkness outside into the glow of the lantern his mother carried with her.

"Benji! *O dị kwa mma?*" she enquired apprehensively, pulling closer to him with the lamp and examining his scar. Benjamin had also grown a bushy beard. He wore steel-toe-capped boots like a military man, and the clothes he had arrived in smelled faintly of urine.

Bizarrely, Benjamin first action when he got through the door was to squat and then eventually sit on the fading, swirly-patterned carpet in their living room. Kalu could not remember the last time he had seen his brother do this. He looked tired, and drank tumbler after tumbler full of the refrigerated water that his mother poured for him from a plastic container, while Kalu and his father sat on the sofas around him.

"I was in an accident," he finally said, after he had taken the first gulp of cold water from the fourth tumbler presented to him. "Chief Alusi was in the car ahead of us. I was behind him with his second driver. We were on our way to the airport on the Lagos expressway when it happened. Our driver died." This drew gasps of horror from his mother. After another gulp, Benjamin continued.

"The car rolled three times and I got slashed by broken glass *here*. I was cut again *here* and across *here* when I tried to crawl out of the wreckage." Benjamin pointed dramatically to injuries on his face, thigh and stomach. He told them that he had been in hospital for three days, but that he was just returning from the driver's burial in his native Gongola State.

"Why did you not have someone call Tobenna's shop when it happened?" his mother enquired. Tobenna was one half of a couple who ran a telephone-calling business on the main road minutes away from their bungalow. It consisted of about five small booths fitted with telephones. People would pay to make international calls or receive them. They would pay extra if a call was received and either Tobenna or his wife had to sprint and fetch whoever it was who was being called. Benjamin had called Tobenna's shop to inform his parents of his safe arrival in Lagos.

Chief Alusi had taken care of everything, Benjamin responded: his hospital bills, the delivery of food from restaurants. He had even sorted out the driver's burial, and had given the driver's family a cash lump sum. A really unfortunate experience, but other than that, everything else was well, Benjamin reassured his family.

Kalu knew his brother was lying. The over-gesticulation, the sparse details, and his brother's pauses and stares mid-sentence, to check if what he was saying was being bought: he had seen him do this many times before. Amidst his mother's outbursts of "praise Jesus!" and "God is merciful!" Kalu also noticed that his father did not ask Benjamin a single question and remained quiet the entire time, a sure sign that he hadn't bought Benjamin's story either, or that he knew far more about Benjamin than he was letting on. Instead, Kalu's father focused his gaze on the strained smile of a young woman holding a toothbrush and a toothpaste tube who looked out at him from a folded newspaper lying on their rusting metal-and-glass coffee table.

23 SANKARA IS NO MORE

"E gbuo dike n' ulo, o ruo n'Ọgụ aga echeta ya"

"Kill a warrior during skirmishes at home; you will remember him when fighting

enemies"

(Traditional Igbo proverb)

15 October 1987

Iwuagwu was lying on his back on his raffia bed, recovering from yet
another bout of influenza, when Nwachukwu called at his house to give
him the bad news.

    "Gịnị?"
"They have killed him, they have killed Sankara."
"I knew this was too good to be true."
"Nwachukwu, we will never get up."

24 THE VULTURES ARE CIRCLING

"Peace does not make a good ruler"

(Traditional Botswana proverb)

21 October 1987

All roads led to Umuwe Secondary that Saturday morning. By ten o'clock, the expansive staff hall, often converted into a town hall meeting area, was full to capacity. Residents of Umuwe who were not able to get a seat on one of the long benches arranged in rows instead perched on the ledges of the bank of windows that flanked the room. Others stood in the adjoining passageways.

Lolo Adanna Akuoha and Iwuagwu sat alone at a table in one of the rooms adjacent to the staff hall. Noises from the jostling and conversation outside filtered into the classroom.

"Iwuagwu, the vultures are circling," Lolo Adanna Akuoha said in an almost-whisper, sinking back into her seat and exhaling loudly. Apart from the fact that Iwuagwu could not remember a time when he had ever seen her afraid or vulnerable, he knew that she was not well. She had lost a great deal of weight and she looked tired.

"Have you visited Dr Ejike? I am concerned," Iwuagwu said.

"Not yet, but I will," Lolo Adanna responded.

"Everybody knows that the accusations are unfounded and that the threats to your life are ridiculous and out of order."

"You are kind as ever, Iwuagwu, but both you and I know what they are after. And with all these military boys in power, all that people now know is how to take things by force. Okoro and Ogazi are very dangerous men."

They both fell silent. Iwuagwu was already aware of how dangerous his distant cousin Okoro was. Henry Ogazi, on the other hand, was not someone he knew much about. Iwuagwu had heard that he was living in Lagos, was a very wealthy man, and was now eyeing the position of Eze of Umuwe. Iwuagwu had been present at the very first kindred meeting where the allegations against Lolo Adanna Akuoha had started. This was about a month ago, when Okoro had attended a scheduled Ama Egwu kindred meeting, bringing along with him a letter of petition signed by a number of Umuwe people, including Henry Ogazi and others who were living in the diaspora in Owerri, Enugwu, Aba and Lagos.

"We have reason to believe Lolo Adanna Akuoha is embezzling Umuwe funds placed in her care as Chair of the Umuwe Welfare Association for the water project," Okoro had read out from the letter, before continuing, "For three years, Umuwe people have been taxed, a lot of donations were collected from people at home and abroad, and we do not yet know how much money was received from the government. You have managed to build a water tower, the borehole has been sunk and we know you have bought the pumping machine, but we are also aware that they are all substandard, bought for a fraction of the money reported."

Iwuagwu knew that copies of that same petition had been read out in kindred meetings up and down Umuwe and, even though it did not speculate on exactly what Lolo Adanna Akuoha had allegedly used the embezzled money for, rumours circulated that the money had already been spent on flights and a down-payment on a house in America for Lolo Adanna's first son, studying in America. Other rumours referenced the recent lynching of a motorcycle thief in a neighbouring autonomous community, the suggestion being that Lolo Adanna's transgressions were far greater than the thief's and it would be unjust if she did not suffer the same fate.

Despite the fact that two muscular men now followed Lolo Adanna Akuoha about and were at that moment sat outside the classroom on guard, there were fears for her life. That was why HRH Eze Anthony Osondu had not hesitated, when asked by Lolo Adanna Akuoha, to send out the town crier to travel up and down Umuwe inviting people to hear Lolo Adanna Akuoha address the allegations directly.

A loud knock on the door interrupted the silence that had settled over the room where Iwuagwu and Lolo Adanna Akuoha sat. After another knock, a man who looked to be in his late thirties poked his head from behind the door: Paul Obi, the Treasurer to the Umuwe Welfare Association.

"Lolo, the van has arrived," he announced.

Lolo Adanna Akuoha hesitated before she stood up and limped her way to the door, towards Obi. Iwuagwu followed closely behind her.

HRH Eze Anthony Osondu was already in the large staff hall with two of his aides. Lolo Adanna Akuoha made her way past the gathered hordes of people to where he was sitting at the high table. He too looked weary. Iwuagwu watched from the sidelines, amongst the many who now stood in the aisles that flanked the long rows of benches in the meeting hall. After Lolo Adanna had performed a curtseyed greeting to the Eze and taken her seat at the high table, the Eze stood up and cleared his throat.

"UMUWE, *KWENU!*" the Eze greeted the crowds, repeating himself several times to louder chants of "*Yaah*" all around. When he felt he had the attention of all in attendance, he concluded with his final greeting: "UMUWE, *KWEZU O' NU OOOO!*" This prompted a momentary rapturous cheer, which died as quickly as it had begun, until nothing but the bleating of nearby goats could be heard. A young man approached from the crowd with a saucer laden with kola nuts, which he handed the Eze, stooping as he did so.

"Our ancestors say that he who offers kola nuts brings life, goodwill and peace, and with peace once again challenged in Umuwe we urge these same ancestors to join our effort in facing up to these challenges." As he spoke, the Eze gripped the large saucer in both of his hands, craning his neck as he projected his voice into the microphone held by one of his aides.

When he had concluded his prayer, the Eze placed the large saucer on the high table and selected a kola nut, which he tentatively bite into and chewed. As he did so, he beckoned the young man who had brought the saucer to him to come forward from the crowd. As the young man, accompanied by number of others, diced the kola nuts into fragments that would eventually make their way into the palms of all in attendance, Eze Anthony Osondu cleared his throat for a second time.

"A hand in the pockets of our welfare association is a hand dipped into the pockets of everyone here, and an unwarranted threat to the reputation and life of the head of our welfare association is a threat to each and every person here.

"We have all heard about the petition read out at your respective kindred meetings and the rumours circulating around.

"I appointed Lolo Adanna Akuoha head of Umuwe Welfare Association. Over the last few weeks, I have looked at the allegations with my council of *nzes*, and I can say that I see no wrongdoing." Here the Eze paused, and a rumbling murmur settled over the crowd in the large hall until he continued to speak again.

"I have invited you here to listen to Lolo Adanna Akuoha's side. As your Eze, I urge you to listen carefully."

There seemed to be some hesitation going on in Lolo Adanna Akuoha's mind. She remained in her seat for a few awkward moments after the Eze's aide offered her the microphone, prompting another murmur amongst the crowd in attendance. Even when she did stand up, and seemed poised to speak into the microphone cradled in both her hands, she remained silent for an uncomfortable moment longer. Some shuffling was heard from the back of the hall.

"*Oya*, make road," a few voices could be heard saying, as the people in the aisles of the hall began to step aside for Paul Obi, who was carrying a large box, flanked by two uniformed police officers each carrying a heavy sack. Two more uniformed officers followed closely behind, cradling automatic firearms.

Lolo Adanna Akuoha remained silent, holding on to the microphone as the treasurer set down the box he had been carrying and tore it open. He retrieved reams of paper from the box and started passing them out to people in the hall. As he did so, the police officers emptied the contents of the sacks on the bare mahogany high table: many thick wads of naira notes held together by multiple rubber bands.

"Every kobo that was donated or collected in taxes, and all of the money provided by the government, is recorded in the paper you have in your hand." Lolo Adanna Akuoha eventually began to speak and the pandemonium amongst the crowd that had greeted the arrival of the officers was suddenly reduced to silence.

"Every kobo of your money that I have ever spent in your name, including what I spent it on, and to whom it was paid, is written in the same paper you are holding," she continued, her voice quavering as her eyes began to fill up with tears.

"Every kobo that is left, that belongs to you, is on that table.

"And there is one more thing I need to place in front of you. This is my son, my firstborn whom it has been rumoured I sent to America with your money," Lolo Adanna Akuoha said, as a man in his late teens approached the high table.

25 OYA, GET UP

"Anaghị ewe 'ekweghịm' mbu nwanyị kwuru"

"If you ask a woman for a favour and you ask and ask again she may say yes and grant

you your request"

(Traditional Igbo proverb)

1990

The morning that Obioma turned seventeen came and went without much fanfare. This was because by his sixteenth birthday he had already grown taller than both of his parents, had developed a deep voice and had sprouted a sparse scattering of fine hair over his upper lip, which, thanks to his great care and nurturing, had begun to resemble a moustache.

At that point, just over a year ago, parents in his neighbourhood had begun to point at him when he walked by, acknowledging his ascent to adulthood to misbehaving children in their care, saying things like, "If you don't behave, I will have that man over there flog you and put pepper in your eyes." Around this time, Obioma had also ceased having the old thoughts about barefoot chases around town, the raggedy ball of cloth used in the tag games that both terrified and excited him, or the exhilarating leaps from school buildings, all now very childish thoughts to him.

Nneka still continued to feature prominently in his mind, but not in the same way she used to. After years of playing Nneka's surrogate brother, things were now different. They were officially girlfriend and boyfriend and, in his new-found grown-up perspective, Obioma often gazed at her with the same sort of pride and accomplishment shown by owners of the new air-conditioned Peugeot 505 saloon, taking in her breasts that rivalled her mother's, an attractive backside, the large almond-shaped eyes and bow-contoured lips, and a smile even more mesmerising than it had been before.

Even so, things were not entirely well.

"No, I'm not into all that nonsense."

This was Nneka's usual one-line response to Obioma's sexual advances, delivered while she loudly sucked the air between her teeth with great annoyance. If there was one thing that hadn't changed about Nneka, it was that she was still a person of very few words. She refused to look at any of Obioma's growing collection of pornographic magazines, which he had acquired at great effort and expense and to the detriment of everything else. She would not join him on his trips to video bars to watch 'blue films', a new pastime of his. And Nneka was not interested in his sworn testimonies about other girls who were currently 'doing it' with their boyfriends.

Obioma believed that Nneka's latest foray into bible meetings had something to do with her resistance. Even though she had not quite swapped her miniskirts and midriff-exposing tops for the all-covering ankle-length dresses or the permanently welded-on headscarves worn by the fanatical – 'nde deeper-life', as they were popularly known – Nneka attended bible and prayer meetings at her all-girls' school at least three times during the week. Obioma imagined this to be some sort of phase, something his mother would have also gone through.

As unpleasant as the thought was, Obioma reasoned that his mother, the most dedicated bible person he knew, must have had sex at least twice for both he and his sister to have been conceived. This reasoning led Obioma to the confident conclusion that Nneka would eventually come round to his thinking. So he continued to be content with the odd opportunistic glance down Nneka's top and the chance squeeze of her buttocks and breasts, all facilitated by an array of mishaps which he regularly orchestrated. These staged incidents sometimes bordered on the farcical. The simpers of amusement or embarrassment which appeared on Nneka's face on these occasions disappeared as quickly as they appeared. Obioma would let his hand linger for as long as practicable, but invariably things ended with Nneka delivering sharp smacks to the offending limb, followed up by swats to the back of his head. Any more direct attempts to grope her were met with even greater aggression.

These 'issues' with Nneka, as Obioma termed them, featured highly and frequently in a long list of predicaments that Obioma believed he faced. It bothered him too that he had never seen what lay beyond the thick mat of curly pubic hair which he only very occasionally caught sight of. Even so, even for these very rare sightings, Obioma routinely appeared at Nneka's home after school.

Nneka still lived in the bedroom she shared with her mother in the large face-me-i-face-you bungalow which they shared with various other families on the other side of town. Nneka always went home to change out of her uniform and to bathe before continuing on to help at her mother's stall. Obioma found that turning up at Nneka's home at these times presented his only opportunity for naked sightings of her.

Obioma calculated that her living situation meant that Nneka would either have to change out of her uniform and into new clothes in the all-in-one bedroom and living room, or do so in the bathroom they shared with other families, which was cramped and always soaking wet. He knew her choice of place would always be the room, unless of course it was a cold, rainy day, in which case there would be no bathing at all.

Obioma painstakingly computed an optimum see-all-angles vantage point for himself in relation to the mirrors in the room and, despite Nneka's stringent demand that he avert his eyes, his efforts occasionally paid off, as Nneka sometimes struggled to conceal herself during her elaborate towel-aided changing routine.

These glimpses of her naked frame fuelled Obioma's thoughts, mingling with the more explicit pornographic images displayed on the old cathode-ray-tube televisions that were mounted on high tables in the dimly lit video bars he often visited.

Obioma would often simulate the rhythmical movements he believed Nneka's large breasts would make if he ever got the chance to be on top of her. He imagined her nipples jutting out, even more than they usually did against the fabric of her blouse on cold, rainy days. He fantasised about squeezing one and putting his lips around the other as he thrust himself deep into her.

Obioma felt unsure of what sounds Nneka would make in the hypothetical world he had created. The soft moans and groans of pleasure he had imagined over the years had now become the loud convulsive squeals the women made on the screens in the dark rooms he visited, noises that occasionally made him question the authenticity of the ardent fantasies he was constructing. He hated the fact that the pleasures he gained from his simulations of her were increasingly short-lived and, in an epiphany one ordinary afternoon, he realised that he needed to make his imagined sessions with Nneka more authentic. He now set out to painstakingly predict what Nneka would do, and what he would never get away with. He concluded that he should not slap Nneka's buttocks or yank at her hair. He believed things would surely be over between them if he ever suggested anal sex, but he was optimistic that he would be allowed to ejaculate on her face, as this always seemed to be genuinely well received on the films he watched. He had also heard a woman in one of these films remark about how good for the skin it was, as she massaged the splatter of semen across her face, with the tips of her fingers.

Obioma was not always confident about the long list of conclusions he had come to, and would often revisit and alter the items on it. But this made little difference to his dreams of her, each becoming more raunchy than the last.

"OBIOMA, *OYA*, GET UP!" Obioma heard the thunderous roar of his mother's voice ringing in his ear. He believed that he had only just shut his eyes, but it had actually been a full four hours since he had collapsed onto his bed in a heap, paralysed by a long shift at his mother's eating house which had ended at midnight. Like a mantis mimicking a dead leaf for camouflage, Obioma remained still in his bed. He heard rustling and the and clanking of pots and pans. His mother's voice, now fainter, reverberated against the walls, doors and ceilings of the flat as she spread the very unwelcome news of the break of a new day to his younger sister.

Obioma squeezed his eyes shut, his eyelids useless against the two newly fired-up 400-watt industrial electric lamps dangling over him from the ceiling. He turned his face and pressed it against his pillow and in seconds he was off again to sleep, only to be smacked back into Monday morning minutes later.

"Obioma, get up; get up now, *oya*, get up!" The repeated light tapping of his mother's palm against the side of his face felt like out-and-out slaps, causing the blurry, smutty images of Nneka he had managed to reinstate in the seconds he drifted back to sleep to vanish into thin air.

The temporary blinding sensation from the glare of the electric bulbs hanging over him cleared and Obioma took in the bleak, cold, not-yet-light morning he would soon be thrown into. His mother scrambled off to rattle and clatter more pots and pans. Images of his mother's wooden comb planted firmly into her unkempt hair, the stump of a week-old used chewing-stick sticking out of her mouth, all unwelcome morning thoughts, eventually motivated Obioma to roll up his pillow in his wafer-thin mattress, and stow them away behind the three-seater couch in the far corner.

With that, his bedroom morphed back into the family living room. More minutes went by, and Obioma and his sister got washed and dressed for school and congregated in their parents' room for morning prayers, as they always did.

"*Na aha* Jesus," his mother cried out, as she led the Morning Prayer. "Lord father, in Matthew 18, Verse 20, you say that where two or three are gathered together in your name, you are in the midst of them. Lord Jehovah, we have gathered again this morning in your presence to thank you for all that you have done and to call upon your mighty name for protection. We pray that you keep…"

These days, Obioma's mother's prayers were more ramblings than vitriol. There was no more talk of demons and principalities, which Obioma now accepted his mother had actually foreseen those many years ago. Their lives had definitely changed. With Obioma's father long dead, combined with the loss of his mother's stockfish shop, Obioma knew that his mother felt that the demons and principalities had done their worst and moved on. What was now left of his mother, Obioma felt, was the idle flutter of habit, like the twitching of a dead insect.

In fact, the rambling prayers she now said were the most he usually heard from her all day. He would be lucky to get a strung-together sentence out of her beyond, "Fetch the mortar and pestle and pound these cooked yams quick, quick," or, "Go serve customer," things she would say as she stood over her large cooking workstation in her eating house, her eyes firmly fixed on the school of dried and welded-together *ikpọkwa* fish she would be painstakingly disassembling. The meals Obioma and his mother shared together at their home during the weekends were also silent, or when they weren't it would be because there was a need to go through a to-do list for the eating house. Obioma felt a twinge of guilt and regret for his indulgence in his long-established habit of expertly straddling the realms of sleep and consciousness as he, his sister and his mother stood around in his parents' room, eyes closed and head bowed.

"Amen," his mother and sister eventually chorused. Too soon as always, Obioma thought. It was now time to face the day.

26 FIRE

"Onye ite abụghị onye ahịa"

"A pot trader whose fortunes are all invested in her clay pots isn't much of a merchant"

(Traditional Igbo proverb)

Later that morning

The sun not fully up yet, Obioma's mother led the way, charging down the road in the dark in giant, quickened strides. Ogechi was not too far behind her. Both carried large basins on their heads full to the brim with groceries. At some distance behind them, Obioma slackly pushed a wheelbarrow heavily laden with yam tubers and bags of various grains.

They hastened past the various heaps of smelly refuse in mid-decay dumped on the road during and after the last Sanitation Day. A day decreed by the military government for everyone to put aside all their plans and clean their immediate surroundings. A day backed up by marauding soldiers in combat vehicles wielding whips and guns.

Within moments, Obioma and the rest of his family were quarter of the way to their destination, walking past the large mob of dejected-looking tradesmen who now eerily perched quietly at the intersection between Nnamdi Azikiwe Road and Mbaise Road. *They look just as I feel,* Obioma thought. With the austerity and all, Obioma was well aware that by noon the spot they were on would be a no-go area, as the numbers of jobless tradesmen would have more than doubled in size and fights would break out as they scrambled to board the contractor pick-up vans that these days only very occasionally swept by.

As he thought about the weary faces that stared back from the low fencing that had now become a mass seating area, it occurred to Obioma that he and his family now woke up well before most of these tradesmen, as well as traders in his neighbourhood. For the few minutes that his sleep-deprived mind could find the focus to think about this, he wondered what his father would have made of all of that was happening now.

The tectonic plates beneath his family's feet had moved considerably over the past few years. The demons his mother had talked about so much had now carried out their wickedest acts, although they had not materialised in the expected form of demon bats, debilitating plague-like illnesseses resulting from Augustus's many trips to witch doctors, or of his plots with other traders on Obioma's mother's aisle to steal her shop and the treasure trove of stockfish supplies hidden in cellar. But in the end, the demons had stolen Obioma's mother's shop away anyway, on an ordinary February evening seven years earlier.

Obioma had only just arrived home from his usual warm farewells to Nneka and her mother, after another evening sitting with them at their stall and selling *egusi* seeds.

"Mr Nneka, are you back?" Obioma's father quipped as usual as Obioma slithered into his seat at the dinner table, opposite Ogechi's mocking grin. Obioma's mother, back from a trip to the kitchen, had only just set bowls of Owerri soup on the table when a heavily panting neighbour barged into their dining room to inform them that the Old Market was on fire.

"You two, lock the door and don't leave the house until we return." Obioma's father issued the instruction in a panic before chasing after Obioma's mother, who was already sprinting up their cul-de-sac towards the Old Market along with a handful of other traders.

From the vantage point of their fifth-floor flat, Obioma and his sister watched the initial faint stream of smoke in the distance thicken, then broaden, before leaps of raw flame became visible. Every now and again, a handful of neighbours would arrive on foot, on motorbikes, in cars or in pick-up vans to unload various wares salvaged from the inferno. Many were covered in black soot and out of breath. They would hurriedly dump rolls of cloth or bags of grain at the front of their residences and rush back up the cul-de-sac towards the market. As the hours rolled by, Obioma and his sister grew more anxious when their parents failed to show up as some of the other traders had done, perhaps with bales or loose clutches of stockfish.

Obioma remembered how, soon after, darkness had properly descended over the city, emphasising the already enormous orange flames that leaped up in the dark night's sky. As Obioma and his sister stood transfixed on their balcony by the eerie spectacle, along with many in the city and beyond, the thoughts that bothered them now were not of stockfish, but of the lives of their parents.

The fire was still raging through the market just after midnight, when Obioma's parents eventually returned home after they had finally accepted that nothing could be saved. They had grown tired of standing around the perimeter of the vast market with frustrated and complaining firemen. The market was too cluttered, they said, a messy mass of sheds with no network of roads running through them for their large trucks, which were also out of water. The dry network of pipes around the market had not seen a molecule of water run through them for many years. The supposed cavalry of firemen from Umuahia, Aba and Okigwe who arrived with water had eventually just joined them on the sidelines to gawk at the leaping flames, Obioma's father lamented. Some hopeful traders had defiantly darted back and forth between the flames and the cordon, hoping to salvage their wares, with little success.

The growing crowd of idle fire officers had eventually filled their time by demolishing buildings round the perimeter of the market to stop the fire engulfing the rest of the city – a possibility that had terrified Owerri city dwellers, including Obioma. When Obioma's parents arrived home, they had found Obioma and Ogechi slumped asleep on the floor of their balcony. Strewn around them were haphazardly packed bags full of school books, a selection of clothes, a sack of onions, Ogechi's decapitated dolls and Obioma's safe-box, items Obioma had made his sister help him assemble when they feared the fire would spread and engulf the city and their building.

It was only around seven o'clock the following morning that the damage caused by the overnight raging fire could be properly surveyed. Smoke still seeped from under the expanse of rubble. The fire had engulfed the entire market and had only abated in the heavy downpour of rain that had begun just after six o'clock that morning. Like most traders in the Old Market, Obioma's mother lost the entire contents of her shop.

Obioma remembered that everyone he had seen that morning had talked about how the rain had come too late. Obioma's mother had been hopeful that, at the very least, the wads of cash stashed in her safe cabinet in the cellar underneath her shop were protected and safe. But when she had finally managed to open the safe, a thing she considered a good omen, she had been greeted by stacks of cremated paper which crumbled into ash when touched. Obioma knew that it had been at that point that his mother had accepted that she was ruined.

Obioma turned into the remaining stretch of road that led to his mother's eating house, her new business. He decided to quicken his pace in an effort to bridge the enormous gap between the wheelbarrow he carried, and his mother and sister way ahead.

27 MADAM SUCCULENT

"Anya hụrụ nmụọ ga-a nwụ"

"The eyes that see a spirit will die"

(Traditional Igbo proverb)

That morning

"Madam Succulent, morning," chorused the half-dozen shopkeepers and labourers when Obioma's mother arrived to unlock the four padlocked hinges that fastened two heavy iron bars, crossed in an 'X', across the wooden doors of the eatery. Obioma watched his mother strive to respond to the greetings, with a forced smile and joviality betrayed by how quickly her face fell flat.

"The day that woman smiles is the day the world will end," Obioma had once heard one of the diners say to another. He had heard worse. Obioma had once witnessed his mother angrily snatch a watch from the wrist of a customer, a trader called Jolly, on a busy morning. In the all-out row that had ensued, Obioma's mother had accused Jolly of abusing the credit that was generously extended to him by not paying his debts at the end of the week as agreed, and Jolly had called his mother a "hairy-chested witch".

Despite such incidents between Obioma's mother and some of her guests occurring from time to time, customers continued to come in droves. Madam Succulent's *akamu*, the local custard his mother made from maize, was legendary, talked about in stalls up and down the two main markets in the city and the shops around town. Obioma knew this was because his mother put in a lot more sugar than was the norm and added flavours like vanilla and cinnamon, things that only ever appeared in ice creams. Madam Succulent's was also the only place in the city anyone could get a bowl of rare dry-fish pepper soup.

With the two heavy bars hoisted out of their latches and secured in the corner by his mother, Obioma bolted the large double doors open, securing them into place with a pair of small bricks. He darted across the eating area, unhooking piles of stowed-away chairs and tables, positioning them for business. His mother and sister disappeared to the kitchen area at the back of the eating house.

Securing the lease for the eating house was one of the very few useful things Obioma's father had done before his death – at least, so Obioma had once heard his mother say. Obioma knew that his mother continued to resent his father, even in death. For not taking her advice and leaving his driving job with the civil service. For not having agreed, before it was too late, to establish a second stockfish shop in the New Market with the stock and money from the cellar of her shop which was later destroyed by fire. Had he done so, he would have been alive and they would have still owned at least one shop.

Obioma's father's death, which happened a year after the market fire, two weeks after Obioma's thirteenth birthday, had come as a sudden shock. He had died on a very rainy day on the Aba–Owerri expressway on his way to deliver some files to a local government office which was about an hour's drive away from Owerri.

The brakes had failed on the old government car to which Obioma's father had been demoted after the loss of his plum job driving the Commissioner, just as he lost control of the car in the rain. He had driven over a large pothole which he had not spotted and, as he swerved to avoid another, the car careered off the high way, somersaulting several metres down the side of the road and into a ditch. A group of his father's colleagues on a condolence visit to Obioma's home had discussed the details as they perched on various surfaces in the living room and waited for Obioma's mother to emerge from her room. A number of them were there when Obioma's father's mangled and decapitated body was recovered from the vehicle wreckage. Obioma had seen it laid out alongside half a dozen others on the darkened, blood-splattered floor of the viewing room of the local mortuary. He and his mother had been obliged to turn up and identify the body.

That day, as the strong mixture of rotten smells and fumes from chemical cleaning agents oozed from the corpses and the floor, Obioma's mother had stood quietly alongside him with a disappointed look on her face. It was the same sort of look she had worn when she had heard that

Sebastian, the second cousin who had worked for her in her stockfish shop, was now a drunkard, driven to drink by the disappointment of losing his job after the shop fire.

Obioma had realised then that his father had been absent long before his death, because she had constantly worn the same look whenever she had looked at Obioma's father in the last months of his life.

The coup d'état that had lost Obioma's father his prized job of chauffeuring the Commissioner had brought with it significant life changes. In the days, weeks and months that followed the coup, Obioma remembered, the radio and television news programmes had been awash with tales of how billions of naira of public funds had been carted away by politicians up and down the country. Wads of cash that could literally fill lorries were dug up from the compounds and gardens of politicians' sprawling mansions and modest bungalows alike, appearing on television sets in living-rooms everywhere. Prominent politicians had ended up shackled, some stripped naked, and paraded alongside recovered state loot on television. Rumours circulated of billions of dollars transferred from state and federal government accounts to the personal bank accounts of politicians in far-flung places in Europe.

There were also tales of those who had got away with it. Like the Commissioner Obioma's father chauffeured, who had managed to flee abroad hours after the coup. Obioma had heard how, following his father's tip-off, the Commissioner arranged to be driven to and smuggled across the border to Cameroon with his wife and three children, and subsequently to Europe, where it was rumoured he owned several houses.

Obioma knew that the call his father had made on the morning of the coup was the last contact he had had with the Commissioner. The incoming military governor and his appointed commissioners either sacked or demoted staff who had served the fleeing or apprehended political appointees. Obioma's father had been relegated to being a pool driver, with the dishevelled car he later died in.

Obioma remembered the protracted rows his parents got into shortly after his father's demotion: taunts from his mother about how Obioma's father had wasted his loyalty on a man who had not bothered to get in touch to thank him for his freedom, whose wife was probably parading up and down shopping malls in Europe, and whose children would be sent to the best schools abroad so that they could come back and pick up where their parents had left off.

Obioma had heard his father call his mother a bush woman.

"How many banks do we have on Douglas Road?" Obioma remembered his father asking his mother at the top of his voice during one of their many rows, chastising her for preferring to hoard her money in a cellar.

In a matter of weeks after his demotion, Obioma's father's bushy beard resurfaced over his increasingly gaunt-looking face. His frame too became emaciated, his ample pot belly receding. His father was fading away.

Obioma awakened from this unusually long bout of daydreaming probably afforded him by the brief energy he derived from the sugary *akamu* and buttered white bread he had scoffed down quickly. At roughly quarter past seven that morning his shift was over and, although he would be back around six o'clock that evening for the next shift, it was now time to leave his mother's eatery for school.

28 SENIOR

"However long the night, the dawn will break"

(Traditional African proverb)

That morning

Owerri was definitely a mess just after seven o'clock that morning. What seemed like the world's largest gathering of motorcyclists constantly moved up and down the great road. Some thought that this was because motorcycles were now cheap to import and buy, and austerity meant that people were ditching their cars for motorcycles. They were everywhere, manoeuvring past each other and the long tailback of cars on both sides of the road. The strained shouts of "Good morning, customer" and *"I na aga?"* (Are you going?) were barely audible over the higher-decibel rattle from the revving of engines all around. Would-be passengers and keen motorcyclists tried to quickly establish an arrangement. Also high on the decibel count were the torrents of creative insults and counter-abuse unleashed as motorcyclists swerved abruptly and dangerously into cars, pedestrians or each other.

"Fuck your mother."

"You dey mad?"

"Chineke kpụọ gi ọkụ" (May God set you alight with fire).

"Usa ra kwa otu nne gi" (May a squirrel have sexual intercourse with your mother's genitals).

These inventive phrases seemed not to be said with any real malice; it was just everyday roadside etiquette. Most of the incidents were near misses, often when the motorcyclists stopped momentarily to collect or release their passengers, wads of far-from-crisp, small-denomination notes handed to them for their toil.

Every now and again it would not be such a good morning for the poor pedestrian or cyclist either shunted off or thrown many yards clear of a fast-moving motorcycle into one of the large, heaving open-drainage gutters that ran on either side of the great road. It was quite typical to see a growing crowd of passers-by looking on as good Samaritans nervously worked to help pull another unfortunate out of the mixture of stagnant month-old litter and water, all hoping against a serious injury or fatality.

Still wrestling his tiredness, Obioma traced the length of the Great Nnamdi Azikiwe Road past Okwe Street, Mere Street and the succession of other quieter streets that ran parallel to the great road. A mixture of modest bungalows and one-storey buildings flagged each side of the roads, dwellings of civil servants and traders who had long left home for the daily toil.

Obioma's lazy gait matched the pace of the music in his ears, which came from the Walkman that bulged awkwardly in one of his trouser pockets. His preferred slow, soulful Boys II Men power ballads blasted out of his earphones at a harmfully high volume and he basked in the cool, fresh morning and the contrasting calm and quiet of the broad, almost empty tarmac which stretched to the horizon in front of him.

He made his usual pit-stops – the first a ramshackle heap of junk with corrugated zinc-fashioned wings, parked on Mere Street. It belonged to a man whom everyone believed suffered from mental illness, or whom they thought at the very least was rather eccentric. In all the years that Obioma had commuted along that street he had only seen the man twice, most recently when he was climbing out of his mock aeroplane on a particularly debilitating hot afternoon. There was no question but that he had to flee his tin can, Obioma remembered thinking. As the man skipped down the narrow metallic stairs of his aircraft, Obioma saw the crazed look in his eye – the same look Moses sometimes wore, that permanent half-startled glare.

Obioma's second stop was further along the quiet succession of roads, right outside Immaculate Cutz, one of two barbers on the route to school. Obioma had never actually been inside the barbershop, but it was impossible for him to just walk past the expansive mirrors that doubled as its main doors and outside walls. Every morning, Obioma's slow walk would grind to a complete halt as he took stock of his attire in the large body of mirror. His oversized, long-sleeved cotton shirt – he had three which he wore on alternating days – was draped over his large shoulders, making him, as intended, seem a lot stouter than he actually was. All three shirts were religiously bleached and Robin-Blued, giving them an almost ghostly fluorescence, even in daylight.

Obioma also wore loose-fitting trousers almost twice his measurements, with double turned-up hems and extra fastenings at the front. This gave his trousers impressive flutters in the mild cross-winds that passed through the surrounding buildings and street, making his trousers look like boat sails.

"*O' boy, abi*! You wan' win Miss Universe?" A passing classmate of his who had been powering down the same succession of roads mocked him as he swept past.

"Ha, John Boon. *Ọtụ nne gị there*," Obioma retorted a little too late before resuming his slow progress in the same direction, his lanky classmate all but vanishing over the horizon up ahead.

Apart from the warm fuzzy feeling of being in clothes that fitted him, there was one more reason to feel elated that morning. Obioma was a month into his final year, having risen to the sixth and final form of his secondary school. This was a very favourable position to finally be in, considering the intense hierarchical regiments that separated each of the six years that made up the typical secondary school experience, particularly in the all-boys school he attended.

Six years earlier, the walk through the school's ironic pearly-white gates had been nerve-racking. Gone were Nneke's intermittent mesmerising smiles which Obioma had grown so accustomed to. In their place, the unending testosterone-fuelled posturing, pecking order and conflict that came from being in an all-boys school.

The first three years of secondary school had seen Obioma and his counterparts wearing white short-sleeved shirts, green shorts and sandals, a statement of their very minor status in the school's ecosystem. They were at the bottom of the food-chain and fair game for all manner of chores, as well as the brutal urges of the more sadistically inclined senior students – those in their final year, just as he was now, and who in addition had acquired one of the dozen or so official prefect office titles. The elite of the elite.

Obioma recalled how a pack of thrill-seeking sixth-form students would descend like hyenas on the isolated hall at the far reaches of the school compound which housed almost all of the first-form classes in the school. They often targeted that sweet spot before noon, just before the afternoon break, when the entire hall would be free of teachers, leaving the six classes housed in the large hall vulnerable to their attack. They would pounce as soon as the last of the teachers left the hall for the staff-room across the vast wilderness of scanty grass and baking sand.

"On your lockers!" the ringleader would typically cry out, as he and his comrades stormed in like commandos. Similar cries would ring out from every entrance to the hall, followed by a brief kerfuffle as young students mounted their standard-issue one-person desk-chairs.

"Where is the class prefect?" the raiders would demand.

"Where are the names of noise makers?" the class prefect would then be asked. Everyone knew the drill.

The responsibility of class prefect was both a blessing and a curse. You were more or less immune to the *Ụtali*, a kind of springy bamboo stick, that stung like nothing on earth if you happen to get whipped with one. But that immunity meant you were responsible for committing your classmates to several lashings of the cane. All class prefects had the responsibility of compiling a list of students who were noisy and disruptive over the course of the day. This was, of course, everyone, but usually a list of about seven names would suffice for the raiders.

Staying off those lists depended on how much of a friend, foe or threat you were to the class prefects. Anyone who had the misfortune to get onto the list became a sort of uncelebrated martyr for the rest of the students. They would be the ones who would be whipped, providing the raiding pack with enough sadistic entertainment to send them on their way, towards another unfortunate bunch of newbies.

Vulnerability to these attacks would continue until about the fourth year, just after the major school midway exams. At this time, students got to wear trousers instead of shorts, a symbol of how far they had come in the world.

Raids were few and far between then. It was perhaps conceptually and practically problematic for the roving packs to engage teaching halls and blocks housing up to two hundred students who were more or less their size. Such raids did not always go down well.

By the sixth year, sandals were swapped for shoes and long-sleeved shirts replaced the short-sleeved ones. If you were one of the dozen or so adorned with a title, you carried a standard issue *Ụtali*, if you weren't but you had a penchant for cruelty, you would obtain one personally, make do, in chance opportunities, with your belt, or improvise with broken-off tree branches, bicycle chains, or wooden legs torn from rickety school chairs.

That morning, Obioma made a particular point of waltzing his way through the school gates, the flutter of his trousers in a slight gust of wind giving his entry an extra regal feel.

"Good morning, senior," some cowering younger boys in shorts and short-sleeved shirts stuttered nervously, scarpering off ahead along the driveway towards the classroom blocks. So great was their fear and need to flee that Obioma did not even have a chance to respond.

29 THE DEFLATION

"A pretty basket does not prevent worries"

(Traditional Congolese proverb)

That morning

By quarter to eight that morning, Obioma's exuberant mood and elation at being in the top class had fizzled out. He sat hunched over his desk as his classmates wandered in and out of the pale-green classroom with the reverence with which people carried themselves in places of worship. Being in the final year did have its own drawback: final examinations.

"Judgement day cometh." That was how one of Obioma's classmates referred to the two-week-long intense flurry of examinations that was only months away. Obioma and his classmates did not begin the day in their usual jovial and boisterous manner. They no longer greeted each other with bellowing laughter and exaggerated chatter about girls they had chatted up or bedded, or about encounters with tear gas at the stadium on Whetheral Road after an Iwuanyawnu National Football Club match. Instead, they sat and intensely stared into their textbooks and the hand-written notes which were crammed into stacks of thick eighty-leaf exercise books, the approaching examinations burdening their young minds in the same way execution-day might weigh on the minds of condemned prison inmates.

No one felt this more greatly than Obioma, who had literally slept his way through his last three years of secondary schooling. Fatigue from the weeks of early mornings and late nights at his mother's eating house caused Obioma to sit slumped at his desk with a strong expectation of ultimate failure, having only just scraped through into the sixth form, his perpetual dozy state propped up by a concoction of anxiety and a nagging sense of under-accomplishment.

"There is no way I'm passing the finals," he would remind himself, as though the resignation would make him feel better.

Obioma's mental collection of images of Nneka's shapely naked frame did very little, at these times, to dull his awareness of the sprawling decline he believed he was in. He instead revisited old dreams of rolling acres of palm plantations and scenes of hundreds of old women in vast fields, pounding pots of cooked palm nuts. But those dreams had long been crushed, and thoughts of them were as relieving as the inconsequential get-well wishes that came from one who visits an unwell friend.

So far, *ntuntu* had helped him scrap past the succession of promotional exams that saw him reach the final year of his school. Before an exam, Obioma would engrave a series of notes on blank sheets of paper which he smuggled into the examination hall as rough paper. He knew this tactic would not work in the final school exams. Besides the fact that the examiners insisted on supplying all rough paper, the exam hall itself was heavily policed and the notes needed for the entire exam enormous.

Obioma's thoughts shifted to the prospect of somehow acquiring the question papers before the exams. This happened quite a lot, but it was pot luck as to whether they were genuine. He remembered the various people who had wandered into his neighbourhood just before the previous year's exams, touting supposed leaked question papers for sale. He had heard that one of the papers turned out to be genuine, but the rest were get-rich-quick schemes hatched in the back rooms of photocopying shops. There were at least fifteen fake versions for every real exam question paper that appeared, and he would have to buy them all to be sure.

There was only one other way, he thought: paying somebody else, *onye ocha*, to sit the examinations.

Alifor was a supposed old neighbour of Obioma. He had never met him, as Alifor had moved away with his family after the breakdown of his mental health, but people around often spoke about him and his family. Alifor had been a truant and, for his final two-week examination, his father had bribed one of the exam invigilators to courier his answer sheets and exam questions to a boy from Owerri's prestigious Federal Boys College, to whom he had also paid large sums of money stolen from the tills of various traders, to sit and write his papers in an abandoned building adjoining the exam hall. Alifor had got A-grades in each of his nine subjects and high marks in his university entrance exam, which the Federal Boys College boy had also sat on his behalf by impersonating him in the exam hall. Alifor had signed up to a medical degree in the prestigious University of Nigeria Nnsuka but, after a semester of work he could not handle, he had sustained a major breakdown. There were stories of Alifor wrapping himself in cling film and parading around town. He and his family were said to have eventually moved to their ancestral home in a rural area many miles from Owerri, where allegedly Alifor had eventually hung himself.

Obioma had heard various versions of this story, and insisted to himself that they were all totally made up. In any event, Alifor had been stupid to pick medicine, a subject Obioma imagined was fraught with heavy workload and practical assessments that one could not navigate around. Alifor should have considered the extent of his mental capacity, Obioma felt. Settling on the idea of using an *onye ọcha m* to sit his exams, Obioma soothed the niggling anxiety over Alifor's fate with a plan to catch up on gaps in his knowledge in the breaks between the examinations and the start of university. He would put the 3,234 naira and 20 kobo he had saved up over the years in his safe-box towards his plan. He reasoned that this amount would be more than enough to get him a really good *onye ocha*. He would look into it tomorrow, he concluded to himself.

Obioma's bumbling train of thought always culminated in his long-standing feud with Kalu. The last time they had spoken, just over a year ago, they had been very close to blows. Obioma's thoughts travelled much further back in time, to about three years earlier, to another sore point in their relationship: that crushing sunny afternoon when Obioma showed up at Kalu's house to help his best friend prepare for their big move from around the Old Market to a large mansion on the outskirts of the city which Kalu's brother Benjamin had just built.

Benjamin had suddenly hit it big in his work with Chief Alusi. In one fell swoop, he had acquired land and built two mansions in a popular suburb of New Owerri. There he had stood, helping Kalu to pack their family heirlooms, when Kalu had chosen to break the news to Obioma that he no longer thought that the palm oil business idea was viable. He would also inform his best friend that afternoon that he had decided to use the money he had saved up in his safe-box towards buying a car in the future instead.

"For one, we will need machines instead of old women to make the palm oil fast enough. We will not have nearly enough money in a million years to buy the amount of land to produce the quantity of palm fruits we need, let alone the machines. We will need to buy many trucks and employ strong grown-up men to carry and transport the oil to thousands of markets. We haven't even began to talk about how those many palm trees would be planted in the first place."

Obioma listened to his friend glibly reel off a million and one reasons why their plans had to be smothered to death, plans he had clung on to as his family and their fortunes unravelled.

Obioma had believed that afternoon that Kalu was really intending on dispensing with their plans and their close friendship in one fell swoop. After all, Kalu and his family were now very rich. In a matter of days they would be living on the outskirts of the city amongst top politicians, wealthy business people, prominent doctors and lawyers. Kalu would overnight turn into a snob. Kalu would look at him with the same disdain and air of superiority that children of such people showed towards their house helps, market traders and the people like him who lived around the market. Obioma had also believed he had seen their rift coming for a while. Kalu had been growing more and more detached and shedding his notable sensitive and thoughtful nature ever since news of his brother's success had started floating about. Like his elder brother Benjamin, Kalu had also grown into the habit of deliberately setting out to be very flippant and hurtful with his comments.

"Pisces is a rubbish zodiac sign. You guys are basically fucked." This was Kalu's take on the misfortunes that had befallen Obioma's family over the years, and on Obioma sharing the zodiac sign with his deceased father.

"So have you fucked Nneka yet? Shall I have a try?" Obioma remembered Kalu once asking him, a recollection that irritated him so much that Obioma broke out from his musing.

At exactly eight that morning, a tall boy with unusually long arms, wearing shorts, appeared from the dormitory area of the school with a large stick. He walked up to a large rusting truck-wheel dangling from the branch of a tree, suspended by bicycle chains. He proceeded to strike the wheel continually for about half a minute, to announce that it was time for morning assembly.

Obioma joined the rest of the students, about two thousand strong, as they marched out from their various classrooms and took their positions in front of the assembly podium, a narrow one-metre slab of raised concrete at the midway point along one of the lengths of the large football field. The podium marked the exact centre of the school compound and had about half a dozen steps, flattening out at the top, with room for one or two people at most to stand. Students lined up in columns according to their years and classes and, after the final group of year-six students had leisurely shuffled to their positions, the assembly area became an impressive orderly display of green-and-white uniforms.

Teachers trickled out of the staff-room a few metres away and stood in their usual detached spot by the right-hand side of the podium.

'Good morning all,' Kalu said as he appeared on the podium, his copy of the *Ancient and Modern* hymn-book in one hand, his standard-issue *ụtalị* in the other. Kalu was the new Senior Prefect, or SP as the position was popularly known. Appointed just before the close of the previous term, he now presided over his cabinet of prefects and the entire student population.

"Kalu has grown into a strapping young man," Obioma had heard his mother remark. "He looks like the handsome, smiling young man on the billboards, running and jumping with cups of cocoa drinks in his hand."

Manipulative, deceitful, arrogant sociopath like his fucking brother. Obioma was very much alone in his damning assessment of his old best friend. Because of this, it was an opinion he tended to keep to himself, and because it made him seem bitter, jealous and petty. Kalu's sporting exploits as a prolific defender in the school's football team, and his achievements for the school in debating and quiz competitions, made him very popular amongst all students.

The election that saw Kalu sweep into power was a landslide victory, and seemed more like a mere formality. Kalu's mature, effortless poise and prodigious academic brilliance also meant that he was well liked by the teachers. He was especially admired by the school principal, who seemed to relate to Kalu on similar terms as he did to his two deputies. Kalu's status as someone who had transcended his student station was cemented by the fact that, from the start of the new term, he arrived at the school in his own car, which he parked alongside the cars of the teachers and the principal in the school's car park.

'Please turn to hymn 573,' Kalu requested in a voice that floated across the vast sea of heads and green-and-white uniforms. After a brief ruffling of pages, Kalu kicked things off, singing the first line, his voice echoing across the quiet school compound.

"All things bright and beautiful."

The singing voices of the students and teachers followed Kalu's cue and rose floating even above the moderate traffic noises beyond the school's fence on the great road.

Obioma did not sing. His heavy eyes gazed up at Kalu and then closed in quiet despair.

30 THE GREAT CULLING 1

"Return to old watering holes for more than water; friends and dreams are there to meet

you"

(Traditional African proverb)

Lolo Adanna Akuoha was not much of a church person, but on the day of her funeral all members of the Christian Mothers' Association of St Bartholomew Parish Church attended in their full ceremonial attire. The women, numbering close to two thousand, marched with a large portrait photograph of Lolo Adanna Akuoha anchored on two poles, each pole carried by two women at the front of the procession. It started at the church premises, situated not too far from the secondary school, and snaked along Umuwe's dusty main road towards Lolo Adanna Akuoha's compound. Against the usual protocol, Iwuagwu joined them, singing, where he could, the hymns and gospel songs that spurred the women on on that slightly breezy, sunny afternoon. When they reached Iyi Ala, a roadside pond dyed by the red earth that surrounded it and darkened by the shade of the tall ancient trees that shielded it from the sun's rays, Iwuagwu, even with the walking stick that he now carried everywhere, could continue no further. This was the spot that marked the beginning of Lolo Adanna Akuoha's village, and Iwuagwu's mind retreated to when he had last seen Adanna alive.

"I still sometimes feel my leg as if it is still there", she had said those many weeks ago as she pushed a needle into her thigh, eventually discharging the contents of the syringe into it. It was Iwuagwu's fifth visit to Lolo Adanna's house since Dr Ejike's diagnosis of type II diabetes – a diagnosis Dr Ejike had caught by chance, when Lolo Adanna Akuoha visited his clinic about a minor cut on her right foot which would not heal. After Lolo Adanna had had that same leg amputated, Iwuagwu made a point of spending a great many afternoons lounging in one of the large comfy chairs in Lolo Adanna Akuoha's living room. She had increasingly confined herself to the room since the loss of her leg.

"Dr Ejike told me this thing, this insulin I am shooting into my leg is actually from pigs."

"Are you sure you don't want me to go, and give you some privacy?" Iwuagwu asked, wincing.

"Don't worry; we have known each other long enough and my late husband is no longer here to disapprove." Adanna said, with a mischievous but strained smile on her face. "Besides there is nothing you haven't at some point seen. I am far too old to care."

Adanna had slumped back into the large couch after administering the injection into her thigh, but now she sat up again.

"Do you remember when we all used to splash up and down Iyi Ala naked?"

"Yes I do, though it is a little fuzzy," Iwuagwu replied.

"I stopped by Iyi Ala a few weeks ago, and noticed how small it now seemed. It felt like a large lake in those days. I also remember that besides your head seeming twice the size of everybody else's, you always had a runny nose, slime perpetually dripping from your nose, sometimes down to your neck, and your cousin, Chukwuka always seemed to get himself entangled in it," Adanna continued. "I miss Chukwuka."

"We all do."

"When Chukwuka died last year, and Donna and Elizabeth joined him months later, I became convinced that I did not have very long."

"Please don't talk like that."

"Well it is true, I wish I could have done a lot more," Adanna insisted.

"Adanna, you see that wash-hand basin right there in that bathroom of yours? I have one too, and every time I turn the taps on I think of you and what you have done and what you are going to continue to do, even from this chair you insist on lying in these days.

"The treasurer and I are meeting the electricity engineer tomorrow. We have not only got a new school and safe drinking water as a result of your efforts, but very soon homes in Umuwe will all have electricity running through them."

Now, the singing of the procession that paraded Lolo Adanna Akuoha's photograph around town had become an incoherent wave of strained and muffled sounds, becoming momentarily audible as gusts of winds lapped against the branches of the large trees that surrounded the pond where

Iwuagwu sat. He guessed that by now the women were well inside Adanna's compounded. Probably taking turns to gawk at her corpse, which was lying in her mahogany wood coffin, looking up at the ceiling of the living room where she had spent most of her last weeks.

The bare, clay-like ground adjacent to the pond was cold and, as the revving of a motorcycle that had sped past faded into the distance, the surroundings where Iwuagwu had once played games and run joyfully as a child with Adanna and many others became quiet and still. Iwuagwu gripped his walking stick and with both hands stabbed it into the ground several times, until it broke in half. As he did so, he invited Ekwensi to rip apart the lives of the men who filled insulin vials with salt and water and sold them up and down the region to local chemists, who went on to sell them to the three hundred who would lose their lives as a result.

31 ASHAWO 1

"Mbah ana bara dike, bu na az̤ụ ya"

"The brave are only criticised behind their backs"

(Traditional Igbo proverb)

That afternoon

Nneka was still sitting at her dark-brown wooden desk in her deserted classroom just after the clock struck two. She would not be joining her mother in the market that afternoon to sell melon seeds on Nwokorie Street. Instead, she was going to be in the company of a handful of other students at the bible meeting that took place twice a week in the grounds of her school.

As the last of the students caught one of the steady stream of rickety old buses that plied the Owerri–Onisha expressway route, Nneka donned her all-covering head-tie, swapped her thigh-high school uniform skirt for an ankle-length dress, and made her way to the venue of the meeting, in an adjacent classroom block.

Nneka knew that most men who stared at her did so because of her ample breasts. This included Mr Odi, a chemistry teacher, and one of two males in the after-school bible meeting she now attended. She had become used to catching Mr Odi's inappropriate looks, but these were the least of her problems.

The other girls who attended the meetings prided themselves on living

121

the life of their faith on a full-time basis. Their school uniforms were deliberately sewn in a loose and flowing style, they wore their long headscarves throughout the day, and they were never seen without a well-worn copy of the Bible clutched in hand. They believed that Nneka was, at best, a part-timer who would not last the month, at worst an agent of the devil sent to test and undermine their work of winning souls for Jesus. They also believed that Mr Odi, who led the group, and whom they had noticed staring at Nneka's breasts on several occasions, had definitely been compromised.

This was why during prayer sessions, and as they 'spoke in tongues', some of the girls directed their loud, fist-wielding, indecipherable outbursts at Nneka. The majority of the girls never spoke to Nneka, and avoided her when they ran into her during school hours or in rare chance meetings outside school, times when Nneka had donned trousers and shorts like a man, or when the hem of her skirts and dresses had reverted to well above her knees, when her lips had assumed an unnaturally red colour, and when her cleavage, in her low-cut tops, was presented to all who would wish to see it. Nneka was sure that she had once noticed one of the girls mouth "*ashawo*", prostitute, in reference to her on Nnamdi Azikiwe Road.

Nneka would later find out that some of the girls in her group had initially assumed that she had fallen pregnant, and that it was the shame that had brought her to their meetings. They believed that it was only a matter of time before she would have her pregnancy removed in a shed in some alleyway.

"In Luke Chapter 7, even Jesus forgave the many sins of the prostitute who approached him," Mr Odi had read out in a protracted bible discussion about 'sins of the flesh' instigated by a few of the girls in the group. They had, in a private discussion with Mr Odi, questioned his encouragement of Nneka's membership of the group.

But Nneka continued to come to the meetings despite the obvious impression that she was not welcome there by many. As she sat quietly in her usual corner at the back of the classroom, she thought about what one of the women who sat beside her mother on Nwokorie Street had said to her: "You need to stop coming here all the time if you do not want to end up being a market woman."

Nneka did not feel that being a market woman like her mother was an option, and she felt the need to spend less time sitting alongside her mother. She considered the bible meeting a good place to bide her time.

She had settled on the idea of being a nurse a long time ago; that was how far she believed her head would take her. Still, she could not really imagine herself as one. She had never really known anyone who was a nurse, except for one lady who lived on her road, five houses away, whom she never spoke to but occasionally saw walk by her house.

"Neat and tidy." Those were the words that came to mind when Nneka thought about the lady. Her multi-coloured pens and clip-on watch were always fastened to her immaculate white uniform, always in the same spot, like military medals, and her white nurse's cap was always secured on her neatly plaited hair with shiny silver hairpins.

Nneka had heard of how the lady would be called upon during late nights by people who lived on her street, especially those whose kids became gravely ill, and how the nurse would rush over with her stethoscope, syringes and bags of medicine. There was no doubt that she was well respected around her neighbourhood, and Nneka thought that this was why the lady always walked with an authoritative and quickened gait. Nneka also noticed that the nurse was sometimes accompanied by a man, whom she assumed to be the lady's husband. But nurses could never be rich people, and Nneka believed she would inevitably need to marry someone who was at the very least comfortable financially. She had seen the nurse's husband many times, and in all those times he was always dressed in a suit. She had also seen him, on a few occasions, driving an ash-coloured car which looked to be new. These were times when thoughts about Obioma surfaced in her mind.

Lately, Nneka had had many discussions with the woman that sat beside her mother in the market. She had been warned by her against letting boys have their way with her too soon. She had been told how, at their age, boys like Obioma were in a phase where they were no longer in control of their minds. When they eventually came to their senses, and when it was time to settle down, they would abandon the girls that they saw as already used up.

This chimed with Nneka's view that Obioma was currently only concerned with women's bottoms, thighs, breasts and genitals. They no longer had their long talks in which they contemplated adulthood, planning which places they would visit, where they would live and how many children they would have. Instead, these days, she felt she was spending the majority of the time in his company fending off his sexual advances. Obioma had become like those people in the movies taken over by unseen alien entities. Nneka had decided not to give in to his demands for sex. However, she believed that part of the Obioma she knew still inhabited the leering collection of muscle, bone and flesh that turned up religiously at her home in the afternoon, and that this part of him would eventually regain control of his body and mind. This was why she had decided that every now and again she would allow him to see her naked, to make sure that he did not go elsewhere – but this was as far as she would go for now.

32 THE OLD MAN AND THE SEA

"Ngwere si̱ na ya ma otu okpuru afo̱ ya di̱, ya jiri magide ya n'ala"

"The lizard says that he knows the condition of his underbelly: this is the reason he has it pressed against the ground"

(Traditional Igbo proverb)

The day after

Iwuagwu believed that he was now an object of pity, a charity case, when his friend Nwachukwu braved the many potholes and puddles of water to visit him at the height of the rainy season during a week-long downpour of rain.

It did not stop there. Nwachukwu had brought along with him a book that had not even once been presented for their usual review. In fact, Nwachukwu dispensed with their usual chapter-by-chapter dissection and analysis, instead explaining both story and moral as one would to a child.

Iwuagwu was sure that Nwachukwu must have heard about his, Iwuagwu's, latest public spat with Okoro, his distant cousin – a verbal exchange that had bizarrely reduced Iwuagwu to actual tears. Everyone must be talking about it, about how he was losing his mind, Iwuagwu reasoned.

Iwuagwu quietly nursed his annoyance and the remaining palm wine in his calabash cup as Nwachukwu momentarily placed his book down on the

124

ground beside him to attend to his own untouched cup. The book's worn front cover depicting what Iwuagwu interpreted as a giant fish leaping over a small boat manned by a lone sailor.

"Nwachukwu, I know you mean well but, at the end of the day, this book, this *Old Man and the Sea*, is about fishing," Iwuagwu stated with an air of annoyance, momentarily interrupting the protracted silence that had endured as he peered at the book's cover.

"I gain no solace in knowing that my side in all of this may be considered the noble one. The fact of the matter is that we are now extinct," Iwuagwu added, clearing his throat before he continued. "Henry Ogazi, a known criminal in Lagos, is now our Eze, can you imagine? Okoro is now appearing in our meetings in Umuwe acting like a statesman, both of them undoing all the good that has been done over the last decade.

"My father once told me that when he was a boy you couldn't randomly throw a stone in this village, or indeed in all *ala* Igbo, without hitting at least one man or one woman who was upright and honourable. Lucky man, he died feeling that those things would endure.

"They convince us to completely forsake our ways, discredit those who are wise amongst us and empower the most unworthy. Their promises of a better way in the end is a fraud; we continue to die like flies.

"Tell me how many people in this village are older than you and I. Why is that charlatan Okoro prospering, building houses, buying cars, recruiting an army of helpers? I am not even able to successfully train up an apprentice." Iwuagwu came to the end of his diatribe. Nwachukwu remained silent.

33 E GBUOLAM OZU!

"Obere ego ruo ogbenye aka, uche ya agba ụzọ iri"

"When a poor man gets a little money, his thoughts go off in ten different directions"

(Traditional Igbo proverb)

The next day in Owerri

Kalu did a ridiculous amount of thinking for a seventeen-year-old. While other boys his age fretted about how to sustain overinflated or outright false claims of success with the opposite sex, Kalu occupied himself with thoughts about what his great legacy should be.

He chose early Saturday mornings to do most of his thinking and scheming, sitting up in bed for hours, staring expressionlessly at the expensive furniture that cluttered his room. He would sometimes sit at the red veneer desk next to his bed, poring over the stacks of books organised neatly on the ceiling-high shelf that covered an entire wall of his room. It would be many hours before the rest of his family woke up, and all that could be heard would be the uninterrupted buzzing sound that came from the large refrigerator in the kitchen adjacent to his room.

Outside, beyond the expensive double-glazed window, stood his brother's ten-bedroom mansion, identical to the one he was sitting in. Both two-storey mansions had been built in one fell swoop the moment Benjamin his brother came into money.

From the vantage point of his desk, Kalu watched as the emerging morning sun's rays bounced off the mostly glass structure of his brother's house with a stunning brilliance. Their nearest neighbours were nearly a quarter of a mile away. Between their houses were scatterings of trees on which birds and squirrels fluttered and frolicked. Beyond them, in the distance, a quiet stream ran down the gently elevated plain on which the mansions stood and which overlooked the congested heap far in the distance: old Owerri, the fate from which his brother Benjamin had rescued both him and his family, Kalu thought.

Kalu had always been touted as the smart one, the one everyone presumed would be the most successful in his family and indeed his neighbourhood. These days, every waking hour, Kalu was consumed with the question of whether he would ever approach replicating his brother's success, never mind topping it.

He recalled the day he had first learnt of his brother's vast wealth. It had been an ordinary Wednesday afternoon about three years earlier. He had just finished the long trek from his school to the neighbourhood of the Old Market where they used to live, and he was lying on the king-sized bed in the shed his brother used to own when a boy who lived nearby barged in.

"*Benji wane gi tuga ego na Uwa Nkwobi*!" (Your brother Benji is making it rain money at Uwa Nkwobi).

Uwa Nkwobi, a ten-minute walk from Kalu's house, was a beer parlour and popular Nkwobi joint. This was where Benjamin squandered all of the money from the thefts and burglaries he was involved in when he lived in Owerri. It was also where he frittered away his earnings from his vulcaniser business.

When Kalu arrived at Uwa Nkwobi it was heaving with customers, with many more arriving. Benjamin, his brother was not there.

"*E gbuolam ozu*!" (I have killed a corpse). Kalu was told that this was what his brother had been bellowing at the top of his voice from the driver's seat of a Lamborghini Diablo when he arrived at Uwa Nkwobi an hour earlier.

Kalu heard how the car's doors opened upwards like the wings of a large bird, and how it growled and rumbled loudly like an angry lion when Benjamin revved it before he sped off.

"*Nwanne gi akuchiela Uwa Nkwobi*?" (Your brother has closed the bar), Kalu heard from a familiar face, a long-time friend of his brother, who talked with a mouthful of meat while swigging a large bottle of beer gripped in his hand. Kalu now heard how Benjamin had asked the proprietor, an old man called Papa, how much it would cost to ensure that no one had to pay for drink and food at Uwa Nkwobi that day.

It was not quite clear exactly what price Papa had named, but many testified that Benjamin went to the trunk of his new car and retrieved several wads of cash from a large suitcase full of money. He was said to have paid the old man the amount he had asked for in what looked like foreign currency. Benjamin was then said to have thrown two fistfuls of twenty-dollar bills to the crowds of people that had begun to gather around his car.

Kalu did not see his brother that day and neither did any other member of his family. It transpired that Benjamin had checked into a suite at the most expensive hotel in the city, where he entertained a steady stream of women. They next saw Benjamin three days later, when he finally rolled up to the house looking utterly exhausted.

34 DON CHAMPION

"Akụ nwata kpatara, wetere nsọpụrụ"

"The wealth of a child causes him to become a respected person"

(Traditional Igbo proverb)

Days later

Obioma aimlessly wandered the streets around the rebuilt Old Market after the end of the school day in his usual dozy manner. Routinely making his way to Nneka's house was no longer an option. She now stayed back at school till very late, dividing her time between the bible group she regularly attended and the reading clubs that had sprung up in her school, as they had across the county as students prepared for the looming final exams.

Obioma did not attend any of the clubs at his school. He believed that failure was inevitable and attending them would be a pointless endeavour, so he was typically to be found killing time in the streets of Owerri.

At exactly three o'clock, Obioma arrived at the intersection between Whetheral Road and Egbu Road, where according to rumours a brand new Rolls-Royce was parked. He saw it. Even from afar it was truly a spectacle, and it looked out of place against the surrounding shabby buildings and the dishevelled old taxis that fretted by. The pronounced chrome front grill of the sky-blue Rolls-Royce glimmered in the distance where it was parked at the side of the busy road. Other cars that drove by took the extra precaution of manoeuvring into the oncoming cars' lane to ensure that they avoided hitting it.

It belonged to Nda Peter, also known as Don Champion, a former plumber who like Kalu's brother had mysteriously come into a great deal of money, enough to buy the first ever Rolls-Royce to parade the streets of Owerri in recent times, probably in all history.

"Make you no go near the motor!" The small group of boys who gathered a safe distance from the car cautioned Obioma against getting too close to the car. Someone had just done so, and the car had actually spoken, warning them to move to a safe distance. Another reason for Obioma to watch from a safe distance was that Don Champion was emerging from the building he had been visiting.

Nda Peter, as he had been known when he was just a plumber dealing with sewer blockages in Obioma's building and around the neighbourhood, was now a different man. Tripled in size, he emerged from the roadside building wearing a white brocade robe. He had grown so fat that folds of skin rippled from the top of his head to the back of his neck. He clutched under his arm a sizeable man's purse, which he unlatched as he waddled towards his car.

Obioma watched him beckon over the half-dozen young boys who stood transfixed in the spot where they had been standing since Obioma arrived. Obioma hastily joined them as they scrambled towards Don Champion.

"Thank you for watching my car," he said in Igbo with a husky, breathless voice that no longer sounded like that of his old self.

Obioma stuffed the crisp twenty-dollar bill placed into his waiting hands by Don Champion into one of his trouser pockets and crossed the street to observe Don Champion's departure from that safe distance, something that annoyed the group of young boys who had apparently struck a deal to keep vigil over Don Champion's car for the full two hours that he was in the roadside building.

As the automatic glass window panels rode up and the rich roar of the Rolls-Royce's engines ignited, it was too late for the scores of people who appeared from the buildings around for their share of the bounty. The muffled rumbling sounds of Don Champion's sound system, along with the car's engine, could be heard for a time as the car taxied into the distance and to the horizon.

"LA 34758 AT."

Obioma found himself memorising the registration number of Don Champion's Rolls-Royce. It was a well-known fact that most cars driven by the suddenly rich in Owerri had registration numbers with the Lagos LA-AT prefix and suffix. It was also rumoured that it was some sort of club identifier for all who obtained their wealth by tricking white men overseas out of their money. There wasn't a neighbourhood in the city that did not harbour a group of young men working day and night with fax machines to net themselves a gullible, rich white man.

Just a stone's throw from Obioma's house, in an adjacent building, there was a flat on the ground floor that housed a number of young men doing just this. No one could figure out exactly how many men actually lived in the flat; it was an endless parade of new faces. As they exited and arrived at the flat, they clutched chunky fax machines close to their chests with one hand and reams of paper in the other. In the small hours of the night the distinctive bleating of fax transmissions could be heard, sometimes several at a time. It had been rumoured for at least a year that they were close to hitting it big.

35 LOST

"Agwo loro agwo ibeya odu ya ga aputaya n'onu"

"A snake that swallows its neighbour will have a tail sticking out of its mouth"

(Traditional Igbo proverb)

That same day

It took a long time for Obioma to register that the picture of the man who appeared on the missing person's poster, glued with corn starch to an electric pole was indeed Moses. The picture they had used was an old one, perhaps one from the time when Moses was a lecturer in Lagos. Moses wore a plain blue shirt and tie and looked a lot younger than Obioma had ever seen him.

It was not unusual to see missing person's posters dotted about town. In fact, they had begun to appear more and more frequently over the last few years, and there were many more people who had gone missing for whom posters had not been put up.

This news brought a whole new purpose to Obioma's wander through the city that afternoon, and he headed for Moses' store to investigate.

Moses' bookshop was no longer a place where books were sold; it had become a sort of electronics shop, one of scores of places around the market that specialised in selling second-hand fax machines, old telephone handsets, car radios, calculators, watches and clocks. Severed wires stuck out from here and there, looking hurriedly torn from wherever they had originally been. The equipment sat dangerously in untidy heaps on the narrow wall-to-wall shelving and the shelves suspended by cables from the ceiling.

Obioma, dressed in his school uniform, caught the young man who appeared from inside the shop looking at him suspiciously as he stood staring at one of the fax machines displayed on a table outside.

"*Omo wetin?*" (You want?), the man enquired in the sort of tone that could only have been intended to prompt Obioma to move along.

"Where is Moses?" Obioma enquired, deepening his voice, sensing that the young man did not regard him as someone who would eventually be purchasing something from the store.

"Nobody by that name here. You sure say you dey the right store?" the young man responded.

"But this na Moses store," Obioma insisted.

"You see that man there?" The young man pointed to a bald man sitting on a stool in front of another shop, reading a newspaper. Obioma nodded in acknowledgement.

"Go to him. He will explain everything."

After quizzing Obioma about his connection to Moses, the man introduced himself as the General Secretary of Zone 3, the trading locality within which Moses' shop was located. A few months back, neighbouring traders had arrived early to find Moses' shop already open, with Moses nowhere to be seen.

In fact, it turned out, he had gone missing a few days before, and over the course of the night more than half of his stock of books had been stolen. The man explained how the traders' association, which he headed, had locked up Moses' shop when he failed to turn up that day, but that his shop was again broken into at night days later and the remainder of his stock stolen.

The man had led a delegation of traders to where Moses lived, to find that none of his neighbours had seen him for days either. None of his close relatives could be traced. It was decided that Moses' store would be rented out for the remainder of his lease. A portion of money received would be held by the traders' association until his return and another portion used to finance the production of posters declaring him missing.

As Obioma trekked back to his mother's eating house to work his shift, he imagined a deranged Moses wandering amongst the makeshift stalls of some deserted, far-flung rural market, or cowering in a crevice somewhere from being pelted with stones by a handful of cruel children.

Much had changed in the country in the last few years, Obioma mused. For one, there was no way on earth that Moses could still be receiving, by post from abroad, the drugs his brother sent that had kept his madness at bay. These days, even simple letters with cards were intercepted and stolen by post office staff.

36 IKEM UNA

"Nwata nna ya dinyere oshi n'eji ụkwụ agbawa ụzọ"

"The child who is sent by his father to steal breaks down the door"

(Traditional Igbo proverb)

The following weekend

Kalu had strayed further than he usually did during his regular Saturday morning walk after one of his heavy reading sessions. This time, he had followed the zigzag network of paths that cut through the high grass, shrubs and trees which draped the undulating landscape right into the city. He had got about halfway before he decided to turn back. In the distance, on the hill ahead and somewhat obscured by trees, Kalu could finally see the road and the decorative metal mesh gates and high walls that surrounded the two mansions where he lived.

He walked up the last of the hill onto his road, and the remainder of his plans for the day unfolded in his mind – first a shower, some food, and then back to reading – plans that would be overshadowed by what he was about to witness.

Kalu emerged onto the road and through the large gates just in time to witness Benjamin and one of his assistants, a cousin of theirs called Mike, drag the bloodied, lifeless body of one of Benjamin's close business associates into one of the cars in the compound.

The man's name was Ikem Una. Kalu knew him well.

Ikem supposedly worked very closely with his brother and would usually join Benjamin and Mike on the long drives from Lagos to Owerri. Their arrival late at night at the mansions usually meant bouts of feasting and heavy drinking, and sometimes the arrival of a bevy of women from Owerri town centre.

Ikem Una had the kind of stature and manner that prompted laughs whenever you met him. His small nose sat unevenly in his almost perfectly round face, and his pot belly contradicted his tall, gangly frame. He habitually wore immaculate, flowing agbada outfits and brightly coloured safari suits, together with his trademark silver embroidered cap, which was perched at one side of his head in an awkward slant.

"Papa Benji. The godfather, morning sir, ahhh Lolo, a fine morning, oh madam," Kalu remembered Ikem would say in an exaggerated pacifying and reverential tone as he seized Kalu's parents' hands in handshakes, stooping and sometimes humorously prostrating himself, his cap barely staying on as he did so.

"Professor." That was what Ikem called Kalu, a nickname that had stuck amongst Benjamin's associates and friends who visited the house.

"Work hard; play hardestly" This was something else that Ikem said regularly; his sort-of mantra. When he was sufficiently drunk, it seemed to be all he was able to mutter.

Kalu had always felt that Ikem was an unlikely close friend for his brother to have. Benjamin was forever brooding and scheming, and even when he was having a good time it was usually at the expense of somebody else's well-being. Kalu knew Ikem's loud clownish manner and antics irritated his brother, but Ikem was Chief Alusi's nephew, the only relative the Chief had in his organisation.

Now Ikem's lifeless body was clad in nothing but his pair of drawstring agbada trousers, now bloodstained. His bruised and bloodied head dangled down limply between his shoulders as Benjamin and Mike gripped his bare torso and legs and hurled him into the trunk of one of Benjamin's cars.

Kalu retreated back beyond the gates and watched from the safe distance of the trees and shrubs across the road.

The night before, when Benjamin, Mike and Ikem had just arrived from Lagos, Kalu had been sent with a wad of cash by his brother to Uwa Nkobi, to wake up Papa to cook food especially for them. The usual group of girls that graced Benjamin's mansion did not arrive that night and Kalu recalled, after his trip into the old town, the boisterous laughs and loud chatting that seeped from his brother's mansion as he had walked the short distance across his brother's car park to the house he shared with the rest of his family.

Kalu did not emerge from his hiding place until he heard the screeching sounds the tyres of one of his brother's cars before it disappeared down the road. As he approached the gates a second time, Kalu heard his father call out to him from the front balcony of the mansion they lived in, the same spot where his father had been sitting the night before.

When Kalu had scaled the two flights of stairs to the balcony, there was no doubt in his mind that his father was drunk. He sat sprawled in his favourite cane armchair. Kalu sat down in the chair opposite, and his bemused gaze stayed fixed on his father as he sat up in his lounge chair to pour what was left in his large whisky bottle into his favourite chunky square glass, the same glass that Kalu had carried up to his father the night before along with the then-full bottle of whisky. His father spoke as he tipped and held the dripping bottle over the glass longer than necessary.

"Ikem is dead."

For a long time, Kalu had believed that there was nothing more he could learn from his father, who had barely finished primary school. This was about to change.

"*Azụ na-eloghị ibe ya anaghị ebu*" (A fish that does not swallow other fishes does not grow fat).

This was how his father began to explain what he had just witnessed. The slurred words lingered in Kalu's mind long after his father had said them.

Things finally began to fall into place. Kalu remembered that his father had attempted to persuade him to join his mother and sisters that weekend on a visit to his mother's sister's place, an hour's drive away from Owerri. It was clear that his father had not slept that night, and that he had been aware of what was planned for Ikem the night before. Kalu saw his father in an even more grave light than in the past. His father's drained look and bloodshot eyes added to the chilling and frightful aura that now surrounded him.

"Ijele, listen," his father said in an irritated tone, as though he could hear Kalu's thoughts, the pet name he had given Kalu years ago suddenly emerging after years of neglect.

Kalu knew that his father now sat wondering whether he should break the secrecy that protected his brother's activities, whether later that day Kalu would be at their local police station reporting what he had seen.

"Ijele, *lekwa*," his father called out again. Once used as a toast to Kalu's successive school exam performances and when he had landed the office of Senior Prefect, Kalu knew the name was now being used to cajole and pacify him.

Ijele was the largest and most revered masquerade in Igbo-land. It took place at chieftaincy coronations and at the burial ceremonies of dignitaries, and on other major occasions. Kalu had never actually seen an Ijele masquerade, as they only occurred in places like Enugwu and Nnewi in the

North of Igbo-land, but as he sat looking at his father nodding off, he remembered his father's explanations many years ago about how some masquerades were known for their strength, others for their grace or influence, but how the Ijelle was a combination of all those things and more. Kalu had revelled in the fact that his father had never referred to Benjamin or his other siblings as Ijele, something he had seen as a mark of his superiority over his brother.

That morning, Kalu began to see Ijele in a new light; and the more his father used it, the more it began to weigh on him like a sort of heavy responsibility.

"Ijele, listen to me," Kalu's father said again in his slurred drawl. "All that rubbish they teach you in school or that you read in the heap of books in your bedroom downstairs is child's play. What you learn here today will sadly make life a lot less carefree and pleasant than it has so far seemed for you, but you are old and smart enough to handle it. We cannot forever be children."

Kalu found himself listening with a new-found attentiveness as his father went on, sometimes incoherently. He heard about how Chief Alusi's health was rapidly ailing and why it was now critical that his relative Ikem Una, the only real contender for leadership of the business and the inheritance of Chief's vast hidden assets, needed to be quickly eliminated. Benjamin was doing what any sensible person in his position and business would do.

"Game theory, *nwa' m*," his father reeled off, his rare use of English sounding strange to Kalu.

This was how the world worked, his father insisted. Kalu would also learn that his brother and cousin had tortured their former business partner for hours to give up any secrets he knew about his uncle Chief Alusi.

"Ikem was a friendly man, we were all fond of him, in fact we all loved him, but when you need to crush someone, you need to crush them completely or they will return to seek revenge for your actions," his father concluded.

Kalu stared into his father's bloodshot eyes. It all seemed chillingly logical, even sensible, in the most grotesque way imaginable.

37 HEADMASTER

"N'afọ ọ bula nwata nwetara nsogbu, n'otu afọ ahụ ka ọ ga ebu ibu arụ"

"At whatever age a child gets a problem, at the same age she has to shoulder responsibility"

(Traditional Igbo proverb)

A few weeks later

Obioma scaled the fence of his secondary school just before eleven o'clock in the morning, and in no time he was back on the bustling great road on his way to the New Market. Like a sedimentary rock, the brick fence bore signs of having being raised multiple times, presumably to curtail students climbing over it. But the fence still betrayed a tell-tale mark of significant traffic: the thinning down into a bow of the topmost bricks.

This was going to be Obioma's final attempt at hiring a mercenary to take his approaching school-leaving examinations. He had met with four contacts so far, and six thousand naira was the lowest quote he'd had for the job.

"Meet Headmaster at Mama Stella at eleven o'clock," the classmate who had arranged his latest meeting had instructed. Obioma had nagged him for over a week to set it up.

Obioma had never met him before, but when he saw the middle-aged-looking boy in ultra-thick-lensed, horn-rimmed glasses hunched over his meal at Mama Stella's shack, Obioma knew he was looking at Peter, better known as Headmaster.

"Afternoon." Obioma found himself addressing Headmaster as he would a teacher.

"*Omo*, how far?" the young man said, halfway through tearing apart a large chunk of red-stew-stained meat which had been resting on a half-eaten heap of rice on the plate in front of him. Up close, Headmaster looked to be no older than Obioma. This briefly caused Obioma to feel a degree of embarrassment and shame given what he was about to ask of him. Obioma detected the peculiar twang of his accent, and in his mind reckoned that his parents were probably lecturers or some sort of officials from a far-flung state in the country, stationed in the city. He had already been informed by his classmate that Headmaster had just finished a three-year stint at the posh federal secondary school, passing with nine straight As and an additional one in further mathematics.

"My name is Obioma." Obioma felt trapped in his compulsion to be ultra-formal despite Peter's casual manner.

Mama Stella's stall was essentially a few large sheets of corrugated zinc roofing, held up by dug-in wooden pillars and divided in the middle to form a kitchen and eating area. It was not yet noon and hence not yet time for the armada of traders that would besiege the stall tucked away at the far end of the market with nothing more to the horizon than sprawling trees, foliage and slightly raised ground overgrown with grass.

It was just the two of them in the eating area and the isolated location of the shack, coupled with the monotonous kitchen noises that emanated from the other side of the corrugated zinc partition, made Obioma feel that he had picked the right place and time for his business with Headmaster. The incessant pounding of mortar and pestle stopped, and a gaunt overworked-looking middle-aged woman appeared.

"*Wetin* you wan' chop?"

"I beg rice and stew, two fish."

"And I go pay for am," Obioma added, pointing at Headmaster. Headmaster was only able to nod in gratitude, having just scooped a large spoonful of stewed rice into his mouth.

Obioma sat on one of the rickety stools opposite Headmaster and waited patiently for him to finish the mouthful.

"*Omo*, this is the thing." Headmaster began to speak in hasty fragments as he neared the conclusion of his latest stint of chewing. "I have four other guys already interested in me. I have whittled them down to two because the others are taking the external GCSE. I am not around then, you see." Headmaster paused. "*Shebi na* WAEC you dey take?" Obioma, struggling to follow, nodded nervously.

"Good, because I should be in the United States during GCSE exams, so it's you and another guy that I am going to see later this evening at Pre Fab. I already saw him yesterday, but I told him you came to me first and I must give you first refusal, so you need to talk well, you understand?" Headmaster finally concluded with a stern look on his face.

"How much the guy offer you?" Obioma asked apprehensively.

"Twelve thousand k," Headmaster said glibly. Obioma knew he was lying, but he guessed it was around 10,000 naira, still twice as much as he could stretch to afford.

"You fit take 4,500k?" Obioma enquired, already knowing what Headmaster's answer would be.

"How many subjects?" Headmaster responded. Obioma knew he was making small talk and thinking of how best to let him down gently; after all, he had just eaten a meal paid for by him. Despite being sure of this, Obioma still held out some hope for a miracle.

"Only nine subjects: English, Mathematics, Commerce, Government, Biology, Geography, Igbo, Agricultural Science and Economics." Obioma waited for Headmaster's response apprehensively. "*Abi* you fit? Just do five subjects for the money, I pay you cash right now, I beg?" he added nervously before Headmaster could respond. As Obioma watched Headmaster formulating his let-down in his head, he quickly retrieved a plastic bag full of notes and coins from his school bag and placed it on the table beside Headmaster's plate – in all, the full contents of his safe. This was his last gambit.

As he did so, he caught sight of the very first note to grace his wooden box, the crisp twenty-naira note placed under his pillow by his father years ago. Obioma wrestled away the thoughts he associated with that morning, his father's beaming smiles as neighbours complimented him on how nice the Commissioner's car looked.

"Exactly 4,457.20 kobo. Please," Obioma pleaded again. He sensed his eyes filling up. He was not sure whether this was because he felt that the rest of his life hinged on the outcome of that particular moment, or because he had suddenly begun to wonder how he had come to find himself at such a low point.

38 HEIR TO THE THRONE

"Onye hụrụ anụ na ngụpụta, amaghị ihe ahụrụ gbuo ya, na ihe ahụrụ sie ya"

"A person who arrives at a feast when the cooked meat is being pulled out of the pot does

not know what was endured by others to catch and cook it"

(Traditional Igbo proverb)

Two months later

Anyone who saw Chief Alusi knew that his death was approaching fast. He was gravely ill. He had long since stopped attending the high-profile ceremonies and events which wealthy men like him typically went to on a regular basis, mostly to show off their wealth. After almost a year abroad visiting various hospitals, Chief Alusi had retreated to his ancestral village in far-away Arochukwu, where he conducted his business.

Benjamin invited his brother Kalu to join him on the long helicopter ride from a patchy field on the outskirts of Owerri to Chief Alusi's vast thirty-acre compound, a haven surrounded by forests, built miles away from his actual ancestral village.

For a while, Benjamin watched his brother, who was on his first ever helicopter ride, his gaze tracing the handful of dusty, erosion-ravaged roads, far beneath their aircraft, which appeared and disappeared in the dense landscape of green trees.

Theirs was a new kind of relationship now. Benjamin was almost certain

Kalu no longer felt the distance in ideology that had separated them all their lives up until the past few months. His little brother now worked for him. A rush of pride jolted through him as he thought this, the kind of pride he had only felt in the past when Kalu had helped him with chores and errands when he was a vulcaniser. But, even then, he had known Kalu's involvement was disingenuous and his participation largely for the cash rewards Benjamin had offered him.

This time it was different. Benjamin believed Kalu had now fully ascribed to the notion that only family truly mattered and that the world was a cesspit of treacherous snakes that needed to be approached ruthlessly.

Even as he mulled over Kalu's conversion, Benjamin noted in his mind the contradiction in his thoughts. He remembered how he had seriously considered killing his brother.

Kalu had really kept Benjamin, his father and his cousin in great suspense. It took an entire fortnight following the death of Ikem Una for Kalu to speak to them. During that time Kalu stayed in his room and avoided contact with everyone.

Benjamin had feared the worst, and he and Mike spend those passing weeks watching and monitoring his brother's movements very carefully. Even though his father kept reassuring them that Kalu would eventually come around to their way of thinking, Benjamin knew well that for Kalu the option of eliminating his older brother was on the table and very real.

As the helicopter gained even more altitude in its flight towards Arochukwu, Benjamin's thoughts about his brother continued to twist. Kalu is a smart boy, surely he must have picked up that his life was under threat, Benjamin now thought. Particularly since during that period Benjamin and Mike had cancelled their trips back to Lagos on two successive occasions. For some fleeting moments, Benjamin wondered if Kalu's sudden co-operation was largely for fear of his life. Benjamin recalled how, about three weeks after Ikem's killing, when most of the family were out, Kalu had suddenly appeared in his room.

"When the time is right, when Ikem has been missing for long enough to prompt a lot of concern, you should go above and beyond all of Chief Alusi's other associates in assisting in the search for him." This was one of the first things Kalu had said to him that Sunday evening.

Even though they had never discussed the day Ikem died, Benjamin knew that after Kalu's two-week self-imposed isolation, his father had been regularly conversing with Kalu. Benjamin knew this was his brother's way of signalling his position.

When the right time did come, Benjamin and Kalu sparked the biggest ever missing person's hunt in the history of the state. Posters bearing Ikem Una's picture appeared on every street in Owerri and in every major city in the country; other versions of the poster were placed in local and national newspapers and shown during local and national television stations' missing-person announcements.

Kalu joined in with the grand scheming that took place over Benjamin's dining table. Presided over by Benjamin, Kalu, their father and their cousin Mike hatched and laid out plot after plot. Another of Chief Alusi's associates was to be sacrificed. A fictitious account of his torture would reveal that Ikem had been taken by Don Champion, a rival of Chief Alusi who was planning a stealth takeover of the Chief's territory and business structures. This would of course be lapped up by the ailing Chief, his personal bad history with Don Champion making him even more susceptible to the ruse.

Benjamin knew that this was partially why Chief Alusi hid out in his newly constructed oasis in the midst of the forest, surrounded by a handful of men with assault rifles.

A large red-roofed mansion and various other smaller buildings were strewn across Chief Alusi's vast compound. The six-seater helicopter approached Chief Alusi's helipad at the furthermost corner of the compound from the mansion. Beside the helipad sat a windowless bungalow, which Kalu and Benjamin were told by one of the AK-45-wielding guards housed a large back-up generator. Another armed guard and a driver in a dark Mercedes Benz saloon car were already at hand to pick up Benjamin and Kalu as they disembarked from the helicopter. They were driven the short distance to the mansion and, as the car navigated the modest network of private roads, a handful of men could be seen trimming the various vast patches of landscaped grass and flowerbeds.

Benjamin had made a point of making an audit of all of the Chief's properties and assets, working out those that he could easily appropriate and others he would have to hand over to the Chief's relatives. He knew that this particular property was off limits to him.

However, there were several others he had his eye on. Easy pickings. In the end, the Chief was just another criminal who laundered a great deal of his wealth through registering these properties in various people's names, half of whom were oblivious to this fact. Benjamin had already counted at least thirty-six properties he knew he would be gunning for.

The bay-windowed reception room where Benjamin and Kalu met Chief Alusi had essentially become his bedroom. The frail Chief lay under an immaculately made-up king-sized bed placed in the centre of the room. It seemed out of place amongst the curving settees and glass side-stools dotted about on the diamond-encrusted marble floors. The Chief had gone on about them when he was installing them in his other mansion on the outskirts of Lagos, which Benjamin had his eye on.

It was on these diamond-encrusted marble floors that the Chief was now recovering from his latest stroke, which had left him bedridden.

Benjamin would later gather that he and Kalu were the only guests the Chief had entertained at the house in over six months. For close to a year, Chief Alusi had been conducting virtually all business through his personal assistant, a portly middle-aged man called Marcus, his second cousin, who would periodically meet Benjamin and Chief Alusi's other associates and attend their joint meetings.

Benjamin knew Marcus would also need to be dispatched with. He felt a momentary twinge of paranoia and curiosity as to why Chief Alusi would send for him.

"Benji, *kedu*," the frail Chief Alusi said in a slow, slurred whisper as he caught sight of them entering the room, his already drooping and disfigured face further contorting with the effort of speech.

"*Oga kedu ka imere?*" Benjamin responded, approaching the bed and seizing one of Chief Alusi's cold limp hands with both of his in a handshake.

"This is my brother, Kalu, you remember him. He is with us now," Benjamin said, noticing Chief Alusi's eyes wander towards where Kalu stood. It soon became apparent that further contortions on the Chief's face were attempts to smile, and the shift of his gaze to a bank of settees in the room an invitation to both Benjamin and Kalu to be seated.

"Ikem is no longer alive, I know it… Don Champion has finally killed him… I have no doubt in my mind that Ikem was severely tortured before he was no more… We need to be vigilant…"

Chief Alusi spoke in between drawn-out and strained breaths as Kalu and his brother settled in their seats. They waited patiently as his train of thought faded in and out.

"We will go after them when we are strong enough," Chief Alusi continued. "But for now, I am going back abroad for medical treatment. I invited you here today so you can meet my son, who has come back from America and is keen on taking over while I am away. He should be on his way back from Port Harcourt any minute now. He needs to be shown the ropes, you understand me?"

Benjamin's annoyance at Chief Alusi's latest order, which he struggled to conceal, was spared by the muffled sounds of a helicopter approaching which could be heard just as the Chief finished his sentence.

"That's him," Chief Alusi informed them as enthusiastically as his condition would allow. A protracted silence ensued as they waited for the Chief's son to appear. The sound of the helicopter eventually become a sustained thunderous roar before finally quenching, giving way to the sound of a convoy of cars.

Chief Alusi had five daughters and one son from his three successive marriages. His only son, his second child, had in his teenage years moved to America with the Chief's first wife. Twice in the past, the Chief had indicated that his son would be joining his organisation with a view to eventually taking over, but Benjamin had largely considered this to be an aspirational wish on the Chief's part, and it had never seemed likely to transpire. Benjamin had never met Chief Alusi's son, could not even remember his name. The boy had hardly visited the country on account of his mother not wanting him to do so. Now, apparently, things had changed. The Chief had spent considerable time abroad with his son since becoming ill, and this might have been a factor, Benjamin thought.

"Wud up, my nigga?" Chief Alusi's son, Frank, swept into the reception room flanked by two bodyguards, greeting first Benjamin and then Kalu with these words.

He was definitely no longer a boy. Sprawling snakes tattooed onto his skin crept well beyond the collar of the button-up short-sleeved shirt he wore which showed off his muscular physique. Benjamin studied him closely, trying to ascertain whether, with his towering frame and the pair of black ear-piercing tapers that stuck out from the lobes of his ears, he would be more at home playing guitar in a rock band, or overseeing a complex web of organised criminality and managing psychopaths.

"Call me Bullet. That's what everyone who knows me call me," Frank said as Benjamin and Kalu introduced themselves. "I hear you are my father's right-hand men. I will be taking over from him immediately. But don't worry, your position is secure with me, as long as you stay loyal that is, you understand?"

As both brothers smiled and nodded in unequivocal agreement, Benjamin mused about how aptly Chief Alusi's son had named himself. Benjamin was in no doubt that Bullet would be joining his father in the afterlife much sooner than he thought.

39 THE GREAT CULLING 2

"The death of an elderly man is like a burning library"

(Traditional Ivorian proverb)

Two weeks later

Obioma was preoccupied with his observation that his uncle Iwuagwu had lost a lot of weight, but this was an understatement of Iwuagwu's condition. He was, in fact, dead. And on the morning of his funeral, Iwuagwu's shrunken body lay in state on his cane and raffia bed, which had been dragged out from his room into the living room of the main bungalow in his compound.

Obioma sat in the corner of the room for hours, gawking at how stiff and wood-like his uncle's skin was; how it had now turned a dark shade of purple; and how cotton-wool buds now stuck out of the nostrils of a face that hardly seemed like his uncle's own. The grey hairs that lined his uncle's eyelids were more plentiful than Obioma remembered them being. But it had been a long time since he had seen him.

The agreements that had been struck between Obioma's mother and Iwuagwu for Obioma to become a traditional healer alongside qualifying as a doctor had been well and truly extinguished years earlier. Iwuagwu had insinuated weeks after Obioma's father's funeral, that his death and the loss of his mother's stockfish shop were probably part of a punitive curse by the Agwu deity for yet-to-be resolved sins. This did not go down well with Obioma or his mother, and consequently Obioma's regular trips back to the village ceased.

146

The last time Obioma had seen his uncle had been about a year and a half ago. Even though it was a fleeting visit, as Obioma sat looking at his uncle's corpse he felt he should have guessed then that his uncle was on his last legs.

Iwuagwu had latterly become even more bitter than he had been in the past. Obioma had noticed that even his good friend the Professor did not visit him as often as he used to. He was now the type of old man who yelled angrily at loud playing children, chasing them, waving his stick and confiscating footballs and other items that happened to stray onto the compound.

Back then, Obioma had returned after almost two years' absence to cart away the remaining items in his father's little hut at the edge of Iwuagwu's compound: the turntable player and the stack of vinyl records his father used to listen to. They were to be sold at the rebuilt Old Market and the money put towards running the eating house, which needed better dining furniture.

"Evil man. You are a fake Dibia, fake." People suspected Iwuagwu of being demented or having had a breakdown as he cultivated the pastime of sitting by the front entrance of his compound on his small cane chair and launching unprovoked verbal attacks at Okoro. Obioma had avoided staying in any of Iwuagwu's four bungalows and spent the handful of nights he stayed in Umuwe in his father's hut. Obioma had regularly walked up to the entrance area of the compound to watch his uncle barking at Okoro's compound, even though no one was in sight.

Iwuagwu's attacks had no apparent impact on either Okoro's popularity or his prosperity. Okoro had become the toast of the newly rich, the OBT boys. They travelled from near and far in their flashy cars to his traditional medicine practice. Okoro was known for performing special wealth-protection rituals. This meant an array of luxury vehicles belonging to his rich clients parked, at all hours, alongside Okoro's own ash-coloured Mercedes Benz VBoot car. Okoro's two-storey building towered above all the other bungalows in the area and eclipsed the tall trees that surrounded Iwuagwu's compound.

Obioma had noticed that Iwuagwu now wheezed incessantly, spoke in a laboured way and moved around with the aid of a walking stick.

"Okoro, are you still continuing this facade, this lie that your brothers and sisters are paying for?" Iwuagwu would say strenuously at the top of his voice, which now croaked and often failed him.

Every now and again, Okoro or someone in his household would emerge at the entrance of their compound, usually to receive or see off visitors, clients and patients. Iwuagwu's shouts at these times would grow louder and more vitriolic.

"You are fraternising with an evil and destructive man," Iwuagwu would assert, declarations that did not illicit the sheepish, tail-between-your-legs reaction or the shuffling embarrassment which Iwuagwu clearly hoped to cause.

"*E gbuo dike n'ụlọ, o ruo n'ọgụ echeta ya!*" This was Okoro's enigmatic response, delivered in a calm manner and with a conceited smile, on one occasion when he appeared at the entrance of his compound to confront Iwuagwu. Obioma had watched from afar as Iwuagwu's fuzzy mind scrambled to make sense of what Okoro had said. And when he finally worked it out – "Kill a warrior during skirmishes at home; you will remember him when fighting enemies" – it caused Iwuagwu to have a convulsive fit of agitation.

"You are not a warrior! You do not represent us! You are a nobody!" Iwuagwu blasted out, standing unsteadily and waving his walking stick once again at Okoro's bare compound, too late with his retort, as Okoro had long slinked back into his mansion.

Now Iwuagwu lay peacefully on his bed, cut down by a sudden bout of pneumonia and not helped by the fake antibiotic medicine that his daughter-in-law had spent a fortune on. At the not-so-grand old age of sixty-eight, Iwuagwu was already the eldest in the kindred of over five hundred people.

"Iwuagwu was not an old man. This useless government and their selfish evil packed with the IMF, this is how our best people are dying," Obioma heard the Professor say to a handful of men who stood around the bungalow where Iwuagwu lay in state.

Obioma felt a rush of guilt engulf him. Along with SAP and all the other atrocities heaped on the people by the military dictatorship, Obioma believed that he, too, had had a hand in Iwuagwu's death. The end to their apprenticeship arrangement must have broken him. He remembered how Iwuagwu had avoided him over the course of the two days when he had last visited the village.

Iwuagwu's son and daughter dashed around the compound with other relatives, making final preparations for his interment later that day. His young grandchildren, Obioma's second cousins, and their mother were sheltered in one of the bungalows in the compound, away from the streams of visitors that besieged the compound.

Earlier that morning, Obioma accompanied Iwuagwu's son in calling at Okoro's house to inform him that Iwuagwu had on several occasions explicitly instructed that Okoro was not to be allowed to attend his funeral. They were there to politely ask him to respect Iwuagwu's wishes by not showing up. Obioma nodded in support as Iwuagu's son spoke. From the look of irritation on Okoro's face, Obioma thought, he looked like the type who would have quite liked to attend if only to gloat at his supposed nemesis.

When Adolf Obiora and his son arrived that morning, things took a more hasty turn. It now felt as though Iwuagwu body's peaceful rest in his favourite room, as people shuffled by, had been taken for granted. The large windows that circled the room Iwuagwu's corpse lay in were now suddenly bolted shut. It suddenly dawned on Obioma that he was seeing the last of his uncle.

Obioma was handed cotton-wool dipped in mentholated ointment to stuff up his nose. Adolf and his son were well known across Umuwe and beyond. It was their job to cut out Iwuagwu's lungs – the organ that had been responsible for his death. This was to ensure Iwuagwu was given a new set of better-working lungs in his next reincarnation. His old lungs would be buried separately. Obioma reluctantly joined Iwuagwu's son and daughter to watch Adolf and his son perform the special task they had been paid to do.

By mid-afternoon that day, Iwuagwu's funeral was in full swing. Nwachukwu, Iwuagwu's dear friend, had dusted off and powered up his old Mercedes Benz days earlier and embarked on a two-day journey to Arochukwu to inform a number of traditional healers there, whom he knew Iwuagwu had held in high regard, that their colleague had passed on. He had then gone back the day before the funeral to shuttle a delegation of the traditional healers to Umuwe, accommodating them in his own house.

Obioma felt that Nwachukwu was avoiding him, just as Iwuagwu had done a year and a half ago. There were none of the hearty greetings or the radiant smiles that usually accompanied his painful, gripping handshake. At the occasional times when Obioma caught Nwachukwu's eye, Nwachukwu gave him the sort of disappointed look that came in response to a woeful school report. This exacerbated Obioma's feelings of guilt.

It was no consolation, but Obioma knew that Iwuagwu would have found his own funeral befitting. Two days earlier, Obioma had joined Iwuagwu's son in the market, personally picking out the two medium-sized dogs that were to be killed, cooked and made available to the medicine men that attended the funeral.

Iwuagwu's interment itself was a spectacle. The four traditional healers who had arrived with Nwachukwu were dressed in full cult regalia: bare-chested and barefoot with ornamental charms draped around their necks and long shotguns slung over their shoulders, which they fired intermittently into the sky as Iwuagwu's body was carried from where he lay in state to where he was to be buried.

A large grave now gaped open beside the mound of earth under which Iwuagwu's wife was buried. With palm leaves tucked between their lips, the four visiting medicine men unravelled their raffia sling-bags bulging with their trade paraphernalia. They poured libations and made invocations to various deities to consecrate the burial area. Then they gyrated to the various songs and war-chants which they spontaneously broke into as Iwuagwu's body was lowered into his grave. The cacophony of gunfire that broke out as the first heaps of sand were thrown onto Iwuagwu's coffin drowned out the rapturous crying all around that had been provoked by the thud of Iwuagwu's coffin finally reaching its final resting place.

Obioma felt more strongly than ever that he had let down his uncle considerably.

40 GLOBALISATION

"O na-abụ ahụ ihe ka ubi, eree ọba"

"If one who farms encounters something bigger than the farm, they sell their barn"

(Traditional Igbo proverb)

Three months later

Kalu knew his brother Benjamin was pleased that he could now publicly indulge himself in his friendship with Don Champion. Chief Alusi had died exactly a month after Kalu and his brother visited him. Frank, or rather Bullet, had joined his father shortly afterwards, following an armed robbery that saw his body and that of his uncle riddled with bullets along with the Rolls-Royce Phantom they were riding in.

The sky was now the limit; Benjamin was sitting on a fortune, as well commanding a network of some of the most dangerous people around, all ready to do his bidding.

"You too are part of this now," Kalu remembered his brother occasionally saying to him in his bedroom as they chatted.

At these times, Kalu was sure Benjamin that detected the hesitations he had over his new life, the dithering that he managed to conceal by applying himself with a cold and calculating, Machiavellian approach to the new world in which he now operated. Kalu had fallen into his role of muse to his brother almost too perfectly, so much so that Benjamin made a point of consulting him before he took any major decisions.

"It must look like an armed robbery gone wrong – one or two casualties on our side. Someone new, a loner with no ties to the boys. It must look very random." These were some of the things Kalu found himself saying when the deaths of Chief Alusi's son and brother were being planned.

The night after the deed was done, as they debriefed each other, there was now no doubt in Kalu's mind that this was how the world worked.

"This is CIA shit, boy, KGB runs," Kalu had once heard his brother brag. "We do enough of this and you don't even need to carry a gun anymore, you just rock up anywhere in your suit and demand shit and people will comply."

"Even if you rock up with shorts and slippers, no *whahala*, the result will be the same," his cousin Mike concluded.

For Kalu, his brother's continued success was vindication enough. The impact of the threat of violence was combined with the streams of dirt they had about the private lives of the great and the good in public life – information Kalu was now privy to given his brother's network of noble and highly esteemed businessmen and politicians. Many were addicted to his brother's quick-turnaround assassination service, which seemed to come into greatest demand during election time. Others were hooked on the underage teenage prostitute ring that Benjamin managed and which he personally indulged in. Drugs, counterfeiting, armed robbery and extortion; it was all symbiotic and the actors linked to every part of the ecosystem. Every now and again, there would need to be a purge, the burning of fodder; people like Chief Alusi, his relatives and other hangers-on.

Kalu had rightly guessed the state of things even before he joined his brother's organisation. In fact, in the almost-dead silence of his regular early Saturday morning reads, Kalu had found himself scouring through books that revealed the world he now inhabited. Books about people like his brother. Cartel leaders in Europe, Asia and South America, even motorcyclists in North America were at it, along with respectable suited bankers in large skyscraper-infested cities, quiet dainty hamlets in Switzerland and others on picturesque vacation islands, all helping them hang on to their money. Globalisation was something Kalu found himself increasingly fascinated with. He had worked out that their access to cheaper guns for robberies and money-counterfeiting equipment, and the ease of moving drugs and money around, had all been made possible because of globalisation– better and better technology and more and more people knowing a whole lot more than in the past. Money, people and things moved around the world faster and in greater quantities than they had ever done in the past, and authorities around the world apparently did not have a clue how to keep track of them. Automatic guns, kilos of cocaine and grains of rice and beans travelled in the same containers and people could not tell real from fake money.

"Surely this could be exploited," he had pondered, but when Kalu brought his observations to Benjamin and his associates all it did was draw blank looks, and they resorted to pelting him with jovial banter about how Kalu was overthinking things as usual.

For Kalu, the realisation that he actually understood Benjamin's world far more than his brother ever could was quietly comforting. There was finally potential for him to upstage his brother. Kalu was confident; sooner or later he would hatch a plan to exploit his knowledge and overtake his brother's achievements. But all this was many weeks ago. A more recent development in Kalu's dealings with his brother and his brother's associates had caused Kalu to seriously question his association with them.

What used to be Chief Alusi's favourite helicopter hovered over the city, and Kalu sat alongside Benjamin and their father on their way to attend Owerri's society event of the year, Don Champion's wedding. In fact, Don Champion, over the course of two months, hosted eight ceremonies to mark his wedding – one in London, another in Lagos, another at his bride's maternal home and two at her father's village. He then paid for two separate evening events in the two most exclusive hotels in Owerri for his close associates and friends and, to crown it all, a massive white-wedding ceremony at the city's main stadium, which was open to the public to attend.

The luxurious AugustaWestland Koala helicopter touched down on the luscious carpet of grass that spanned the football pitch in the middle of the stadium; and Kalu, his brother and his father alighted and took their seats in the executive seating area as ordinary folk looked on from the packed stands. Helicopters arrived and departed as more of Don Champion's moneyed friends and associates arrived. Kalu and his family sat only a few aisles away from the military governor and his wife, along with scores of men and their wives rumoured to be worth millions or billions of naira.

Stewards ferried chilled bottles of refreshments up and down the rows of throne-like leather seats, and adjusted the scores of standing and rotating fans warding off the humid, stagnant afternoon heat and mixed scent of expensive perfume. Soon the bride and groom appeared, stepping out of a luxurious Sikorsky aircraft to cheers from around the stands. Speeches, food and more drink were consumed and then the first dance ensued in the executive enclosure, away from the baying crowds in the stands. Don Champion's friends rallied around the happy, dancing couple and showered them with unravelled wads of dollars, pounds and euros carried in big boxes by their aides. Kalu joined his brother in the executive enclosure with their own box of cash for the frenzy of cash throwing. He was sure he could spot classmates looking on at the spectacle from the surrounding stands. But in his mind, Kalu could not help but revisit what he had discovered three days earlier.

Touted by his brother as yet another milestone in Kalu's introduction to the business, Benjamin had announced that it was time for Kalu to "meet the boys on the ground, the people that made it all happen". In fact, this particular group was one of a few discrete groups that his brother maintained in various parts of the country.

These men resided in a large three-storey building that his brother had swindled from Chief Alusi. About an hour's drive south of Owerri, and about mid-morning on a Tuesday, Kalu and his brother found themselves wedged uncomfortably into the low hull of Benjamin's brand new 1994 Porsche 911, which scraped painfully against the network of potholed roads they navigated that morning.

The building itself was a narrow tower block that had only just been completed and was yet to be painted on the outside. It was located on an isolated spot amongst acres of partitioned farmlands and bushes strewn with rows of tall cassava plants, corn stalks and overgrown weeds. Small footpaths criss-crossed each other, extending for miles in all directions to shabby settlements of bungalows and sheds. The air carried the muffled, distant sounds of bleating goats and screeching children in the substandard sheds they used for classrooms.

They settled the car alongside two others parked in the unkempt compound threatened by the encroaching weed and shrubs that flanked the road for miles. Kalu followed his brother closely as he swept through the compound with the familiarity of someone who lived there. Kalu concluded that he must have done so at some point.

"Martin, Armour, Aka Egbe," Benjamin called out at the top of his voice as he unlocked the front door with a set of keys he carried in his pocket. This prompted a number of sleepy groans and sighs from within the building. Kalu accompanied Benjamin as he called at rooms one by one, like a doctor on a ward round.

"Mrs Don born again this year."

"Una need to try use rubber to fuck now."

"How many magazine remain?"

Kalu watched in silence as his brother made small talk, checking the condition of his stock, with those who asked inquisitively about planned new raids and weapons and others who needed to visit the doctor in town over some STD.

The men were as Kalu expected, half-witted, battle-scarred, drugged-up, not-so-smart versions of his brother. Their peculiar Igbo and pidgin-English twangs placed their origins at the periphery of the state and beyond. Perhaps some of them hailed from neighbouring countries like Cameroon and the Republic of Benin, Kalu thought. Perhaps they, too, were telling their families that they were away in Lagos working in the tall buildings in Marina or Victoria Island, shuttling between there and the shipping port, importing and exporting *tokunbo* cars.

Apart from "showing Kalu the boys," there was a side reason for Benjamin's visit. Martin, one of Benjamin's men, had impregnated one of the girls, a runaway he had picked up a few miles away.

Kalu watched Martin, dressed only in his stained underpants, explain how out of the kindness of his heart he had allowed her to stay a while in the house with them. No one was sure exactly where she had run away from. She had helped clean around the building. This was before the dozen or so men living in the building coaxed her on multiple occasions, sometimes forcefully, to sleep with them. However, it was Martin who had brought her to the building and according to the way things worked, consequently it was he who carried responsibility for her. That had been Benjamin's judgement on the matter a few weeks earlier when it was brought to his attention. Benjamin had paid for a man to visit the building and abort the pregnancy.

"So that situation has been sorted, right?" Benjamin's repeated questions drew blanks from Martin. Apparently it had not.

"*Oga* Benji, she bled quite a lot, sir," Martin eventually explained in a sort of half-hearted nonchalant defence of the man, whom Benjamin apparently knew well. In between early-morning swigs from a brandy bottle clutched in his right hand, Martin detailed the 29-minute-long failed abortion procedure that he claimed he had witnessed.

"Where is she now?" Benjamin finally asked. The question opened a whole new side of Benjamin's operations of which Kalu had had no previous reckoning.

"She is at the Business Centre," Martin responded coyly, knowing it would draw Benjamin's wrath.

"What the fuck is she doing there?" Benjamin barked in rage. "The Business Centre is for business, for *business*! I have warned you boys not to take your personal affairs there."

Until he finally saw it, Kalu did not know about the place referred to as the Business Centre; another building, just a few miles north of where they were. It was a place where people kidnapped for extortion purposes were held as their release was bargained for. This was also where any torture would happen. Kalu learnt that day that Ikem had not been killed that Saturday morning, but had actually been alive for several days afterwards. Benjamin and Mike had been concerned that his screams would be overheard during their interrogations, so they had drugged him and carried him to the Business Centre to conclude things properly.

41 FELICIA

"Mmiri mara ohu, n'ama onye n'achʊ ohu"

"The same rain that drenches the slave also drenches the slave driver"

(Traditional Igbo proverb)

The place they called the Business Centre was an exact replica of the building that Kalu, Benjamin and Martin had just left, although it was in a much less completed state and was virtually in the middle of nowhere.

They squeezed out of the dirt-covered Porsche 911 after twelve miles of dusty road. Martin led the way as they waded through the overgrown shrubs that concealed the shabby and abandoned construction site. With the claw of the hammer Martin carried in his pocket, he dislodged the handful of nails which fastened a few wooden boards across the main doorway of the building, before unlocking a thick metal mesh gate welded into the door-frame from the inside.

Felicia looked no more than fifteen years old. She cowered in a crouching position in the corner of one of the many bare rooms in the concrete house. Her dozy eyes were visible in the modest mid-morning sun-rays that seeped through the gaps in the wood panels and metal mesh that barricaded the windows. She did not speak or move, but Martin assured Benjamin and Kalu that Felicia was still pregnant; he had examined her himself the day before. He said this as he nailed back the boards of wood across the main door, the stench of urine and faeces necessitating a prompt exit. The odour seemed to penetrate the wooden barriers and stay with them as they talked outside the building.

"Dibia go. Come around two for the thing, sir," Martin said as he checked his watch and took another swig from his bottle of brandy. Benjamin remained quiet. Kalu knew too well that Benjamin's silence meant he was seething with anger.

"*Oga*, as we get operation tomorrow, I thought we might as well, eh? Go solve two problems, sir," Martin added, drawing a reluctant nod from Benjamin.

Benjamin often told Kalu that the men were difficult to manage. That afternoon Kalu would accomplish more than his brother had planned for him that day. He had met the boys alright, but he would soon find out what drove them.

The young Dibia, who looked no older than Benjamin, arrived at exactly two o'clock in his *tokunbo* Mercedes Benz along with the young man who chauffeured him. To Kalu, it was as though the Dibia was making a particular effort to look twice his age, wearing a red traditional Igbo hat, a heavily patterned wrapper tied around his waist, his bare torso heavily adorned with charms and beads. The Dibia took measured, seemingly painful steps from where his aide parked the car to where Benjamin, Kalu and Martin stood. His helper followed closely behind him with a large bag clutched in one hand and a heavy industrial flashlight in the other, items which he had swiftly retrieved from the trunk of the car.

"Okoro, *kedu*," Benjamin called out as the medicine man approached them and seized their hands in handshakes. Martin grasped Okoro's right hand with both of his, with the sort of reverence usually reserved for royalty. Kalu still remained clueless as to why Okoro was present, until Benjamin began to explain.

A hit on a bank security motorcade in a neighbouring state was scheduled for the following day. Benjamin had received a tip-off from one of his highly placed contacts, as he often did, about the movement of a large sum of foreign currency. A dozen men, including Martin, most of whom lived at the house that they had just visited, had been designated to carry out the robbery. It was customary for them to perform protection ceremonies.

It's all bullshit, but the men needed to feel safe, Benjamin would later confide in Kalu. *It actually makes them a lot more daring.* Standing beside his brother, Kalu watched with quiet alarm as Martin, Okoro and Okoro's helper made their way back to the uncompleted building, Martin once again prising open the planks of wood barricading the main entrance with the claw of his hammer. A few short moments passed. Kalu heard the muffled screams of the pregnant girl, along with loud, indecipherable bursts of incantation, as Okoro decapitated her alive and performed his ritual, aided by the two men with him.

As the notes continued to rain down on Don Champion and his new wife, their laughter and the cheers of their guests were not quite enough to drown out the screams and chanting that still echoed in Kalu's head.

42 CANCER

*"The anya h*ụ*r*ụ *anagh*ị *ach*ọ *onye aka-ebe"*

"What the eye sees does not need witnesses"

(Traditional Igbo proverb)

Two weeks later

On the last day of exams, Obioma half-heartedly joined in the exuberant, carefree horseplay, which culminated in students defacing each other's school uniforms. The remnants of ink that had survived the two-week-long frenzied writing was put to use in drawings of various takes on genitalia and boastful epithets of the sort usually found defacing public toilets. Desks and chairs were securely wedged together and balanced on students' heads.

Obioma and the other boys eventually vacated the school, setting off on their final trek home, but not until there were no more junior students to taunt, until they felt the live-in principal's dog had been tormented enough, and until the principal had threatened to call the police when the protracted ogling at some of the younger female student-teachers had gone too far.

Obioma was finally alone with his thoughts on the last stretch of road to his building,Obioma reflected on the ghastly two weeks of examinations. Four days ago, the heavens had complemented his feelings by opening up. It had rained continuously since then, but on that final day it had stopped. Arriving home, Obioma looked out of his window and saw Nneka approaching his building. It was the first time he had seen her in weeks.

Nneka had also spotted Obioma looking out of his window, and her brisk pace quickened even more. As Obioma raced down the seven stairwells to the front entrance of his building he appraised his situation. His mother would not be home until late, he did not have to be at the eating house until later, and Ogechi no longer lived at home.

It would finally happen. She was coming to fuck.

He did not have a reason to associate the end of their secondary school days with Nneka finally giving in to him, but he was sure that the universe had finally aligned itself.

"I can't stay," Nneka said tearfully as she met him at the foot of the stairs. "My mother is ill, and I am going back to the hospital. I just wanted to let you know."

Obioma accompanied Nneka to Owerri General Hospital that afternoon, because that was why she had come all the way to his house, even though she had played it down.

The raggedy taxi stopped on Orlu Road, and Obioma and Nneka alighted and made their way up the sloped road in the hospital compound. At the end of that same road, at the top of the hill, lay a gated compound with a sizeable building – the hospital's mortuary which Obioma had twice visited, first with his mother to identify his father's mangled corpse, and then, later, in the company of his relatives in a motorcade to retrieve the body for burial.

Obioma remembered the putrid smell that had hit them when he and his mother first stepped into the main reception room of the building. A smell not too dissimilar, he thought, to the smell that now greeted him and Nneka as they arrived at the overcrowded ward.

Nneka's mother lay on one of the spring beds in the corner of the ward, shrouded in her all-black wrapper, which was pulled ominously over her face. Nneka's mother moved a little, allaying Nneka's brief apprehension as they marched down the hall-like ward towards her.

"Mma," Obioma greeted her in a low and sombre tone befitting the bleak setting and complementing the dejected look on Nneka's mother's face as she sat up in her bed.

Her voice was faint and crackling, as though it had been put to a great deal of use. She had good news, she claimed. After a two-day wait, a doctor had finally appeared and looked at her and at the results from samples of tissue drawn from her by injection. She had breast cancer, she said, just as one of the nurses had reckoned when had she arrived and disrobed to reveal a small wound, a few lumps, and discharges of blood and pus from her right breast. Whatever else the doctor had said had gone over her head, but she understood that both of her breasts needed to be removed quickly, and that it would cost a great deal of money. Obioma quietly searched for the good news in what Nneka's mother had just said.

"What do you mean, they have to cut them off?" Nneka said initially, looking at her mother in petrified disbelief. Obioma watched silently as Nneka pressed her mother further on what else the doctor had said. This did not yield any more information, leading Nneka to scour the ward for more information, Obioma in tow.

"I am busy. Come back tomorrow morning when the doctor is around," was all the first nurse Nneka accosted at the entrance of the ward had to say, after she had made Nneka wait while she finished the newspaper article she was reading. Their brief encounter with another nurse in the corridor joining the male and female sections of the ward yielded nothing more. She reminded them that it was already past visiting hours, before briskly walking off.

"The fat ones are the worst." The old man who had spoken had been sitting idly in the corner long enough to see Nneka and Obioma's hopeless dashing around. "You're best off lying in wait for one of the slimmer younger ones, the trainee ones who haven't been desensitised and hardened against the smell of sickness, helplessness and desperate people like us."

It took another three hours and a shift change before they found a nurse whom they considered slim and new enough to fit the advice, a young male nurse who could not have been more than three years older than Obioma, and who looked eerily to them like Mr Success, though much shorter and younger.

When they initially saw him, he was briskly walking through the ward towards the office, his head rapidly swinging from side to side in a mechanical manner, like a robot wheeling across the room, rapidly conducting sweeping sight checks.

Minutes after they approached him, he had them sitting in the ward office with Nneka's mother's file spread open on his desk. After words and phrases like "malignant tumour", "aggressive and deadly", "private hospital", "surgery" and "radiotherapy", he finally said "eight hundred thousand naira".

"Find that money quickly if you want your mother to live," the nurse gravely warned a stunned-silent Nneka and Obioma.

The nurse led them into one of the handful of private rooms attached to the ward. A woman who looked to be in her forties lay half naked, her eyes closed, her bare left breast now shrivelled and a dark purple shade. It reminded Obioma of his uncle's dead body. The nurse explained that she had received the same sort of news Nneka's mother had been given just under a year ago, and neither she nor her family had the money to follow things up.

"She will be dead in less than a month. Cutting them off six months ago would not have saved her," he advised, as he closed the door to the private room.

Later on that evening, Obioma left Nneka and her mother at the hospital for his shift at his mother's eating house. He personally knew of only one person who could arrange that sort of money.

43 AKAMU

"Ụwa dị ka anra ewu: Ọnaghị enye mmiri anra ma a na-apịghị ya"

"The world is like a goat's udder: it does not yield any milk, unless you punch and

squeeze it"

(Traditional Igbo proverb)

Twelve months later

Obioma's mother always found eleven o'clock in the morning to be a lull period at her eating house, more so now that she had two helpers pounding bits of boiled yam and chopping heaps of vegetables for the impending swarm of traders and civil servants who would besiege her establishment at noon. She availed herself of this rare stint of free time and scooped a generous portion of her critically acclaimed *akamu* pap into a bowl: breakfast, which she dawdled with, sitting at one of the tables in the almost empty dining area.

It was incredibly fortunate that a portion of the New Market had recently been gutted by fire, she found herself thinking. Had that not happened, Obioma would still be wandering about town aimlessly. It would only be a matter of time before that took its toll.

The New Market was not as congested as the Old Market had been, and the fire had been caught quite early. Nevertheless, it had destroyed a fair number of shops. But many of them were not doing well anyway. Obioma's mother knew of a number of traders, particularly those who sold clothing material, who saw the fire as an unfortunate but welcome push to finally end their long-running, fruitless ventures. They sold what was left of their trading spaces and found something else to do.

Obioma now sold stockfish out of one of the renovated shops in the market. His mother had sunk all of the accumulated profits from Madam Succulent into buying the shop and stocking it up, close to one and a half million naira in total. A resurgence of the glory days of her old store would soon be a reality, she thought, as she stirred the thick, yellowish pap in her bowl.

Her mind continued to wander. She planned how she would take charge of the store once things picked up. She would open a second one in the renovated Old Market which Obioma could take charge of. In less than a year, Madam Succulent would bring in the money for that, she was sure.

She considered which of her cousins she would send for to help run the eating house, and which other relatives would be suited to running a third store in Aba. She would need to build stronger ties with the Icelandic and Norwegian sailors who shipped in the stockfish if she was to eventually become a wholesaler. But first things first, she thought. Before all that she needed to jolt Obioma out of his sulking; he was very crucial to her plans but he was now taking after his father a bit too much, she thought.

Obioma had been unable to pick himself up after failing most of his school-leaving exams. *Trying hard to be something he is not*, she felt, something that had taken both her husband and his brother to their graves. Her appetite for her pap disappeared as her worry grew that Obioma now spent his time hiding away in the shop reading textbooks instead of engaging with customers.

But at least there was a silver lining. He had also stopped talking about that dreadful girl he had been so long obsessed with, even though it had taken months for him to get over the fact that she was no longer interested in him. Still, his new delusion had to be tackled. He needed a good talking to, Obioma's mother finally resolved, before rising to her feet as the first of her lunch-time customers walked into the eating house.

44 THE TRAP

"Bad friends will prevent you from having good friends"

(Traditional Gabon proverb)

"Sorry, still no vacancy," the lady sitting in a small office cubicle under a stairwell said to Nneka. The young lady was the university housing officer for a collection of single-storied buildings scattered around the university, all aggregated under the banner 'Hall B'.

"Why do you even want to be in Hall B?" Rose, one of Nneka's roommates, had queried earlier that day, as she stuffed a handful of clothing into her travel bag for yet another overnight trip to a friend somewhere.

Nneka remained quiet, her legs swinging back and forth as she sat with her head in a novel on the upper portion of a bunk bed crammed in with three others in the small single-windowed room. She watched Rose lying on the floor as she wriggled impossibly into the tightest pair of jeans, and it somehow reminded her of how snakes shed their skin. Nneka had never intended for Rose to catch her wandering into the housing office of Hall B. She had planned to vanish from Hall F, her current lodgings, as stealthily as she had arrived only a few weeks earlier.

Rose put on a plunging crop top, no more concealing than a bra, and when she was finally standing up she doused herself in a shower of perfume.

"All those girls at Hall B are all butty," Rose continued, temporarily unbuttoned the latches at the front of her jeans to breathe. *Butty; 'big city girl' indeed. This one only just started going to Lagos yesterday and 'Ajibo' has already become 'butty'*, Nneka thought to herself.

And this was partly why she wanted to leave Hall F. Every one of her other six roommates was an exact replica of Rose, a 'runs girl', and so were most of the girls who found themselves in Hall F. And in E, G and H, for that matter. This was no accident.

Nneka had found out that it was customary for the university to assign halls according to the performance results they had for students. All the academically bright girls, those with exam scores just above the JAMB admission requirements, and others whose privileged background had bought them a decent enough education found themselves in Halls A, B, C and D. This was apparent even to those who had impersonators take exams for them or who managed to cheat some other way and achieve a high score. They soon found themselves in unfamiliar company and many sought to change their living situations. On the day that Nneka realised that her lacklustre marks had brought her to Hall F, she decided against going to any of her lectures. She went back to her bed and quietly sobbed for hours. That was when it also dawned on her that she was no better than her roommates and that perhaps she had spent far too much time in bible study.

Despite her fretting over her school work, she had landed with the not-so-bright. They, above all others, had to survive by bribing lecturers with cash and sex, by managing a string of sugar daddies and resourceful 'friends' in various far-flung cities, to whom they travelled at their beck and call. When night fell or the weekend approached, around Hall F and others like it there would be all manner of cars parked up, and the corridors swarmed with so many middle-aged men that Friday was jovially termed 'father's day'.

"Jesus Christ, *omo*, nice fucking boobs, girl. When my sugar daddies come here, please make you hide them under this oversized blouse as you dey hide them so, because if they come out, there is no competition, you win hands down," Rose had said to Nneka the very first time they met each other. Almost a month on, Nneka did not even know what courses most of her roommates were taking. She had never actually seen them around the university.

"You this girl, you have not said a word, abi that book sweet so?" Rose said to Nneka.

"Ah sorry, you still dey here?" Nneka responded, her gaze momentarily lifting from her book.

"Please don't make the mistake of joining all those butty and deeper-life girls in Hall B. You know that stupid girl from Hall B and those *yeye ajibo-*wanna-be ganster boys are not going to make it past this semester. The lecturer is an ex cult guy. I am going, oh *jare*." Rose flung her all-carrying handbag over her left shoulder and left the room, sucking in the air between her front teeth in annoyance as she did so.

Nneka knew that Rose was referring to the shamed lecturer who had picked on the wrong girl to pester for sex. He had already failed the girl twice and, in an ambush that involved a camera and two of her cousins who were also at the university, they lured the lecturer to the girl's off-campus flat and captured audio and video recordings of the lecturer naked and poised for sex. This was right before the boys gave the lecturer a severe beating.

As Nneka stared helplessly for the fourth time into the eyes of the Hall B housing officer later that day, she knew she would be moving back to live with her mother in town. Not because of Rose or her other classmates, but because Kalu's impromptu visits to her halls had now increased, and with each visit he was getting more and more clear in his motives.

45 CHALET O'BRIEN

"Whether it was the tenant who seduced the landlord's wife, or the landlord who seduced

the tenant's wife, it is the tenant who will leave the house"

(Traditional Igbo proverb)

One month later

The wide, cracked concrete aisles of Owerri New Market were awash with water as the heavy late-May rain gushed down. It was a full three hours into the downpour and it showed no signs of abating. Apart from the threat of another devastating flood, this was very good news for Obioma. There would definitely be no more customers calling at the store to disturb him.

Obioma had already barricaded the entrance of his shop with sandbags against the ominous but expected rising tide of floodwater which meandered through the network of aisles. Surrounded by hanging bales of stockfish, Obioma planted himself on his old chair and desk from school, which he had moved to the shop, and buried his head in a biology textbook.

His mind wandered off elsewhere. It went where it had always gone for the past nine months: to that dreadful day when an old classmate informed him that he had spotted Nneka and Kalu going into Chalet O'Brien, a place in town where you could rent a room with a bed by the hour. His long-accumulated bank of fantasies about Nneka's naked form now worked against his well-being, as he helplessly imagined their liaisons at Chalet O'Brien in graphic detail.

Chalet O'Brien also had an eatery, but there was no doubt as to what they would have been up to there. *Anybody who goes to Chalet O'Brien goes there for one thing only.* Obioma's mind recited the slogan which was never really written anywhere but which lived in the minds of all who knew of the place.

Obioma also thought a lot at this time about his dead uncle, with his cautionary tales about the perils of going against the Agwu deity. At the tail-end of his torturous montage of thoughts, Obioma would typically liken himself to Prometheus, his regenerating liver being pecked at and devoured by an eagle over and over again.

Obioma had seen Nneka's transgressions coming, almost as clearly as he had foreseen his woeful performance at his school-leaving examinations. It was clear that it had been a huge mistake to approach Kalu and his brother for the money for Nneka's mother's treatment. If only he had stuck with his uncle's programme he would have had the full amount to give Nneka to get her mother treated. On several occasions, he had seen Iwuagwu's huge stash of cash hidden in the base of his raffia-and-cane bed. That cash would have been handed to him following his uncle's death, he was sure.

Nneka had approached Kalu the day after the nurse warned them about her mother's impending death, and she had come straight back to Obioma with the good news that Kalu and his brother were able and willing to help. It was going to be a loan. It would take some time but eventually they would be able to pay it all back from her mother's stall profits and the nursing placements Nneka would be able to secure as soon as two years into her undergraduate studies. A repayment plan had already been drawn up.

"Kalu is not as he used to be." Obioma remembered rehearsing how to begin to explain delicately his disagreement with the decision to involve Kalu. But no matter how he said it, he knew that he would end up at the receiving end of Nneka's angry, steely stare and the accusation of putting his petty jealousy and insecurities ahead of her mother's life. He kept his mouth shut.

Obioma's involuntary recollections continued, even as the storm raged violently outside his shop and dusk fell over the city prematurely in the rain.

He remembered how he had been sidelined the afternoon Kalu arrived at the hospital in one of his brother's flashy cars with a boot full of money. Just under one million naira. Kalu had paid the full amount of eight hundred thousand, in cash, to the hospital cashiers. They had had to organise a special escort to take the money to the bank. Kalu had then proceeded to hand out personal cash gifts to all of the nurses and attendants on duty that afternoon. Obioma remembered the look of adulation in Nneka's eyes as she watched Kalu hovering around the ward. This was when he truly believed it was over.

"You don't need to worry about us," Obioma remembered Nneka

saying on many occasions as he fidgeted about news of yet another impromptu call by Kalu at her faculty at the campus in town. Kalu would drop by under the pretext of having great news of a potential job with some doctors he knew who ran private hospitals. He had told them about her, and they owed favours to his brother.

Initially, Obioma was grateful that Nneka gave him a running commentary of her contact with Kalu, because it soothed his anxieties, especially when she finally admitted that she believed she was being pursued by him.

They agreed that they would handle him delicately, not so harshly as to prompt a demand for an immediate repayment of all the money they owed him and his brother. Obioma would not go calling at Kalu's house to warn him to keep away from Nneka, as he had planned to do on various occasions.

Obioma was just about to take custody of his mother's new shop then. It was planned that, between the money Nneka made from her evening placement with a clinic and a portion of Obioma's eventual profits, they should be able to repay Kalu and Benjamin much sooner than arranged.

Then Nneka arrived at Obioma's shop one afternoon with news.

"I ran into Kalu again on my way back from lectures. He said he has some contacts in Lagos, an American hospital which caters to expats. He said he had pulled some strings and they want to get me enrolled into the University of Lagos and take me on at their hospital."

"How can they want to do all that for someone they have not met?" Obioma asked her.

"He gave them my CV and picture."

"And where did he get your CV and picture from?"

"I gave him copies a week earlier," Nneka responded hesitantly.

Obioma had guessed right that the Lagos arrangements would suddenly hit some sort of complication as soon as Kalu learnt that Obioma had offered to join Nneka to meet the people at the private hospital. Kalu sent feedback from the hospital, who were apparently in a rush for an answer, and the offer was withdrawn.

Obioma knew Kalu well enough to realise he would not give up. Only days later, Obioma heard that Kalu had dropped by Nneka's campus again, asking her to come by his house later that week to discuss her repayments. This was the first time the repayments had been brought up. They had stepped on the snake's tail. Obioma feared the worst.

When Kalu opened his front door to what he thought was a sole visit from Nneka, Obioma was there, standing beside her.

"Obioma, what are you doing here? You were not invited to this meeting," Obioma remembered Kalu saying. He appeared drunk.

"I asked Obioma to come with me," Nneka explained as tension grew,

Kalu staring menacingly at Obioma.

"He is not welcome here," Kalu retorted as Obioma remained calm.

"If you want to discuss the loan, let's discuss the loan," Obioma remembered saying, trying hard not to be belligerent. There was no point being aggressive when he could not back it up with money. At least, not yet, Obioma reasoned.

"This has nothing to do with you. As I said, you were not invited to this meeting," Kalu insisted, followed by the ultimatum, "Nneka, are you coming in or not?"

Nneka and Obioma embarked on the long walk back to town. Obioma had won for now, but he feared that his victory would be short-lived. There were no further running commentaries about Kalu's calls to Nneka's campus, and for a time Obioma rested easy in the mistaken impression that the exchange outside Kalu's front door had finally warded Kalu off for good.

Obioma broke out of his deep thoughts as water began to seep through the sandbags lining his shop's door. He knew that before long he would be back to those thoughts.

46 ASHAWO 2

"Onye gburu enyi ya abụghị dike"

"The killing of a friend does not show strength"

(Traditional Igbo proverb)

A week later

Nneka heard the first strains of thumping music coming from outside her room. She paused her beauty routine and sat transfixed in front of the dressing mirror in the room that she shared with her mother.

The sound grew rapidly and seemed to settle just outside her window, along with the deliberate frenzied revving of an engine and finally the toot of a car horn. Nneka's eyes began to fill up almost immediately.

She hastily completed encircling her eyelids in dark eyeliner before the next toot of the horn, which forced her out of the room and right outside her shared bungalow's front door. There, she struggled to tame her riding micro-mini skirt while balancing on her six-inch nail-sharp white stilettos, but she managed the short walk to the waiting car despite the burning gaze of neighbours and passers-by, drawn to the spectacle of the gold-plated convertible Maserati, blasting out thumping club music.

Kalu sat slouched and waiting behind the steering wheel of the car, with streams of smoke gushing out of his mouth and nostrils. Nneka knew he was drunk the moment she sat beside him in the passenger seat.

As the car pulled away, and as Kalu's hands wandered up her thighs and under her skirt, her eyes interlocked for the very first time with those of the nurse who lived up her road. Like many who lived in the neighbourhood, the lady stood peering into the car from the elevated vantage point of her roadside balcony.

She looked a lot older than how Nneka usually saw and imagined her. No longer the immaculate and pristinely dressed nurse whom Nneka had gawked at years ago, who hurried past Nneka's house to work with the quickened pace of somebody going to do something very important. She looked chunkier, and streaks of grey hair peppered her plaits. The tiny arms of the rather sickly looking child she was cradling clung to the woman's bosom. It, too, seemed to peer at Nneka with a mixture of pity and disgust.

The eardrum-busting thump of the music could not silence the loud thoughts of revulsion painted on the faces that looked into the car that evening.

"*Ashawo*," Nneka saw a young girl mouth to another, but the disheartening look of the lady and her child stayed with Nneka long after Kalu's car had pulled into the grounds of his brother's mansions, long after she had ingested the drink and pills she was plied with, as she drifted in and out of consciousness, as bodies with grimacing faces, some recognisable, others not, mounted and dismounted her.

PART 4

47 ROAD TO REDEMPTION

"O chọrọ iri awọ, rie nke gbara agba"

"If you decide to eat a toad, you should at least select one that is big"

(Traditional Igbo proverb)

Four months later

Nowadays, Kalu drank less and was not as indulgent in partaking in the array of medication that his brother Benjamin had on tap. The increased periods of lucidity that resulted brought with them burdens of their own, burdens that would see Kalu berate himself as he sat at his veneer desk in his room in the early hours of the morning.

Of all the deaths, pain and suffering that Kalu felt he was implicated in, all of those who had to fall as part of his grand schemes, and all the young girls he had handed over to his brother never to be heard from again, Kalu was particularly haunted by the fate of Felicia, the young girl who, months ago, he had seen cowering in the uncompleted building overgrown by bushes. He could still hear echoes of her agonising squealing just before she died and the permanent look of anguish on her face as Okoro the medicine man shuffled out of the building carrying her severed head.

Her constant presence around him was bizarre, considering his very loose connection to her death. Kalu was sure that this meant he had only begun to experience the tip of the iceberg when it came to penance for his actions and deeds.

"How many have there been?" Kalu once asked his brother.

"Quite many, but you never forget your first." Benjamin's supposedly reassuring comment offered no reprieve.

In fact, Kalu had already dug deeper. There were many people out there who believed that the rituals by themselves turned over money, the corpses and body parts literally coughing up wads of cash on command. Others believed that these things offered some form of protection for their risky endeavours – so much so that some of Benjamin's boys were in the business of killing and selling parts in their spare time to earn extra money. Kalu had heard how some had left Benjamin's employment altogether for this line of business. The city and beyond was littered with posters of missing people as a result.

Felicia often visited Kalu in his dreams, lying right there next to him silently, all the time gawking at him expressionlessly. When he could, Kalu reasoned that this was perhaps some sort of important turning point. Perhaps the day he had seen her had been his last chance to reconsider his involvement with his brother. Kalu also thought about his decision to defer his admission to study law at the University of Nnsuka.

His mind now often harked back to the simpler days, when all that occupied him was the growing collection of books he gathered and his plans to build a palm oil factory. Inevitably, this meant thoughts of Obioma and Nneka and of his treachery and cruelty to them, thoughts he had made extra efforts to suppress, fearing that otherwise he would be even more tormented than he currently was.

This was why, earlier that week, he had invited himself over to his brother's mansion, sat with him during dinner and waited for the appropriate time to consult with him on plans to build a palm oil factory and a noodle-manufacturing plant. Far from the old, childish ideas of scores of old ladies pounding palm seeds, Kalu drew up a business plan – there really was a great deal of money to be made. Besides the obvious food markets, palm oil was now sought by large foreign companies for all sorts of stuff, from fuel for running engines to napalm. Everyone nowadays ate noodles and it was really nothing but flour and water. Fertile land was still abundant and cheap on the fringes of the state and across in neighbouring states. They could produce noodles cheaper than the Chinese imports and sell them across the country.

Kalu had felt his mouth dry up as Benjamin sat silent and expressionless across his dark oak dining table; he did not look at the bound book Kalu had placed in front of him. Kalu had done all the calculations, there were billions to be made, and the switch from what they were currently engaged in to legitimate business could be done quite quickly. He had willed himself across the finishing line of his presentation.

Kalu had not prepared for the mocking laughter that his brother broke into when he had finished, and the taunting questions that followed.

"Did our visit to the boys the other day scare you? Are you afraid? Are you turning into a pussy so soon?"

Kalu had said no more.

48 TRADER

"Dogs do not actually prefer bones to meat; it is just that no one ever gives them meat"

(Traditional Akan proverb, Ghana)

7:25am Tuesday 26 May 1993

Obioma would not admit it to himself, but he was increasingly morphing into a caricature of a typical New Market trader. Only just a full year into his trade and he had already bulked out in frame from the lifestyle: the morning, afternoon and evening trips to Mama Stella's *buka* at the far end of the market and the impulsive snacking on *moi moi* whenever hawkers called at the shop with small tins of the steamed bean pudding balanced on trays on their heads. Sitting around in the shop virtually all day did not help.

Obioma's fluorescent-white long-sleeved cotton shirts from his school days were now replaced by a number of floaty linen shirts, which he owned in a range of colours. The baggy linen trousers he wore were now even baggier and in white, silky, brocade material. He was rarely seen without the signature chunky bunch of keys of a trader, needed for the many locks that secured his shop. Tagged onto them was also the standard-issue miniature metallic shoehorn, which was really an emergency spoon for impromptu purchases of *moi moi*. Together, they bulged out of Obioma's right trouser pocket or swung and jingled as they dangled from his index finger. The unmistakable look of a New Market trader.

With his keys dangling from his hand, Obioma made the familiar walk to work, tracing the ever-bustling Nnamdi Azikiwe Road via the calm streets and roads that ran parallel to it. He would turn off the roads just

178

short of his previous school destination.

He generally now slept well, since he no longer spent his sleeping hours pounding tubers of yam at his mother's eating house. And, although there was now no need to, Obioma continued to carry himself in his slow, lazy, tired gait. Some days he would catch himself and jolt into frenzied power steps, but they always fizzled out as soon as his mind wandered again. Some habits could never be kicked, Obioma conceded to himself, but that was all that was left of the old, he was sure.

Almost a full year of burying his head in books – over his desk deep inside his shop, at night in his room at home, and on the long truck rides he took to and from the suppliers of stockfish – had to pay off. Obioma signed up for external school-leaving qualification exams, starting from scratch. Now only months away, the looming examinations were what occupied his mind, even during his continued but brief pit-stops outside Immaculate Cutz. That morning was no different, except for the unusually large numbers of people – traders, uniformed students and teachers – who began to trickle in from the adjoining Nnamdi Azikiwe Road on to the quiet road.

49 ZONE 5

"Onye arụrụala liee onwe ya, otu aka ya n'apụta"

"If a deceitful person buries himself, one of his arms will stick out"

(Traditional Igbo proverb)

4:46am, the same morning

Very early that morning, well ahead of dawn and before the city had been alerted to the horrendous news that was about to grip it, Kalu grasped tightly on one of the telephone handsets in his brother's living room and listened intently to the conversation that his brother was having with a policeman. This was the second conversation that had occurred with the same policeman within the last ten minutes.

"*Oga*, we no even fit enter the cell block," the calm voice at the other end informed a dejected-looking Benjamin, who squatted down in the corner of the living room.

Across in the other mansion, in the dead-quiet and dark early morning, lights began to come on as his father began the process of telling his mother and sisters that they had to get up and quickly pack their bags for an impending journey.

"*Oga*, I don' try. Constable Kofi and Sergeant Raymond also don' try as well. We no fit reach Mike, na Zone 5 matter now," the police officer concluded.

Kalu recognised the names, police officers who were regularly in his

180

brother's pay and who carried out all manner of favours for Benjamin. From tip-offs of impending police raids, to helping destroy evidence, to facilitating the release of arrested associates, their help had been invaluable. This time, Benjamin was asking for a favour of an even graver nature.

"*Meela* the man, it is already too late, there is no point, Mike will not survive this, eliminate Mike," Benjamin barked frustratedly down the phone to the silent police officer.

Getting to Mike to carry out the deed was not so easy, the policeman reiterated, along with the misfortune that it just happened that the officers who had arrested Mike were actually an out-of-town squad from Calabar on an exchange assignment in the city. They had initially flagged down the car Mike was driving because it looked expensive and they hoped to wrangle out some change for beers later. However, when they came across what he was carrying, they radioed their regional Zone Command immediately, prompting the involvement of the Zone Commander. This was no longer a station or city command matter, the police officer emphasised over the phone. Mike had effectively been quarantined away from local police officers.

The noose was tightening around their necks. Kalu felt it.

During the policeman's earlier call, Benjamin had been informed that Mike had already been severely beaten by his captors in an interrogation conducted minutes after his capture. He was now talking to the police, and had already mentioned Don Champion as an accomplice. Officers were on their way to arrest Don Champion.

Kalu knew Mike was only buying them a little time. Perhaps it wasn't as selfless as it seemed. Maybe Mike was harbouring hopes of getting out of this alive, and was waiting for an intervention by Benjamin through his highly placed contacts. It remained unspoken, but it was clear that Mike would eventually point the finger Benjamin's way.

Kalu listened as the police officer signed off with advice he had already given Benjamin in his previous call: "*Oga*, leave town now."

Kalu watched his brother slump down on the floor as the phone was hung up at the other end, the long, dead tone of the telephone the only sound.

50 CHANGE OF PLAN

"You may be clever but you can never lose your shadow"

(Traditional Igbo proverb)

5:30am

The farm roads on the outskirts of Owerri offered the best cover to move inconspicuously. The 4x4 Porsche Cayenne that Kalu and his brother selected at random from Benjamin's fleet of cars sped down the narrow, meandering roads. The silence as they rode along was punctuated by the thumping sounds the car made as it grazed over potholes, and by the strained morning calls of cockerels on the farms strewn across the terrain.

Benjamin's grim gaze bore down on the road ahead. He had not said a word since their departure from the mansions. Kalu had noticed the handgun he quickly retrieved from his bedroom, which now sat in the glove compartment of the SUV.

"AK also dey for back. We might need it if there is trouble," Benjamin eventually stated. He had apparently glanced at Kalu and seen Kalu's gaze settle on the glove compartment's handle. Kalu did not speak. His mind hovered over the recollection of his mother's mortified face when she was told that morning what Mike had been found with.

"Jesus Christ, you say they found Mike with *what?*" she repeated, her voice trembling. "Benji, did you know about this? Kalu, did you know about this?" His mother extended her frantic enquiries to their father. "Rufus? Are you hearing what your children have been involved in?"

Kalu's father, as expected, maintained his usual passive silence and his feigned stoic calm, though this was betrayed by two bouts of near-fainting and an actual minor fall in the kitchen.

Earlier that morning, as Benjamin sat slumped in his living room and his father lay in bed to get back his composure after the fall, it had been clear to Kalu how much of a sham their assertions about life were, and that he had made a grave mistake. The air of accomplishment, invincibility and omniscience which had already faded with the slaying of Felicia was now firmly replaced by dread, and the pure and certain knowledge that the worst was yet to come.

As the SUV swerved around the many bends that peppered the country road, Kalu recalled the fleeting goodbye hugs he'd had to give his father, mother and sisters before they scrambled and squeezed themselves into the seats of another of Benjamin's impractical cars.

Ominously, the staff had failed to show up, as expected, at the crack of dawn. Benjamin's gateman was quickly handed a few wads of bank notes, deputised to drive staff and given his first task: to drive Kalu's father, mother and sisters to Port Harcourt Airport en route to one of Chief Alusi's villas in Gabon, which Benjamin had stolen.

"We will all meet there, make you no worry." Kalu watched Benjamin's pathetic attempt to reassure their weary-looking mother as their new driver drove off towards the gates of the compound. The mortified look on his mother's face was like a stain that could never be rubbed off.

Benjamin remained silent as he drove, and Kalu anxiously pondered the prospect of taking on a new identity and having to go into hiding for a very long time, perhaps never being able to see Owerri again. He faced the very real possibility of being lynched or publicly executed by firing squad, the fate he had, many years ago, presupposed that his brother would meet. He began to entertain the thought of abandoning his brother and finding his own way out. When they got to Gabon he would vanish, never to contact any member of his family again, he concluded.

A ping from Benjamin's phone, which lay on the car's dashboard, alerted them to an incoming text message. Kalu read aloud as his brother drove: "I am here now and ready. When are you arriving?"

"On our way now," Kalu tapped out his brother's dictated response. Benjamin stopped the car a short distance away from the clearing where the helipad was, and they approached on foot.

In minutes Kalu and his brother had the helipad in their sights. However, they arrived to find, instead of a deserted patch of field, that a cluster of dark-blue police vans surrounded the six-seater helicopter and a few men in uniform were staking out the sizeable grounds that served as Benjamin's helipad. Further along the highway, the detained pilot lay on the bare ground with a few assault rifles trained on him.

Mike had finally sold them out, Kalu concluded.

"Are you close?" Another text message arrived, supposedly from the pilot. Kalu saw his brother's response, just before he sent it.

"Change of plan. Going to drive instead. On the Owerri–Onitsha road at the moment. Fly to Onitsha and wait. I will contact you when I arrive."

Seconds later, Kalu and Benjamin watched from amongst the tall shrubs they hid in as a few uniformed men scrambled into one of the police vans and speed off into the distance on the highway. It was clear there was no way they could get past the scores of checkpoints that were undoubtedly being placed on the various roads leading out of the city. The decision to run back to the Porche Cayanne, dump it at a secluded spot off the farm road, and board the first rickety public commuter bus back into town, was swiftly taken.

51 VERSACE

"I gaghị agbagide ọsọ, gbafere azụ gi"

"A person can never run so fast as to run away from his backside"

(Traditional Igbo proverb)

6:12am

The ramshackle Hiace minibus heading back into town could not have come soon enough.

Earlier, on two occasions, Kalu and Benjamin had found themselves taking cover behind the tree trunks at the roadside as more unmistakable dark-blue police vans sped down the highway in both directions.

"*Oga* Benji sir." These were the driver's first words when the minibus pulled up by the side of the highway where Kalu and Benjamin were waiting. The bald-headed, bare-chested driver could have been at any or all of the public events that Benjamin graced religiously. *Throwing money to the crowd and flaunting his wealth, just like the rest of the fucking rich idiots*, Kalu thought to himself. It all would backfire now.

With a beaming, fawning smile, the driver ordered the two passengers sitting beside him to the back and, after frenziedly patting the worn upholstery as though to transform it into a more befitting state, he invited Benjamin and Kalu to take a seat.

"*Ogas*, please sirs," the driver beckoned, gesticulating to the empty seats.

A rush of anxiety gripped Kalu. The driver, his conductor and the half-dozen passengers in the minibus were apparently not aware of what was happening, particularly as they were only now heading into town, but Kalu knew things would change quickly.

Their glaring conspicuousness had already been a worry to Kalu: the Porsche Cayenne had now been dumped, but the silky Versace shirts, expensive watches and floaty linen trousers that Benjamin had insisted on wearing were also grave mistakes. It became clear to Kalu that his brother was a significant liability and he would need to abandon him sooner than he had planned.

"*Oga*, your moto break?" the driver said, intermittently flashing his gaze across to Benjamin and Kalu, trying to make small talk as his van crept frustratingly along the expressway. He drew nothing more than nods from both.

Kalu felt his legs going to sleep, as he was tightly wedged between his brother and the front side door of the minibus.

After they had lodged the Porsche Cayenne in a hidden ditch just off the farm road, they had each taken their time stuffing wads of dollars from the box Benjamin had stashed in the trunk into the pockets and inside lining of their trousers. Kalu felt a persistent numbing ache at the side of his leg from the loaded handgun, which Benjamin had taken from the glove compartment and which was now protruding from Benjamin's trouser pocket, along with the wads of cash stuffed there.

Soon, the slew of overgrown shrubs and bushes lining the potholed highway road became fewer, replaced by roadside shops and shacks, dwellings in the shape of bungalows and one-storey buildings, many still in their building phase. A lone woman who looked to be in her forties stood by the roadside, flagging down the bus. A quiet panic was set off in Kalu's head as the minibus pulled up alongside her and a rush of wariness filled the woman's face when she caught sight of Benjamin. It was clear that the events of that early morning had now become public knowledge.

52 HEADHUNTER

"Anaghị ezo anwụrụ ọkụ n'ala"

"You cannot bury smoke in the ground"

(Traditional Igbo proverb)

8:10am

In less than an hour, the trickle of people Obioma had observed on the way to his shop became a baying crowd, drawn from all corners of the city, and all headed in one direction: towards the central police station situated at the western end of Whetheral Road.

Obioma joined the stream of traders and school children who navigated the streets and roads west of Nnamdi Azikiwe Road. Soon he found himself squeezing and clawing his way ahead of the mass of bodies surging towards the fence that surrounded the police station.

At this point progress became slow, and every now and again someone would squeeze past, swimming against the tide. The latest was a middle-aged man, and Obioma smelled the unmistakable rancid smell of puke as the man brushed passed him, his clothes caked with vomit.

Up ahead, the mesh of metal fencing that partitioned the police station from Whetheral Road bowed forward from the strain put on it by the surging crowd. Obioma continued to force his way through, his determination increasing with each stride.

Gasps of horror could be heard up ahead, increasing as he drew nearer.

From his vantage point, he could see people throwing their arms in the air as they cried out in shock. He knew something terrible lay ahead. It was typical for the police to parade the fruits of their latest raids and adventures, showing off fleets of recovered stolen luxury vehicles, guns and ammunition, and sometimes the lifeless and bullet-ridden corpses of overcome bandits at the front of their compound. But nothing could have prepared Obioma for the sight that awaited him.

He got only a momentary glimpse, but it was long enough. Obioma thrust his head through the arms of one of a number of people who had decided to permanently plant themselves at the front of the police fencing. At first he was not sure what he was looking at. An apparently badly beaten-up and handcuffed man, stripped completely naked, his eyes bloodshot and vacant. Then Obioma recognised him. It was Kalu's cousin, Mike, the one who had driven the big van during Kalu and his family's move from the Old Market to their mansions on the outskirts of the city.

Mike now sat silently bare ground with a number of old plastic shopping bags scattered around him. Some in the baying crowd on Obioma's side of the fence hurled abuse at him, past the four heavily armed police officers who stood a few yards away, their automatic rifles trained on him, at the ready.

Obioma focused a bit more, forcing his eyes to confront directly what they had apparently been avoiding: about a dozen severed human heads in the partially rolled-down plastic bags strewn around Kalu's cousin.

The story of Mike's capture had spread around town like wildfire. Mike had been stopped at one of the checkpoints as he made his way out of the city and the car he was driving searched by the police. It had been a routine nuisance-stop by a group of new policemen, to prompt a bribe. They asked to search the boot of the car, and in it they found the decapitated heads of nine grown men, their eyes shrivelled and their skin darkened and shrunken like old wood. The larger bag sitting alongside him in the front passenger seat was found to contain four smaller bags, wrapped around the heads of three girls and a young lady. Unlike the men, they had clearly met their deaths in the past few days or even hours, their wide-open eyes glassy and distant and their braided hairdos still very much in place. A dazed Obioma panned helplessly from one bag to the other, until it became apparent to him that one of the severed heads was that of Moses.

53 OSO NDU

"The Stream says that it is because it has nobody to direct it that it goes in a zigzag

way"

(Traditional Igbo proverb)

10:10am

Obioma's laboured run quickened when he turned into the street that Nneka lived on. His decision to look for Nneka after seeing Kalu's cousin sitting amongst the decapitated heads had been instinctive. It had been almost two years since Obioma had last visited the room Nneka shared with her mother. After he had knocked on their door for the twelfth time, along with that of their neighbours, he was none the wiser about Nneka's whereabouts.

There were only three other places Nneka could be, Obioma reckoned. At her university – that is, if she still attended. He had heard rumours that she had dropped out. Then there was Nneka's mother's stall, but Obioma could not imagine she still went there to help her mother out. Finally, there was Kalu's house, which was a good few hours' walk away.

Obioma resumed his sprint, heading for Kalu's house, his pace quickly deteriorating into a breathless jog.

As he navigated the streets and roads leading out of the city, Obioma recalled the last time that he had seen Nneka. She had turned up at his doorstep 'to say goodbye properly', and to hand him back gifts he had given to her over the previous years: a pair of shoes, heaps of cassette tapes he had dubbed with her favourite songs, and a fake leather purse.

Recollections of the time before last were even more humiliating. Obioma had been left in a crumpled heap of despair outside Chalet O'Brien. After the tip-off from his old school friend, Obioma had rushed to Chalet O'Brien just in time to catch Kalu and Nneka leaving the hotel.

Obioma soldiered on, dropping out of his recollections of that dreadful afternoon. The mix of shop-fronts and home terraces, tall blocks, shacks and bungalows eventually gave way to wild-growing shrubs, grass and trees, which lined either side of the main road. The whizz of fast-travelling cars on either side of the road kept Obioma to the narrow crevasse between the bushes and the tarmac. With the intensifying rays of the sun bearing down on him, Obioma tortured himself with the nagging fear that maybe Nneka had been reduced to the shrivelled and decapitated body parts he had just seen.

Obioma's mind harked back to what he had heard around the police station that morning. About a dozen men gathered in one of hundreds of impromptu conversations that had broken out around town. This one had formed around a man who was claiming to have known one of the dead girls.

"You mean the one in the bag at the far left?"

"Yes. Her name is Chidimma. She was in my class in primary school. In fact, back in the day, she lived just a few houses from my former house," the man had explained.

"*Ewo* fine girl," a man sighed.

"Very fine girl," another added.

"Fine girl, fine girl, shut up! You guys acting like you did not know!" another man passing by cut in angrily. He looked to Obioma to be in his thirties, and there was no doubt in his mind that he was a trader. Like Obioma, he clutched the end of a mini shoehorn, from which a heavy bunch of keys dangled.

"You, you and you, even me. We were hailing these bastards, hailing their money, their Lamborghinis, Ferraris, Porsches and Cadillacs, while they were busy fucking these girls and killing people," the man continued.

"The going rate amongst these 419 boys was two thousand naira to fuck any girl in Owerri without a condom. We all knew it. We were too busy tracking the parties where they spread money at, so that we could hopefully pick up dollar bills to change at Ama Hausa. Well, this is the result now. This is the result now! This is the result now!" the man continued in a loud bellow, attracting the attention of other huddles of people.

Obioma had heard the rumours too. The spiked drinks, drug-induced coercions and blackmail that turned a number of young girls and women in the city into full-time prostitutes and sex slaves. Girls were paid a finder's fee to convince their friends to take part. People like Kalu and his brother passed them around like neighbours passed pruning shears to each other. An infamous and growing list of girls on speed dial was said to be in circulation amongst the exclusive clubs of 419 money-men in the city. A growing guilt began to form in Obioma's mind.

54 MANSION

"Udu mmiri anaghị amasị elu-igwe"

"The rainy season does not please the sky"

(Traditional Igbo proverb)

12:50pm

Obioma strenuously hoisted his frame up one more branch of the tall, barren mango tree that grew a short distance away from the high walls encircling Kalu's compound. The imposing electric gates at Kalu's home were locked shut, and Obioma's incessant banging on their ornamental metal plates yielded no results. He had already held down the button of the electric bell on more than three occasions for almost a minute at a time. He had ignored the tell-tale sign of the police tape that was pasted across the large gates, and which stretched each way to the corners of the tall fence walls.

From his new vantage point, Obioma now peered directly and intently into the rooms of both mansions, looking for signs of movement. He climbed even further up the tree. After close to half an hour of carefully observing each room in the two buildings he concluded that there was no one there and his trip had been a total waste of time.

Obioma embarked on the relatively easier downhill walk back to the grey mass that was the city.

"How did they get money out of people's body parts?" Obioma found himself questioning as he took the direct approach of heading down small paths that cut through bushes and shrubs.

His mind wandered through old folk stories, rumours of dead kings who needed to be buried along with the heads of some of their subjects as monuments to their high status, stories told in villages to stop children neglecting their chores and wandering off into the forests in search of wild fruits and insects.

Lately there had been new tales, of strange and diabolical people roaming through markets snatching people's genitals with simple taps on shoulders; rumours about the fate of close relatives of wealthy people; stories that melded into scripts for Nollywood movies, about secret cults that demanded the ritual sacrifice of their members' relatives in exchange for enormous wealth; whispered accounts about entranced captives prompted, under the spell of incantations and elaborate rituals by witch doctors, to literally cough up money in dark, dingy mud-huts.

The migraine that now gripped Obioma did not abate, even as he left the direct glare of the sun for the alternating shade of the stalls in the market.

Owerri was now a changed place in a matter of a few hours, Obioma thought to himself. The market road, usually crammed with people and traders, had literally been emptied out by the events of that morning.

Obioma heard that the display of Kalu's captured cousin and the decapitated heads found with him had stopped at around eleven that morning, but people continued to besiege the police station. An undercurrent of tension now gripped the market and the city, as small groups of traders continued to form and break away from impromptu conversations about what had just transpired.

Small transistor radios were now permanently pressed against ears for more news as the local radio stations ran updates on the story. Parents who bothered to come out could be seen clutching on to their children more tightly than usual as they moved through the market. When Obioma reached the usual spot, he was not surprised to discover that Nneka's mother was not trading that day.

55 DRIVER, STOP

"Anaghị ezoro ala ozu"

"One does not hide a corpse from the land"

(Traditional Igbo proverb)

Earlier that morning

Whatever was responsible for the distress on the face of the woman who waved down the minibus, it also caused her to be initially reluctant to board. This drew puzzled looks from commuters already on the bus. The impatient conductor had already slid the door back well before the minibus had actually ground to a complete halt next to her.

From the front seat, Kalu anxiously watched the middle-aged woman as she nervously wrapped and unwrapped the outermost layer of the rolls of lacy cloth around her ample frame. She still hesitated in her decision about whether to board the bus, in a sort of silent dance back and forth from the door of the vehicle. It became apparent to Kalu that the woman was averting her gaze from the front of the van, where he and his brother were seated, and there was no doubt in his mind that she was well aware of the horrendous news that was now taking hold of the city.

The woman did eventually board, taking one of the spare seats at the back, after being persuaded by the conductor to make up her mind quickly. Kalu monitored her in the rear-view mirror. She kept her eyes tightly closed and, with her head tilted down, she launched almost immediately into bouts of inaudible mumbled prayers.

At least she was not making conversation with the other passengers or with the conductor; Kalu felt some reprieve. His glance across to his brother found Benjamin also staring intently into the rear-view mirror. At the same time, Kalu saw his brother's hand reaching into his pocket for his handgun, persisting despite Kalu's discreet head-shaking.

Kalu knew his brother well enough to know that he was seriously contemplating the slaughter of everyone on board that bus, something Kalu, to his own surprise, found himself not entirely disagreeing with, if it were necessary. But Kalu doubted Benjamin had enough ammunition to carry it out.

"Driver! Stop us here," Kalu shouted out to the driver, before pressing a crumpled hundred-dollar note that he blindly retrieved from one of the wads of cash in his pocket into the waiting palm of the driver.

Kalu felt a tentative relief as the minibus disappeared down the road, and as he and his brother slunk through the quiet outer back streets of Owerri. He knew that anyone and everyone was a potential whistle-blower, now that it was clear that news of Mike's capture was floating through the city.

This was why they headed for Chalet O'Brien, which was only a few streets away. Benjamin had suggested hiding out there to his brother earlier as they stood concealed behind trees on the highway.

Bob, who ran Chalet O'Brien, was well known for his discretion. It was a skill he had turned into a thriving business. With well over twenty years' experience of running the place, he held the infidelity secrets of probably thousands, Kalu reckoned.

Bob was a 'no questions asked' kind of guy, but even though Kalu had himself used Chalet O'Brien, he had reservations, which he kept to himself. Persuading Bob to look beyond the grim rumours that were bound to be circulating around the city was a tall order. But Kalu could think of no alternative plans.

56 GUILT

"Ihe egbe riri na alaghachi n'afọ udele"

"The thing that the hawk ate returns to the vulture's stomach"

(Traditional Igbo proverb)

1:17pm

Obioma arrived home to find Nneka's mother sitting on the bare ground, slouched against the side wall of his building. Her bloodshot eyes and tear-stained face stared dismally into the distance, and a group of children who lived nearby had gathered around to gawk at her from a safe distance.

She abruptly sprang to her feet when Obioma walked into her field of vision. As she seized him in a locking embrace, Obioma realised that it had been at least a year since the last time he saw her, just after she had been discharged from hospital. Back then, her conspicuous bosom had already been, strikingly, completely gone, but now she looked even more gaunt and drained than she had then. But she spoke to Obioma with the same familiarity she'd had with him when they sat side by side selling melon seeds in the middle of the market road years before.

"I can't find Nneka! Have you seen your sister?" she screeched, her expectant gaze searching Obioma's clueless face.

"I haven't seen her in months," Obioma eventually said, initially shaking his head until he felt ready to force the disappointing words out of his mouth.

"I have not seen Nneka in three weeks," she said, with burdened tone of one who felt she had neglected her child.

"Three weeks?" The words involuntarily left Obioma's mouth. He realised they sounded judgemental, like a stab in a wound of guilt. This forced Nneka's mother back into another bout of silence. When she began to speak again, she explained how she had been told by Benjamin that Nneka had ended her relationship with Kalu and was away in Lagos, with a doctor who was arranging for her to continue her nursing training there. He had suggested that she must have been promised a job in his hospital. Nneka had left some contact details: a phone number, which Benjamin said Nneka had passed on in a recent telephone call to Kalu. Nneka's mother rummaged through the contents of the tied end of her wrapper cloth, eventually retrieving a crumpled piece of paper with a phone number written across it.

"I called the number, from the call shop at the top of the market, for almost a week, before someone, a man, picked it up and said that Nneka did not want to see or speak to me," Nneka's mother told Obioma. "He said that she was angry with me, but it made no sense. What would she be angry with me about? We have always been close. She is all I have."

More tears began to collect in her eyes. "They have killed her, haven't they?" she finally concluded.

Obioma did not want to tell her that he did not believe Nneka would be found alive, but she somehow knew that this was what he was thinking. A few moments passed, then her quivering body slumped onto his.

Nneka's mother eventually regained consciousness. Obioma and one of his neighbours had laid her out on his living-room sofa, having carried her up the seven stairwells to Obioma's flat.

After she had gulped down two full glasses of water, she began to speak about how she, too, had clambered with the surge of onlookers at the police station to see for herself, after news had reached her that the man who had been caught with severed heads was a relation of Kalu.

"I have lost her." Nneka's mother resumed her weeping. They were words that also tugged on Obioma's own sense of guilt. He had let his feelings of rivalry with Kalu get in the way of looking out for Nneka, and now it was probably too late.

57 NDO

"Arụsị kpakarịa ike anyị egosị ya osisi e siri pịapụta ya"

"If a carved idol becomes very destructive, we will show it the tree from which it is carved"

(Traditional Igbo proverb)

11:40pm

As midnight approached, images of the severed heads Obioma had seen earlier that morning still hovered around the mosquito net draped over his single four-poster metal-framed bed. The routine nightly prayer session of Obioma's mother was unsurprisingly lengthy that night and her murmurs floated through the walls into Obioma's room.

The city of Owerri was on tenterhooks, particularly after footage of Mike and the severed heads had featured on the local television station's news programme at eight o'clock that evening. The shock that had gripped the city earlier that morning had now rejuvenated itself, and people gathered in groups to discuss the latest rumours well into the night. Mike was dead, killed in custody by corrupt police officers keen to cover the tracks of those who paid them, but it had all been too late. A number of people had already been implicated by information that had been extracted from Mike in the torture interrogation sessions he was subjected to before his death.

At around midnight, Obioma gave up trying to fall asleep and joined one of many groups congregating up and down the city. At the entrance to his cul-de-sac, people gathered under the rays of light that beamed from the security lamps hanging over the balconies and verandas of the buildings and shacks that lined the cul-de-sac and the adjoining road. The strained sounds of their loud conversations filtered their way into his room and coaxed him downstairs to join in. Just in time; new information about events around town was being relayed by a small group of men who had joined them from the next street. About a dozen in number, they brandished bruised and sore hands from their latest expedition: the digging up of Don Champion's vast gated compound.

"Sixteen decapitated bodies! Can you imagine? Can you imagine?" one of them repeated to the swelling, baying crowd.

"Some of them fresh as if they were killed yesterday, others already decaying, smelling," another added.

The stories carried by the men filtered through the crowd. Obioma moved around, straining his ears as small sub-conversations formed around each of the returning men.

The dig had been instigated by a handful of police officers who had retained the services of some local building contractors: a follow-up to various interrogations that had taken place that afternoon. One of the men described how people had initially gathered at a distance to watch, but how things had descended into a free-for-all the moment the first mutilated bodies had started appearing. Random members of the public joined in with spades and shovels, others digging with their bare hands.

Obioma noticed an old man, a neighbour whom he had seen totter out of his shack by the side of the road earlier. He was now being held up by the shoulders by two young men, who gingerly carried him over the wide gap of the gutter to sit him down by the foot of some stairs. Others begin to gather around him with words of sympathy. Obioma followed suit: a comforting hand on the man's shoulder and "*Ndo*" (sorry), just as everyone else had done.

"James was an easy target. Body parts of albinos go for a lot more money," Obioma heard someone remark about the old man's son.

"He was a sufferer of albinism: that is the correct way you say it. Please don't insult the man in death as well," another retorted.

Obioma had seen the old man's son on several occasions. He drank a lot and was known to regularly visit a drinking house at the other side of the city. He would stagger home late in the night drunk, sometimes singing songs. He had vanished about six months ago. Parts of his body had now been dug up in the back garden of Don Champion's house. One of the men in the crowd had to lift the headless torso out from a shallow ditch. Still draped in the clothes he had been seen in last, there was no question it was him; he always wore that outfit – it even appeared in the missing person's poster that his family had pasted all around town over the months since his disappearance.

A seething anger began to fester in the crowd.

58 ARA AGWU!

"Mgbe ndịmmadụ na -akpọkọta nkume, nkumeghọọ chi akpaalaokwu"

"When people gather stones, the stones become deities"

(Traditional Igbo proverb)

1:15am Wednesday 27 May 1993

The sounds of pounding feet, along with stirring church hymns and renditions of gospel songs, things normally reserved for Sunday masses, now serenaded the usually dead, sleepy early-morning streets of Owerri.

Obioma joined one of the swelling crowds of hundreds marauding through the city. Toppled burning cars lit up the sky in their wake. Obioma as if he sat on a comet, perhaps somewhere around its tail, observing the collection of loosely connected people flow forward in such destructive harmony that they acquired their own gravitational pull, drawing others in.

The road eventually straightened and it became apparent where they were now headed. Obioma he sprinted ahead, side-stepping the broken bottles and other debris that littered the great Nnamdi Azikiwe Road. He imagined the mass digging that would ensue when they got to their destination.

What would they find this time?

What if all that was left of Nneka was a headless torso?

Obioma's mind pestered him. It had been weeks since she was last seen; she would surely be in a decomposing state. When he could no longer bear thinking of Nneka as a rotten corpse, Obioma thought of other things that would happen at Kalu's house. For one, all of Benjamin's cars would be set alight, he thought.

"In this fucking austerity, do you see anyone other than those *yeye* boys buying these flashy cars?" a man clutching a car-radio ripped from a roadside car said, as he emptied the contents of a small jerry can over the seats of the car. The can contained fuel that had been syphoned from the same car seconds before.

The digging up of the back of Benjamin's compound, the only portion not paved with concrete slabs, started minutes after the mechanical gates had been prised open by the mob. Obioma soon got tired of hovering over the diggers who were randomly excavating portions of the compound by torchlight, and later by the beams of headlights of hot-wired cars parked nearby. He took over from one of the diggers and, as he took hold of the shovel, Obioma caught himself casting an inquisitive eye across Kalu's long, narrow compound as he wondered where Kalu would have buried Nneka's body.

"*Bia nu eba!*" a man digging at the far end called out. Obioma had heard earlier how this man's twin teenage daughters who had hawked soft drinks around the city had gone missing six months ago. Everyone in the city had seen the striking missing person's poster of them sitting side by side. That night, he was reported to have been anywhere and everywhere, and told tales of trawling through the putrid mess of flesh and bone and hovering over the gory finds of headless, dismembered and decomposing bodies which he frequently stumbled on in the half-dozen compounds he had already helped to dig up.

Obioma, along with some others, rushed towards where the man stood. The man's latest find turned out to be the carcass of a dog. After about an hour and a half of digging, Obioma and the few still left wandering Benjamin's compound conceded to themselves that there were no corpses to be found there, a decision that was influenced by the downpour of rain that began just after the dog was discovered.

59 STOPOVER

"Anaghị ekpuchi afọ ime aka"

"A pregnant stomach cannot be covered with the hand"

(Traditional Igbo proverb)

At the same time

The room was a good size, with blinds across the large bay windows which remained tightly drawn and apparently newly painted pale-green walls. It was big enough to have a bed, a mini settee arrangement in one corner and a work desk and chair in another. Benjamin's handgun rested on the round glass coffee table that sat in between an old floral-patterned couch and two similarly upholstered chairs. Beside it rested an empty bottle of Jack Daniels whisky, which Benjamin had drunk dry.

Kalu sat in an armchair in the far corner of the room, as his brother staggered to the door to hand Bob yet another fat wad of hundred-dollar bills to buy another few hours of his discretion, together with a new and unopened bottle of Jack Daniels, which Bob claimed he had to travel across town to buy.

Bob was just as expected, his thin, drawn, unassuming face decorated with equally thin bifocal glasses, which sat midway on his nose. He seemed to be forever glancing into a notepad which sat on his desk, and which he carried with him whenever he left the desk, giving him a comforting air of detachment. But every now and again he would flash a knowing look that suggested he was well aware of what was happening. He did this with a calm which signalled that his silence could be bought.

This time, just before Bob closed the door to slink back into the corridor, Kalu saw the façade of his face momentarily fall away, his look of concern as Benjamin staggered back to the settee swigging large gulps of liquor from the bottle Bob had just handed to him. His hospitable smile returned almost instantly, but Kalu recognised that they were on borrowed time.

All through the day, Kalu watched his brother's downward spiral into despair. He believed Benjamin was preparing himself for capture and death, in the same way someone on death row approached their final hours.

At first, Benjamin was full of boisterous talk of getting to one of his many properties in neighbouring countries, laying low until they could take retributive action on anyone and everyone who was involved in the crisis they now faced. This was just after Bob had first led them into their room, agreeing to close all other reservations for his remaining rooms, for a fee. Bob had also laid out a lavish spread of food shortly after they settled in.

But then came the relay of images of Mike on the eight o'clock news programme, a video clip of the mass of people that had gathered that morning to gawk at him and the severed heads propped up around him. It was apparently the news programme which inspired the strained sounds of crowds of people chanting that Kalu and Benjamin heard coming from outside from time to time, well into the night and early the next morning.

Just after ten o'clock that night, Benjamin had received a call on his mobile phone from the policeman he had spoken to earlier that morning, a last favour he would pay him, the policeman said. It would also be the last phone call Benjamin would receive on his mobile phone before his batteries finally died.

The policeman had confirmed that Mike had identified him as the ringleader behind the spate of ritual killings before he could be silenced, and that Benjamin was now officially a wanted man. Don Champion and a number of his associates had been rounded up and arrested, and had all pleaded similarly, not that it would help them to stay alive, the policeman reckoned. Pictures of Benjamin had already been recovered from a search that was conducted on his mansion and distributed to law enforcement officers across the country.

The policeman had reserved the most devastating news for last, reports about a shoot-out that had occurred not far from Port Harcourt Airport when the car carrying Benjamin's family had been stopped by police at a checkpoint. His father, one of his sisters and the driver were said to have been shot dead on the spot. Benjamin's phone had died just as he pressed for news about the rest of his family. Benjamin had kept this piece of news from Kalu until just now, and Kalu seethed with a concoction of anger and trepidation at the chain of events he had allowed to occur.

He gazed at the handgun that sat on the table.

60 THE BENIGN

"Amaghị ịhe, bụ ọrịa"

"Ignorance is a sickness"

(Traditional Igbo proverb)

2:35am

Obioma found himself sitting in Kalu's living room, running his fingers across the gold-coloured façade of the sofa he had once sat in years before, when he had helped out with Kalu's family's big move.

How significantly things had changed. Now the luxurious seats were slashed wide open, his host nowhere to be seen. Many more had joined from across the city in the storming of the mansions, and amongst the marauding mob were those whose intentions were to cart away expensive television sets, washing machines and other valuables. The enormous vases, ornaments and various kitschy gold-framed mirrors, paintings and photographs which were once placed here and there either were broken or had vanished. The majority of the rampaging mob, now taking shelter from the rain, were next door in Benjamin's house, which had comparatively more valuable furnishings.

As Obioma rested on the sofa, his fatigued mind working on where next to look for Nneka, he remembered how the now slushy and heavy carpet underneath his feet had once felt lusciously soft, like standing on a large fluffy pillow. The relentless downpour which had cut short the fruitless digging had found its way into the house through the large brick-shattered windows. An exhausted Obioma remained planted on the sofa, his guilt-stricken mind reflecting on what he would do if he were to come across Kalu, what he should have done those past few months, and how his deceased uncle Iwuagwu would have reacted to events in the city and the great purge that had ensued.

"Agwu's madness can overcome a city," Obioma remembered his uncle once saying.

"If the disproportion of bad people to good people is too great the Agwu deity will surely step in," his uncle would insist.

"*Udi mmadu ano no n,uwa*" (There are four types of people in this world), Iwuagwu had once announced those many years ago, doing so as though results from an elaborate survey he had conducted had just come in. His lecture, part of Obioma's education, had come following one of Iwuagwu's verbal clashes with Okoro earlier that day. Obioma's memories of that afternoon were vivid.

"*Ndi oma*, the good. Like your cousin Ejike, who despite being intelligent enough to obtain a medical qualification neglected the allure of escaping to the big cities to a guaranteed better life, and instead set up shop here helping ordinary people, sometimes with little or no payment for his good work.

"Ejike is a good person. He is not naive or stupid," Obioma remembered his uncle insisting. "His parents lived and died in that small mud-hut in wretched poverty, yet he remains here. Your mother is a good person, deeply flawed in her tact, temperament and approach, but fundamentally a good person."

"*Ndi miri miri*" (Then we have the benign), Iwuagwu had continued. "Easy-going, nice men like your father. They do not necessarily do bad. They maybe even be keen on being fair-minded and reciprocating good deeds, but, like seedless palm trees, they serve no real purpose. Nothing greater than providing shade on a hot day."

"'*Ndi nkemu nkemu*" (Then the indifferent and selfish), Obioma's uncle declared. "Akwuna is a very selfish person, lying, dishonest and self-absorbed." Obioma did not know exactly who Akwuna was. "This type of person would never do good for its own sake and cares even less for those who get harmed by the bad of others.

"It is always only a matter of time and opportunity before these people eventually worsen and finally become *nde ojo*" (bad people), he continued. "This final group of people are vile and entirely disconnected from the positive forces of life; people who take actions that hurt others and would never dream of preventing harm, but rather only of causing it."

"Okoro, *I bu onye ojoo*" (Okoro, you are a bad person), Obioma remembered his uncle howling at the top of his voice, as his index finger made stabbing gestures towards Okoro, Obioma's much older distant cousin.

Obioma could not help but think of Kalu when he recalled what, at the time, seemed to be another of his uncle's long and rambling monologues, suddenly now poignant and relevant. As he sat in the rain-flooded living room, he wondered which of the four groups of people Iwuagwu had listed he belonged to himself.

"The benign are never present," Iwuagwu's voice reverberated in his thoughts, as if to answer his question.

Just then, the stench of petrol filled Obioma's nostrils as it engulfed the dimly candle-lit living room. Obioma felt tapping on his shoulder. One of two middle-aged men, who had been dousing rooms in the buildings with petrol, spoke to Obioma in a voice filled with caution, his comrade at the same time emerging with an empty jerry can at the foot of the stairs leading to the upper level of the mansion.

"It will not be safe to be here in a few minutes. All these ill-gotten gains and blood money have to go."

Obioma thought of how, in the months that had passed, those rampaging through the building would have been out cheering the likes of Benjamin as they sprayed money at public events, and how, like him, they too had waited too long to be good.

61 DEATH ROW

"Nwata na-erughị eru chọọ ihe mere nna ya, ihe mere nna ya emee ya"

"If a child is not prudent in seeking what killed his father, what killed his father may

also kill him"

(Traditional Igbo proverb)

3:40am

Kalu continued to sit silently in the armchair, watching his brother Benjamin take laboured breaths as he slept across the room, his snores echoing across the quiet corridors and vacant rooms of Chalet O'Brien.

Kalu hadn't moved at all from his seat since Benjamin broke the news about the death of their father and of one of their sisters, over two hours previously.

The policeman who informed Benjamin about their deaths did not say which of his sisters had died. There was no mention of the fate of their mother and remaining sister, whether they were injured, imprisoned or set free. Benjamin had guzzled down a full bottle of Jack Daniels and moved on to his second in a matter of minutes after the news arrived, taking swigs from the second bottle as he had from the first until he got just over halfway through the bottle. Then he had collapsed in a heap on the bed in the room they shared.

Kalu stewed in his thoughts, brooding over the contempt he had for his brother, his father, and himself. He recalled the frightened look on both of his sisters' faces that morning shortly before the gateman-turned-driver set off with them to Port Harcourt.

Benjamin liked to stash guns in all of his cars, Kalu remembered. The driver may have tried to use one of Benjamin's weapons to confront the police when they got cornered. But it seemed more plausible that his father would have been the one to gamble on challenging the police with a firearm. After all, he was given to rash and foolish instincts. Or, maybe there were no guns, just his father's annoying and provoking nature. He did not really need a gun.

Kalu decided not to mourn the apparent death of his father, blaming him for all that had transpired, from Benjamin's disposition to criminality, to manipulating him into joining Benjamin's business, and for ultimately destroying their family.

In the room, lit up only by the red glow of the standby light that shone from the base of a wall mounted television, Kalu rested his gaze on his brother, who laid sprawled out awkwardly across the bed, his gaping mouth quivering as he snored. This made Kalu hark back to their childhood days, when they lived near the Old Market. He thought about the concealed looks of pride and reassurance his father would beam towards Benjamin whenever he had got into trouble. The callous snatching of a neighbour's bike, the burst lips of boys Benjamin instigated altercations with, visits by neighbours whose windows had been broken, whose young daughters had been groomed and violated.

"The building of a monster," Kalu concluded to himself. "Two monsters," his mind suggested as the train of thought continued.

Kalu began to recount his own recent transgressions: drugging and raping Nneka when she finally succumbed to his invitations to visit his house alone, along with the subsequent abuses that followed, not to talk of passing her on to his brother and to Mike. This was when Kalu accepted that he had morphed into his brother, Benjamin.

Sudden unfamiliar clinking sounds outside awakened Kalu from his deep and chaotic thoughts. He remembered seeing Bob lock the gates to the compound just after eleven o'clock that night, just before Bob had retired back to his bedroom at the top level of the guest-house.

Now, the bedside digital clock-radio on the chest of drawers in the room registered 03:49, early in the morning. From the silhouettes Kalu could see outside on the street, Bob appeared to be having a conversation with two other men as he unlocked the compound gates.

Kalu watch them discreetly around the sides of the blinds drawn across the large bay windows of the room. Watching closely as the men disappeared down the street after their conversation with Bob had ended, Kalu then followed Bob's walk across the short distance between the vacant guest parking spots to the front of the main building. Seconds later he heard the sound of knocking on their bedroom door.

"*Biko bịa ka any sụọ*" (Come let us discuss), Bob said when Kalu tentatively opened the door to him.

Much of Bob's nonchalant disposition had now disappeared, and Kalu felt the brunt of the look of distain and disgust which his face now wore. Bob led Kalu further down the dimly lit corridor before he started to speak, an action Kalu read as his intention to be out of earshot of Benjamin.

"Your brother is officially a wanted man," Bob said in a grave and solemn tone. "By tomorrow, police posters with his picture will be pasted all across town and in newspapers. You guys have to leave before sunrise."

Bob's forceful tone suggested he expected an argument, a reaction that did not immediately materialise from Kalu, who in his contemplative silence had latched onto a glint of hope that he read into Bob's words. Neither the police tip-off nor Bob himself mentioned any reports of Kalu being considered a suspect.

"Who told you this?" Kalu asked.

"Are you hearing me? Police are raiding places indiscriminately, 'area boys' are everywhere burning houses anyhow. If they discover you guys here I will be in the same situation as you, and this building will be burnt to the ground."

"Was it those two men you were just speaking to who told you this?"

"Everyone knows this. The posters are already going up on the main roads."

"Do those men you were speaking to know we are here?"

"It's none of your business who I speak to."

"My brother gave you at least ten thousand dollars cash for a week's stay and to keep your mouth shut," Kalu said sternly. "Are you setting us up?" Bob bolted hurriedly down the corridor towards and out of the main door. Kalu became gripped by panic as he become aware of what was about to occur.

He rushed back to the room, calling out to his brother to wake up, delivering several slaps to Benjamin's face, which yielded no results. He rolled his brother off the bed and onto the floor with a thump. Benjamin briefly uttered some slurred and indecipherable mutterings before settling back into his slumber at the foot of the bed.

Kalu heard the clinking sounds again. He rushed to the window to find Bob unlocking the gates from the outside, accompanied by the silent silhouettes of at least five men who appeared from the shadows across the dead quiet street.

62 THE FORETOLD

"Ọkụkọ na-ajụgbu ajụgbu tụpu o rie"

"The chicken pecks a thing to death before eating"

(Traditional Igbo proverb)

4:02am

Kalu scaled the multiple flights of stairs leading to the top floor of the building that housed Chalet O'Brien, eventually emerging at the very top just by Bob's single room.

Bob's door had been left ajar, and Kalu found himself clambering dangerously out of one of the windows in Bob's room and up a drainage pipe leading to the roof of the building.

Now on all fours, Kalu crawled delicately across the slanted and partly corroded corrugated zinc roofing sheets that shielded the building from the elements. He could hear the growing commotion on the ground, a twenty-five-metre drop away, along with the sounds of pounding feet racing up the stairs in the building. He pressed his palm against one of his pockets and felt the reassuring bulk of his brother's handgun.

The half-moon cast its moderate light across the dark early morning, against the backdrop of a moderate spread of stars in the clear sky. Kalu knew they would not immediately think to look for him on the roof. Even so, in minutes he had made his way onto the roof of an adjoining building and then on to another, safely out of immediate reach.

As he paused to catch his breath, in the distance on the street below, Kalu saw what he had always thought he would see one day: the lynching of Benjamin, his brother.

Vicious silhouettes of at least ten men rallied together, keeping a moderate distance away around the sobbing, staggering figure aimlessly on the move in the middle of the street. Kalu knew that the thin protrusions in the hands of the many menacing shadows were machetes and knives. Kalu watched as they each took turns to deliver stabs and blows, slowing Benjamin down to a standstill, the once sleepy street awakening to his bellows and squeals. As bedroom and balcony lights across the street lit up, Kalu saw his brother fall to the ground and tumble into one of the stagnant, garbage-littered gutters that lined the street.

63 THE GRAVEDIGGERS

"Ọkụkọ mmanya n'egbu ezutebeghị mmanwụ ara n'agba"

"A drunk fowl has not met a mad fox"

(Traditional Igbo proverb)

Four months later

From the skies, Owerri looked in more of a state than it had ever been. The blanket of rusting corrugated iron rooftops which covered almost all forty square miles of the city looked even more tarnished than they had in the past. The formerly luxuriously shiny rooftops of duplexes and mansions which were concentrated around the city's very few high-end suburbs were now peeled back to reveal nothing but burnt-out carcasses of buildings. Equally hollow and charred cars littered the landscape, and staunch armed police patrols now roamed the city.

But Owerri still bore some sense and feel of normality, with its roads pumping vigorously, as the clock struck seven in the morning. Traders still trooped to their shops before dawn, civil servants and others who earned a living sitting behind desks still strutted around their secretariats and about town in two-piece suits in the scorching heat, and students and teachers continued to besiege gates of school compounds all across town and beyond.

As usual, Obioma traced the quiet side roads that ran parallel to Nnamdi Azikiwe Road on his morning commute to his stockfish shop in the New

Market and, as he did so, he searchingly panned across the horizons in front, behind and to the sides of him. He no longer stopped as he always had in front of Immaculate Cutz to admire his attire and appearance, and purposeful and conscious strides were now substituted for his former lazy gait. But his mind still wandered about as he powered down the quiet roads.

The dark and rainy night of the purge that had seen so much carnage, destruction and death had failed to resolve questions about the fate of Nneka. All of Obioma's free time was now consumed in meeting up with like-minded souls in uncompleted and abandoned buildings purported to have been owned by Benjamin, Don Champion or any of the dozen or so suspects who had managed to flee the city and country. They would meet bearing shovels and other digging implements, and with Tupperware crammed with food to sustain them as they dug up compounds in various remote places, hoping to find closure.

THE END

ABOUT THE AUTHOR

Ibeh Liedstrand-Nwokocha is of Nigerian, Barbadian and British heritage and has lived in Nigeria, the United Kingdom, Sweden and Norway. Ibeh's screenplay *High* was shortlisted in the BBC Talent Drama Writer competition. Ibeh has a working background in policy and business development and holds a first degree in law, advanced legal training and a Masters of Business Administration degree. *Medicine Man* is Ibeh's debut novel. Two more works of fiction – *Particle*, set in London, and *Nobel*, which plays out in Sweden and Norway – are planned for release in late 2016 and 2017 respectively.

www.ingramcontent.com/pod-product-compliance
Lightning Source LLC
Chambersburg PA
CBHW030824020726
47499CB00006B/2063